T0021941

PRAISE FOR SIMO

The Last Protector

"Gervais's brisk series kickoff, which jumps around the world, is built on the tension underlying the tenuous alliances among the sort of power-hungry villains who will stop at nothing. Well-modulated action scenes alternate with showdowns that reposition the pawns."

—*Kirkus Reviews*

"[A] solid thriller from Gervais . . ."

—*Publishers Weekly*

"Gervais has already cemented himself as one of the supreme writers in the genre, and this newest novel only adds to it. This is a book that thriller fans won't want to miss."

—Stuart Ashenbrenner, *Best Thriller Books*

"A thrill ride from the first page to the last! Simon Gervais is coming in hot with *The Last Protector*. Looking for action, intrigue, and suspense? This is your novel! Move it to the top of your list!"

—Jack Carr, #1 *New York Times* bestselling author of *The Devil's Hand*

"*The Last Protector*, by Simon Gervais, is a perfectly built, spellbinding thriller with true heart and depth woven into the blood-soaked and bone-crunching action. Relentlessly paced, authentic, and utterly engrossing, *The Last Protector* knocked me off my feet."

—Mark Greaney, #1 *New York Times* bestselling author of *The Gray Man*

"Simon Gervais writes with an insider's knowledge, putting us in the shoes of someone working close-protection assignments. Tightly plotted and lightning fast, *The Last Protector* is a must-read."

—Marc Cameron, *New York Times* bestselling author of *Stone Cross* and *Tom Clancy Code of Honor*

Hunt Them Down

"In *Hunt Them Down*, Gervais has crafted an intelligent and thoughtful thriller that mixes family dynamics with explosive action . . . The possibilities are endless in this new series, and this will easily find an enthusiastic audience craving Hunt's next adventures."

—Associated Press

"[An] action-packed series launch from Gervais . . ."

—*Publishers Weekly*

"Nonstop action meets relentless suspense . . . The blood flows knee deep in this one as Gervais uses his background as a drug investigator for the Royal Canadian Mounted Police to bring a gritty authenticity to his latest thriller."

—*The Real Book Spy*

"Gervais dishes out lavish suspense to keep a reader glued . . ."

—Authorlink

"Superbly crafted and deceptively complex . . . This is thriller writing at its level best by a new voice not afraid to push the envelope beyond traditional storytelling norms."

—*Providence Journal*

"Another simply riveting read from author Simon Gervais, *Hunt Them Down* showcases his mastery of narrative-driven storytelling and his flair for embedding his novels with more twists and turns than a Coney Island roller coaster."

—Midwest Book Review

"From the first page, *Hunt Them Down* is a stick of dynamite that Simon Gervais hands you, masterfully lights, and then dares you to put down before it explodes. Don't. It's worth a few fingers to read to the end."

—Matthew Fitzsimmons, bestselling author of *The Short Drop*

"Your hunt for the next great adventure novel is over. If Jack Reacher started writing thrillers, he'd be Simon Gervais."
—Lee Goldberg, #1 *New York Times* bestselling author of *True Fiction*

Time to Hunt

"An action-packed thrill ride with plot twists around nearly every curve."

—*Kirkus Reviews*

"Gervais consistently entertains."

—*Publishers Weekly*

THE LAST SENTINEL

ALSO BY SIMON GERVAIS

CLAYTON WHITE SERIES

The Last Protector

PIERCE HUNT SERIES

Hunt Them Down
Trained to Hunt
Time to Hunt

MIKE WALTON SERIES

The Thin Black Line
A Long Gray Line
A Red Dotted Line
A Thick Crimson Line

THE LAST SENTINEL

SIMON GERVAIS

THOMAS & MERCER

This is a work of fiction. Names, characters, organizations, places, events, and incidents are either products of the author's imagination or are used fictitiously. Any resemblance to actual persons, living or dead, or actual events is purely coincidental.

Text copyright © 2022 by Simon Gervais
All rights reserved.

No part of this book may be reproduced, or stored in a retrieval system, or transmitted in any form or by any means, electronic, mechanical, photocopying, recording, or otherwise, without express written permission of the publisher.

Published by Thomas & Mercer, Seattle

www.apub.com

Amazon, the Amazon logo, and Thomas & Mercer are trademarks of Amazon.com, Inc., or its affiliates.

ISBN-13: 9781542038928
ISBN-10: 1542038928

Cover design by Kirk DouPonce, DogEared Design

Printed in the United States of America

To my two children, who inspire me every single day.
Always be the best you can be.

PART ONE
EIGHT YEARS AGO

CHAPTER ONE

Baghdad, Iraq

The rumble of the Dassault Falcon 900's wheels hitting the runway jolted Quds Force major Reza Ashtari awake. Blinking and wincing as he stretched his sore neck, Reza opened the window shade on his left. The sun, which had been shining over Tehran at full wattage when Reza and his team had taken off a little over an hour ago, was now blanketed by low-hanging clouds of varying shades of gray, and a light drizzle darkened the cracked concrete of the runway. While the clouds and the rain had impaired the pilots' visibility during landing, they were nevertheless welcome sights. Only a few days ago, a commercial airliner had been struck by gunfire as it landed here at Baghdad International Airport, injuring one passenger. In response, many carriers had suspended their flight operations. The culprits hadn't been caught, but Reza suspected ISIS fighters were behind the attack. With the Islamic State of Iraq and Syria quickly gaining ground in Iraq, Iran's supreme leader, in consultation with the Iranian president and the Guardian Council, had decided to discreetly send one of their top generals to meet with the Iraqi defense minister to coordinate a military response to ISIS's aggression. Reza's mission was to keep their general safe.

Since it was the Iraqis who'd be providing the bulk of the security forces, Reza had sent a two-man advance team to Baghdad to link up with the Iraqi National Intelligence Service. Reza had reviewed the details of the security package earlier that morning and had been impressed with what the Iraqis had come up with on such short notice. But would they deliver? That remained to be seen.

Rain peppered the wing of the aircraft, and Reza turned his attention to the window. The wind had picked up, and it was driving droplets like buckshot against the fuselage.

In the distance, he spotted a string of fire trucks and an ambulance parked next to a hangar, but still no military vehicles in sight. He unbuckled his seat belt and looked behind him at the eight commandos he had handpicked for today's mission. He zeroed in on his second-in-command, Captain Armeen Sadough, and motioned the officer to come over. While Reza was wearing a dark business suit to match the general's attire, Sadough and the rest wore tricolor desert camouflage uniforms. Sadough, a tall, beefy man with thick black hair and a neatly trimmed beard that didn't do much to cover the scars on his right cheek and chin, took a seat next to his commanding officer.

"Major?" Sadough said.

"Get the men together for a final brief and a comms check," Reza said while validating that his own radio was on the right frequency. "The security package the Iraqis put together for the general looks fine on paper, but I don't trust them. I'm not sure how long we'll be in Baghdad, but I want to be ready."

"Yes, sir. And for the record, I don't trust them either." Sadough's tone made it clear he wasn't a fan of the Iraqi military. "Anything else?"

"Instruct the men to keep their heads on a swivel, Armeen. The threats could come from anywhere, anytime. Including from within the Iraqis' ranks."

While the fall of Saddam Hussein in 2003 and the rise to power of pro-Iranian Shia factions in Iraq had helped normalize relations between the two countries, many inside Iran hadn't forgiven Iraq for invading their country in September 1980 and for using chemical weapons on the Iranian populace. It didn't matter that the war had ended decades ago. The dynamics between the two countries remained complex. It was the supreme leader's hope that if Iran came to the assistance of Iraq in its fight against ISIS, a delicate political equilibrium could emerge and strengthen both countries.

Reza stood and squeezed past Sadough. He moved to the other side of the plane for a better view of what was going on outside. Although Reza didn't spot anything remotely suspicious, there was still no sign of the motorcade he expected for the general.

The Dassault Falcon continued taxiing off the runway and rolled into a large holding area next to a hangar. Concerned about sniper fire, Reza was glad to see that this portion of the airport wasn't visible from the exits leading out of the airport. Certain parts of the main terminal had a direct view, but that couldn't be helped. It was for this very reason that Reza had ordered all external markings that could identify the Falcon as Iranian to be removed.

The copilot, a lieutenant colonel in the Aerospace Force of the Islamic Revolutionary Guard Corps, exited the cockpit. He approached Reza and said, "The control tower informed us a motorcade is rolling in as we speak, Major."

"Thank you, sir," Reza replied. "How much notice do you need to take off again?"

"Three, four minutes, I'd say." The copilot was already walking back toward the cockpit. "There's no need to refuel. When we get clearance from the tower, we can take off at a moment's notice."

A quick glance behind Reza confirmed that Captain Sadough was briefing the men. Satisfied that his second-in-command was taking care of the logistics, Reza approached the front of the aircraft, where the general and his aides occupied the first row of seats. The general was the first to notice him.

"Are we ready to go, Major?"

"Not yet, sir," Reza replied. "It will be a few more minutes."

The general nodded and returned his attention to the file on his lap.

The main cabin door opened, and the high-pitched whine of the Falcon's three Honeywell turbofan engines filled the jet. The pilot turned off the engines, and the noise quickly subsided, only to be replaced by the distinct rotor sound of a Russian-built Mi-28 attack helicopter. Reza craned his neck and looked out through the open cabin door in time to see the Mi-28 the Iraqis had promised land less than one hundred feet behind the Falcon.

Movement at the front of the Falcon caught Reza's eye. A medium-size Mercedes sedan with a flashing yellow light on its roof was leading an eight-car motorcade of matching dark gray SUVs with blacked-out windows toward the airplane. The convoy rolled up to the Falcon, with the fourth SUV coming to a stop a few feet from the bottom of the airstairs. Now that the vehicles were closer, Reza could see that the SUVs were all up-armored. Armed men in nondescript black uniforms poured out of the third and fifth SUVs and formed a protective cordon. The Quds Force soldiers Reza had sent to negotiate the general's security arrangement exited the sixth vehicle. Both were dressed in navy blue business suits and gave Reza a thumbs-up.

Reza turned his focus to the Iraqis, examining their demeanor, as Sadough and the other Quds Force commandos lined up behind him inside the cabin. While the newcomers' uniforms didn't carry any insignia or rank, Reza assumed the men were members of the Iraqi National Intelligence Service. They were lean and fit, with stern, hard-set faces that communicated they were there to do a serious job.

Another man, wearing a white shirt and a pair of dress pants, stepped out of the first vehicle, a small assault rifle strapped across his chest. He waved to Reza, a big smile on his face. The man was stocky and a few inches shorter than Reza's own six foot one, but his hands were the size of small shovels.

Reza climbed down the airstairs and introduced himself in Arabic.

"I'm Major Reza Ashtari, Quds Force," he said, noting that the rain had stopped.

"Uday Majid, Iraqi intelligence. I'm the motorcade commander." The man offered his hand, and Reza shook it.

"I'll let you deal with the motorcade commander, Captain Sadough," Reza said in Farsi to his second-in-command. "But I want you to ride with him at the front and have at least two of our men in the third and fifth vehicles. I'll be in the fourth with the general."

"Anything else, sir?" Sadough asked.

"Ask the commander if he'd allow our men to drive the general's vehicle," Reza said.

"That won't be a problem, Major," answered Majid in perfect Farsi. "I was about to suggest the same. And in case you haven't noticed, the general's vehicle is armored. It has ballistic glass, a plate-steel undercarriage, and run-flat tires."

Reza thanked Majid for his assistance and hurried back into the Falcon, where the copilot was waiting for him with an encrypted satellite phone. Reza used it to contact the tactical operations center in Tehran.

"This is Heaven's Gate," answered the voice of the TOC officer on duty.

"Heaven's Gate, this is Dragoon-One. We're wheels down and about to proceed toward point Bravo."

"Good copy, Dragoon-One. We see you."

The TOC was located more than four hundred miles away, but two second-generation Shahed 129s were in overwatch. The Shahed 129, a single-engine, long-endurance unmanned aerial vehicle designed in Iran, was a capable reconnaissance drone similar to the American MQ-1 Predator. The UAV was still incapable of carrying armaments, but that was a problem Iranian military scientists were working hard to fix.

Reza approached the general, who kept glancing around impatiently.

"We're ready when you are, General," Reza said.

"Any issues I should be aware of?" the general asked, putting on his suit jacket.

"No, sir."

"Then lead the way, Major Ashtari."

Reza adjusted the volume of his radio, which he had turned down prior to reentering the cabin, and reached out to Sadough to get a quick situation report.

"We're good to go, sir," Sadough informed him. "Mr. Majid confirmed we're cleared to proceed and that it shouldn't take us more than twenty or twenty-five minutes to arrive at the Ministry of Defense."

Reza stopped abruptly, steps away from the main cabin door. A street map of the route between the airport and the Iraqi Ministry of Defense complex, tucked in the northeastern corner of the Green Zone, appeared in his mind with hypothetical ambush locations manifesting as blinking red dots.

The Green Zone, an area of approximately four square miles surrounded by high concrete blast walls and accessed through a handful of controlled entry points, was the safest area in Baghdad and the center of the international presence in the city. The only way the motorcade could get there so quickly was if Majid had informed the police to clear traffic along the route they'd be taking. Usually, this would have pleased Reza. But the general's meeting with the Iraqi defense minister, although not a covert mission, was supposed to be kept under the radar. Having the police block the roads would single out the motorcade and make the general an easier target. On the other hand, hostile vehicles would be easier to spot.

"What's the holdup?" the general said with an edge of impatience.

"Nothing, sir." Reza turned his head in acknowledgment. "My apologies."

With the Quds Force commandos already in position around the motorcade, he led the way down the Falcon's airstairs, then smoothly transitioned to the rear of the general. An Iraqi bodyguard opened the armored SUV's door, and the general climbed aboard. Reza followed him in, glad to see that one of his men was seated behind the wheel. The interior was air-conditioned, and a power-operated window separated the front seat from the rear occupants.

Moments after all the bodyguards had climbed back into their vehicles, the motorcade started to roll. The convoy swung east on Airport Street, and Reza twisted in his seat just in time to see the Mi-28 take off. The helicopter quickly gained altitude and speed before gyrating toward the fast-moving motorcade.

"Relax, Reza," the general said, his voice softer now that they were alone and out of earshot. "We're here to help them. Our two countries have finally found a common enemy."

"I hope your assumption is correct, Father," Reza replied, keeping his eyes on the Mi-28.

"The ISIS threat is real for them. Their army is coming, and there's nothing Baghdad can do about it," the general said grudgingly. "The degenerates in charge of ISIS aren't listening to anyone but themselves. I'm here to show the Iraqi government that for the upcoming fight, Tehran is a better ally to them than Washington.

"In the last forty-eight hours, I've shared with the minister of defense a number of intelligence reports that prove beyond any reasonable doubt that ISIS is about to launch a large offensive on Mosul and Tikrit."

"I wasn't aware," Reza confessed, astonished that ISIS even had the strength and logistics necessary for such a sizable operation.

"You're a major, Reza, not a general. These reports are still classified."

Reza smirked. "You have assets inside ISIS, don't you?" But it wasn't really a question. His father, Major General Mohsen Ashtari, was in charge of the Islamic Revolutionary Guard Corps's clandestine military and intelligence-gathering operations. He had his fingers in pies all over the world. Some people considered him the right-hand man of the supreme leader. Knowing his father, Reza guessed that the general had ordered Quds Force spies to infiltrate ISIS a long time ago. To many

Iranians, Mohsen Ashtari was a visionary. State-controlled media had even begun talking about him becoming the next president.

"Do you think ISIS will become a bigger threat to us than the United States?" Reza asked.

"If we can't stop ISIS from taking Mosul and Tikrit, they'll keep expanding and will build a network of affiliates that could take years to fight off. That said, because of their unlawful economic sanctions against us, the Americans remain the most dangerous threat to our national security."

"The American pigs are asphyxiating us," Reza growled.

"Yes, they are, but not for much longer, my dear son. We're about to strike back, and they'll see how unwise their decision to starve our country really was. Trust me on this."

Reza wasn't convinced. "With all due respect, I've been hearing about policies designed to back the Americans into a corner for over a decade, and nothing has ever been done."

His father gave him a devious smile. "That's because we've never had a strong strategic partner before. We do now."

"Russia?" Reza asked.

"Russia's a bully," his father replied. "And they're broke. No, our new deal is with China. They too have had just about enough of the Americans."

China? Reza was stunned. He was aware of the increased tensions between Washington and Beijing, but he hadn't heard anything about a possible strategic partnership between Iran and China. Not a peep.

"What kind of deal?" he asked.

"China is calling it their Belt and Road Initiative. The details are still being ironed out, but its aim is to connect China with Africa and Europe through land and maritime infrastructure networks to stimulate economic growth across the regions. The initiative will soon become the cornerstone of China's foreign policy, and Iran will be at its center. An economic and strategic alliance like this will give us the leeway to wiggle free from the Americans' grasp. I'm flying to Beijing with our president next week to finalize the agreement. Nader's coming too."

Reza raised an eyebrow. His brother was an up-and-coming intelligence officer with the Ministry of Intelligence and Security. For years now, it had been apparent to Reza that Nader was being groomed for higher office within the Iranian spy agency. Reza had to give it to his brother: Nader knew how to make himself indispensable.

"Who else knows about this?" Reza asked.

"Everybody who needs to know," his father said. "And you."

Reza nodded, not taking the rebuttal personally. He was an operator. A shooter. His place was in the field, not in an office in Tehran. And that was perfectly fine.

"Anyhow, today's topic is the rise of ISIS," his father said, handing him a file folder. "Read this, and let me know what you think."

CHAPTER TWO

Fifteen Miles East of Baghdad

Captain Clayton White glanced behind him. The nearest Iraqi soldier was only two hundred feet away, much closer than White would have liked. Impressed by the man's performance, White picked up his pace and jogged between the two water jerricans that marked the finish line.

"Did you get lost, sir?" Technical Sergeant Oscar Pérez said, glancing at his watch. The air force NCO's left foot rested on top of one of the jerricans.

White gave him the finger. "Tomorrow's your turn. Let's see how well you'll do."

"Ten bucks says I'll beat your time by at least ten minutes," Pérez replied between sips of the sugary energy drink he enjoyed so much.

"You're on," White said, slightly out of breath.

Pérez, a fellow pararescue specialist, or PJ, gave White a thumbs-up. White dragged a dusty sleeve across his face and took his forty-five-pound rucksack off his back. The relief to his shoulders and back muscles was immediate. The grueling twelve-mile forced march across the desert had left his uniform drenched with sweat. Pale circles had formed under his armpits from the loss of body salt. The Iraqi soldier who'd been following White crossed the finish line and collapsed face first a few feet past the jerricans.

The Iraqi, who White now recognized as Lieutenant Mustafa Kaddouri, was a young officer assigned to the 1st Commando Battalion. Part of the Iraqi 1st Special Operations Brigade, the 1st Commando Battalion had a role comparable to that of US Army Rangers.

White knelt next to the fallen officer and rolled him to his side. Kaddouri grinned at him.

"I almost caught up to you, Captain," Kaddouri said in accented English.

White's eyes moved to his wristwatch. "Well done," he said, offering his hand to the man.

Kaddouri grabbed it, and White helped him to his feet.

White had started the twelve-mile journey at a brisk pace. Most of the Iraqi commandos had kept up with him for the first six miles but had gradually fallen behind when White had quickened his pace for the second half of the challenging route he'd selected. He had completed the twelve-mile journey in just under two and a half hours, despite the scorching heat and the rough terrain.

White, Pérez, and Kaddouri stood next to the finish line and fist-bumped the commandos as they walked or ran past it—all of them finishing the forced march with at least fifteen minutes of the allotted three hours to spare. White wasn't surprised. The Iraqi soldiers selected for the 1st Commando Battalion were true warriors. The United States had spent a considerable sum of money training and equipping them, and the unit had proven itself more than once in combat, often alongside American Special Forces.

"Your men have done well, Lieutenant Kaddouri," White said.

Kaddouri passed the tip of his tongue over his parched lips. "You've left them no choice," he replied. "None of them is interested in having to walk the eight miles back to base."

Walking back to base was what White had threatened for any man unable to make the time.

"What about you?" White asked. "Seems to me like you could have easily walked another ten miles."

The young officer shrugged. "This is my country. I was born of the desert, Captain. I don't mind walking."

White clapped him on the shoulder. "Good to know."

"Make sure your men are well hydrated and that every man cleans their weapon," Pérez said.

Kaddouri turned toward Pérez. "I always do, Sergeant," he said, a hint of steel in his voice. "Good soldiers under poor leadership have died out here in the sweltering summer heat. Mother Nature has no love or pity for the fool who has an insufficient water supply. I've never lost a man to dehydration or a dirty rifle."

White examined Kaddouri for a moment. The Iraqi officer was several inches shorter than White's six-foot height, but he had a massive torso, thick with muscles. While White and Pérez had only flown into Baghdad two days ago for a month-long training exercise with the 1st Commando Battalion, White had already measured Kaddouri as a capable leader and exactly the type of no-nonsense officer the Iraqi military needed to rebuild its strength.

"The helicopters will be there in twenty minutes," White said, tapping his watch with his finger. "Be ready."

Kaddouri nodded, gave Pérez a last look, and jogged back to his men.

Attached to the 24th Special Tactics Squadron—the Tier One unit of the US Air Force Special Operations Command—White had been summoned to Iraq to lead a four-week training exercise for some thirty men. With Pérez's help, White had been tasked with introducing the Iraqi soldiers to tactical evacuation procedures on the battlefield.

Which made total sense. It was White's specialty.

White, a graduate of the Air Force Academy, was a combat rescue officer. Like any PJ, he was trained to conduct conventional and unconventional rescue operations in combat environments. To join this elite group and earn the right to wear the maroon beret, White had had to endure some of the toughest training offered in the US military. Although he was a skilled deep-sea diver and trained in everything from mountain climbing to free fall parachute operations, White's true job was to lead teams of pararescuemen and other operators in personnel recovery missions.

With the imminent threat of an ISIS offensive in northern Iraq, the Iraqi military commanders had finally woken up and had invited the Americans to assess the capabilities of their only true elite infantry unit. As skilled at warfighting as they were, the members of the 1st Commando Battalion had only a limited knowledge of rescue operations in hostile territory. It was White's job to bring them to the level they needed to be. One month wasn't enough, but with ISIS breathing down their necks, White would find a way to make it work. He had to. The lives of these men might very well depend on White's ability to drill into them the basics of tactical evacuation procedures.

Saving lives. For White, there was no greater calling.

The forced march had allowed White to evaluate the commandos' level of fitness. It was now time to start the actual training phase.

"Did you brief the four youngest men of the unit like I asked you to?" White asked Pérez.

"I did," Pérez replied, pulling out two pairs of yellow earplugs from his pocket. He gave one to White. "You wanna do this now?" Pérez asked.

"Kaddouri thinks the exercise is over," White said, pushing the earplugs deep into his ears. "It's the perfect time."

He grabbed four flash-bangs, four CS gas canisters, and two gas masks from his pack. He and Pérez removed the pins and tossed the stun grenades toward the commandos. Relatively harmless, flash-bangs were designed to temporarily stun and disorient one's targets by producing a maximum of light and sound when they exploded, while the CS gas reacted with the moisture on the skin and eyes to cause uncontrollable coughing and a burning sensation in the eyes and throat. Tear gas.

The flash-bangs landed less than thirty feet away from the commandos. They detonated within seconds of each other, and the four commandos Pérez had briefed earlier went down, each simulating a different type of injury.

"Lieutenant Kaddouri, you're under accurate enemy artillery fire, and your unit has sustained four injuries," White shouted. "You have two minutes before the next salvo. What are you going to do? Report back to me with a plan."

The Iraqi officer barked a series of orders, and, within seconds, the commandos had divided the injured men's equipment and weapons among them and were rapidly moving away from the danger zone. Kaddouri ran to White and pulled a map from a chest pocket.

"Requesting a new landing zone, sir," Kaddouri said, opening the map. He tapped a finger on where he wanted the helicopters to land and gave the coordinates to White. The new landing zone Kaddouri had selected was behind a hill six hundred meters north of their current position.

"Why?" White asked.

"Sir, the hill might not save us from indirect fire, but it will conceal us from an enemy observer directing artillery or mortar fire on our position."

If White had been in Kaddouri's shoes, he would have picked the same spot.

"Very well, Lieutenant," White said. "Make contact with the chopper pilots and advise them of the changes. But what about your men?" he added. "What kind of injuries have they sustained?"

It was a trick question, but Kaddouri didn't fall for it.

"Unknown at this time," the Iraqi replied. "My first priority is to get my unit moving before the next artillery barrage."

White nodded and dismissed Kaddouri, who sprinted back to his men.

"Kaddouri's on the ball," White said. "Why don't you make it a bit more challenging for him, Sergeant?"

Pérez, who'd been waiting for that exact order, loaded the CS canisters into a launcher and fired them toward Kaddouri's men. The tear gas hissed into a thick fog and quickly enveloped the commandos.

"Gas! Gas! Gas!" White heard Kaddouri shout.

White had his gas mask ready, but the wind was keeping the tear gas away from him and Pérez.

For the next five minutes White observed the Iraqis from two hundred meters away. He was impressed with what he was seeing. He and Pérez wouldn't have to start evacuation training from scratch. The Iraqis had a pretty solid foundation.

"What do you think of Kaddouri?" White asked.

"Effective leader," Pérez replied. "Not one to take shit from anyone but takes orders well."

"They need more men like him," White said, pulling a one-gallon jug of water from his rucksack.

White took a long drink and poured some of the lukewarm water over his head and neck, enjoying the tepid flow through his hair and down the back of his uniform.

"All you need now, sir, is some aromatherapy gel and a few slices of cucumbers for your eyes," Pérez said, a smart-ass smile on his face.

White laughed out loud. He liked Pérez. They'd been working together for almost eighteen months, and Pérez was as solid as they came.

"Did you speak to your wife?" White asked.

"I tried, but the connection isn't great here. I'll try again once we're back at base."

Pérez's wife had given birth to their first child the day before. A baby girl. There had been some complications. While the newborn and her mother were now doing fine, the doctors wanted to keep an eye on them. So, out of an abundance of caution, they would remain at the hospital for a couple more days.

"How you holding up?" White asked.

"Thanks for asking, Captain, but I'm not the first guy deployed overseas whose wife has given birth. She's very close to her parents, so I know she's getting the support she needs."

"Glad to hear that," White said, not wanting to push the issue. Sometimes a man had to deal with his challenges on his own, but White wanted Pérez to know that if he needed to talk or vent, he'd be there for him.

"What about you, sir? Did you reach out to the general's daughter like I told you to?"

White sighed, his eyes fixed on the commandos who were now providing medical care to the four men feigning injuries.

"I didn't," White finally admitted with a note of disappointment. "Our schedules didn't allow for it."

"That's absolute bullshit," Pérez said, shaking his head.

White shrugged and took another pull from the water jug. Veronica Hammond, White's childhood friend and the daughter of Lieutenant General Alexander Hammond, was a very special person. White had known her almost his entire life. His father, Brigadier General Maxwell White, had served under her father twice, excluding his current assignment at JSOC. Veronica had been White's best friend until he'd entered the Air Force Academy. They had kept in touch, but the time between their phone calls had gotten longer as the years had gone by. Veronica was now a PhD candidate at Yale University and would soon travel to Greece to conduct research at an archaeological site. She was brilliant, breathtakingly beautiful, and the last person White thought about before falling asleep. During their last phone call, she had hinted at wanting to see more of him and had even wondered if he'd be interested in spending his upcoming leave with her in Greece. Caught by surprise, White had babbled some incoherent excuse before ending the call.

He'd felt like an idiot the moment he'd hung up. Veronica wasn't only the most thoughtful person he knew; she had the ability to make the people around her feel good. It was one of her gifts to the world. She deserved someone who'd make her happy every hour of every day, not some military officer whose job would take him away from home six months a year. Sure, a two-week vacation in the Greek Isles with a beautiful woman much smarter than him would be magical, but it could never work long term. Heck, White's longest relationship hadn't crossed the two-month mark. Veronica was better off without him.

Pérez crushed the aluminum can he'd been drinking from, startling White.

"Where were you, sir? The Greek Isles?" Pérez asked with a knowing smile.

"I knew I shouldn't have shared those details with you," White replied. "It was a mistake."

"Your only mistake is not calling her back," Pérez said, poking White's chest with the tip of his finger. "It's not too late."

White wasn't so sure, but he and Pérez had other things to worry about. Talking chickenshit about his personal life wasn't why they were in Iraq. They had a job to do.

"Enough of this," White said. "What about the next training evolution? Did you set it all up?"

Pérez reached for something in his backpack and said, "Everything is set up like you wanted, and I talked to command less than two hours ago. We're good to go, sir."

Pérez grinned as he found what he was looking for. He pulled out two more cans of energy drink and offered one to White.

He shook his head. "You keep drinking these and your heart's going to pop, brother," White said, only half joking, as he watched the two approaching Russian-built Mi-17 transport helicopters.

Pérez gave him a dismissive wave of the hand. "They keep me motivated," he said, cracking the first can open and slurping the spill off the top. "Stop being such a wuss, sir. Live a little."

CHAPTER THREE

Washington, DC

Lieutenant General Alexander Hammond, commanding officer of the Joint Special Operations Command, wondered what great warfare tacticians like Alexander the Great and Julius Caesar would think of him if they were to see him now. The objective of war was the same as it had been a thousand years ago: to kill people. What had changed were the methods. Career soldiers like Hammond could now sit in climate-controlled headquarters and rain down death without ever getting their boots dirty. The introduction of drones and other precision weapons systems had softened some of the most primitive things about armed conflicts. Hammond, unlike Alexander the Great, wouldn't have to smell the awful odor of a gut wound or hear the screams of the men he was about to kill. But that didn't mean the process of having one's enemies killed was stress-free.

Hammond inhaled a long, deep breath and did his best to remain calm. It wasn't an easy task. He was responsible for the planning and execution of American special operations missions worldwide. As such, he wished he could be in North Carolina, where JSOC's headquarters was located, instead of where he presently was: a small conference room adjacent to the White House Situation Room. Placing a headset on his head, Hammond confirmed he had good comms with the JSOC operations center.

There were about a dozen people crammed into the space. An oval conference table occupied the center of the room. An untouched platter of assorted sandwiches was laid out on the table next to several carafes of coffee. The hushed conversations among the senior White House officials present stopped when the president of the United States entered and took his seat to Hammond's immediate left.

"All right," the president said, his calm voice doing nothing to lessen the palpable tension in the room. "Where are we at?"

On the large flat screen fixed to the wall, the presidential seal was replaced by a live feed from an MQ-9 Reaper drone already in flight.

"The Iranian aircraft touched down without incident, Mr. President," Hammond replied.

"Like we knew it would," added Secretary of Defense Isaac Hughes.

Hammond cringed inwardly at Hughes's words. It wasn't a secret to anyone that Hammond wasn't a fan of Secretary Hughes, a small, shrewish man with an unsmiling face who had never served a single day in the military. If Hughes had lived in the times of Julius Caesar or Alexander the Great, he would have been executed for incompetence. Of course, this option wasn't available to Hammond, so he had to endure the fool.

Hammond understood why Hughes had summoned him. Since it was Hammond who had orchestrated the operation, the SecDef wanted him present. Officially, Hammond was there to answer any question the president might field, but he wasn't duped. The real reason for his presence was to provide Hughes with a culprit in case of mission failure.

Hammond had put a target on Major General Mohsen Ashtari's head years ago, right after the general had authorized the killing of American foreign diplomats by Iran-linked operatives. Although most of the attacks had been thwarted, two American ambassadors had barely escaped with their lives after their official vehicles had been ambushed. In response, Hammond had tried to eliminate General Ashtari three times by sending Tier One operators after him. Twice in Syria, and once in Iran itself. Three missions, three misses. It seemed as though every time the Tier One operators were about to close in on him for the kill, the general vanished into thin air.

A week ago, the CIA had shared with the president its belief that Mohsen Ashtari was about to green-light a second wave of targeted assassinations of American diplomats. Even though the CIA had been unable to provide hard evidence, the president had ordered Hammond to stop Ashtari at all costs.

"I'm done playing with this degenerate asswipe, General," the president had memorably said.

Hammond had gone to work, and for once, chance had been on his side. General Ashtari was scheduled to travel to Baghdad, giving Hammond a prime opportunity to move against him.

Today's gonna be different, he thought, confident that if Ashtari was indeed in the Dassault Falcon they were seeing on the screen, they were all witnessing his final minutes on earth.

The quality of the live feed captured by the MQ-9 Reaper drone's camera was superb considering the weather. An Mi-28 helicopter landed behind the Falcon, and, moments later, an eight-vehicle motorcade stopped next to the plane. Men disembarked from the vehicles and fanned out around the motorcade.

Hammond activated his headset's microphone.

"Zoom in on their faces," he ordered.

Moments later, the drone's camera switched to their faces. Hammond, his throat dry and tight, was at the edge of his seat. It took him a few seconds, but when he found the person he was looking for, a brief smile appeared on his lips.

Uday Majid was there. As promised. As paid for. For the last ten years, Majid had been the CIA's most prized asset within the Iraqi National Intelligence Service. Hammond didn't know how much the CIA was paying Majid, but he was worth every penny.

A single man exited the Falcon and met with the Iraqi motorcade commander. Hammond examined the newcomer's face. It wasn't Mohsen Ashtari.

"Who's that?" Secretary Hughes asked, reaching for the platter at the middle of the conference table and helping himself to what looked like a turkey sandwich.

Hammond was pretty sure who it was, but he opened the laptop in front of him and refreshed the screen. He scrolled down to the bottom of the operational plan. He examined several photos and took the extra second he needed to confirm the man's identity.

"That is Reza Ashtari, sir," Hammond replied, a frisson of excitement running through him. "The general's son. He's a major in the Quds Force, and the Agency thinks he was one of the team leaders involved in the attack on our diplomats in Azerbaijan a couple years back."

The president's eyes were on Hammond. "Did we know he'd be on this trip?"

"We didn't, Mr. President," Hammond said. "The most recent intel we have shows him to be in Syria training progovernment militias."

"I'm not impressed, General," Hughes cut in between bites of his sandwich. "What else did you miss? Anything that could jeopardize the mission?"

Hammond clenched his fists and looked at Hughes with undisguised contempt. But before he could say something he'd surely regret, the president put a hand on his shoulder. "In your opinion, General Hammond, what's General Ashtari's son doing in Iraq?"

Hammond turned his attention to his commander-in-chief. "My guess is that he's being groomed for higher command within the Quds Force, sir. There's also the possibility that he's acting as his father's aide-de-camp, or even as one of his bodyguards."

The president's eyes moved to Jennifer Alleyne, the White House chief counsel.

"Does that change anything for us, Jennifer?"

Alleyne, a red-haired woman in her early forties, shrugged. "Frankly, sir, I don't think so. The Quds Force has been designated a terrorist organization by the US government since 2007. Major Ashtari is a legitimate target, and once this comes out, public opinion will be on our side."

Hammond nodded his thanks to Alleyne. The White House chief counsel had a quiet yet powerful presence that intimidated most men.

Especially that schmuck Hughes, Hammond thought, his eyes moving to the SecDef. The man, his mouth full of sandwich, had his hand stretched out toward the platter again.

On the flat screen, men dressed in business attire disembarked from the Falcon. They rapidly boarded different SUVs before Hammond could confirm the presence of Major General Ashtari. Nevertheless, he was confident he knew in which SUV the general would make the trip to the Green Zone.

"Did anyone recognize Ashtari or see which vehicle he climbed into?" Secretary Hughes asked, shoving a large piece of sandwich into his open mouth.

"I tracked Major Ashtari and another person, possibly our primary target, to the fourth vehicle," Hammond said without hesitation. "It's the only vehicle for which a bodyguard opened and closed the door for the occupants. I'm positive the fourth vehicle is the one being used to transport the general."

"You're positive?" Hughes asked. "Really? What does that even mean?"

Hammond didn't answer but angled his head toward Hughes just as a big blob of mustard fell from the sandwich onto the SecDef's tie.

The president leaned back in his chair and put his hands behind his head, a weary look on his face. "This better pan out, Alexander, because it might be the last chance we'll get to eliminate General Ashtari. If we miss and there's another attack on our diplomats, full-fledged war with Iran is possible."

"I understand, sir," Hammond replied, not remembering the president ever calling him by his first name before. He had done everything he possibly could to ensure mission success. Even the CIA had chipped in and given him access to Uday Majid, their inside man. But the truth was, there were so many variables that despite his best efforts, the outcome was far from being guaranteed.

The mission commander's voice came through Hammond's headset. "It's confirmed, sir. General Ashtari and two other Quds Force soldiers are aboard the motorcade's fourth vehicle. Are we clear to engage?"

"Stand by for permission to engage," Hammond replied.

"Roger. Standing by."

Hammond could feel the president's eyes on him. He pointed to the flat-screen television. "As you can see, sir, the motorcade is presently heading eastbound on Airport Street. And thanks to our asset who ensured that most access points were blocked, traffic is light. If we strike now, we don't expect much in unforeseen collateral damage."

The president took a deep breath and looked around him. "Any last-minute objections?"

Hammond half expected Hughes to say something, but the man kept his mouth shut, which was a good thing since the already small window of opportunity to strike was getting smaller by the second.

"Okay, General Hammond, you have my authorization."

Hammond relaxed as he keyed the headset's mic. "Permission granted," he said. "You're clear to engage."

"Good copy. We are clear to engage," replied the mission commander.

Hammond put down his headset and turned on the speaker so that everyone in the room could hear the exchange between the mission commander and the drone pilot. The Reaper was carrying a contingent of two AGM 114 air-to-ground Hellfire missiles and two GBU-12

Paveway laser-guided bombs. It should take only one Hellfire to destroy their target.

"I have good visual," the calm but very young-sounding pilot said. "Missile away."

It was only then that Secretary Hughes's hand shot up, his finger pointing at the flat screen. "What are they doing?"

Hammond's eyes moved to the live feed, and he had to resist the urge to slam his fist on the conference table. Two security vehicles had suddenly flanked the fourth SUV.

Shit, he thought, knowing that the mission had just taken a turn for the worse.

CHAPTER FOUR

Baghdad, Iraq

Major Reza Ashtari opened the folder his father had given him and started reviewing the impressive strategy his father had put together to stop the advancing ISIS army. There was no way Reza could read it all before their meeting with the defense minister, but it didn't matter. He wasn't the one who'd have to sell it to the Iraqis, and it wasn't as if his father would modify it based on his critique. Nevertheless, Reza appreciated his father's trust in sharing it with him. What struck him most about the plan was how much military power his father was ready to deploy to Iraq. Yes, the Iranian government was concerned about the rise of ISIS, but Reza had no idea that an actual invasion of his country was considered likely if ISIS wasn't destroyed while still in Iraq. The Americans would think twice about starting a war with Iran once they learned about the upcoming strategic partnership between Tehran and Beijing, but ISIS couldn't care less. They were uneducated brutes.

A bump in the road broke Reza's concentration, and he looked outside. Above and to the right of the speeding motorcade, the Mi-28 darted out front, providing top cover and scanning the roadway ahead. The land surrounding the highway was flat and lined with scrubby palm trees, but the pavement was free of the usual scorch marks left by roadside bombs. It hadn't always been the case.

"Did you know this was once the most dangerous stretch of highway in the world?" his father asked.

"Of course," Reza said, still focused on the operational plan.

"Do you know why?"

Something in his father's voice caused Reza to stop reading.

"This road was the most critical line of supply in and out of Iraq," Reza said. "With all the American military convoys traversing it daily, it was a target-rich environment for the insurgents."

His father nodded. "For years militias trained by us owned that strip of concrete, Reza. The militias ambushed American supply convoys almost every day."

"The Quds Force were involved?" Reza asked, surprised. Back when al-Qaeda and other insurgents controlled the 7.5-mile route to and from the Green Zone, Reza was still attending the military academy in Tehran. That tidbit of information about the Quds Force's involvement had been left out of the books at the military academy.

"Not only did the Quds Force supply the militias with weapons, we also took part in many of the raids against American high-value targets," the general said.

"Wasn't that careless? What if the Americans had captured one of us?" Reza asked. "It could have been catastrophic."

A devilish smile appeared on his father's lips. "The Americans aren't the only ones with deniable assets," he said. "You know that, and very soon you'll see more examples of our global reach."

"What do you mean?" Reza asked, intrigued.

"All in due time, my son," his father said, looking away and out the window. "All in due time."

Reza had always seen his father as bold and audacious. The general wasn't one to show fear in the face of adversity. He had achieved much in his long and illustrious career, and Reza still had much to learn from him.

In Reza's ear, Captain Sadough's voice came through the radio, interrupting his train of thought.

"To all Dragoon call signs, this is Dragoon-Six. Be alert," Sadough said. "The Mi-28 pilot just informed the motorcade commander of a red vehicle ahead that is backing down an on-ramp onto the road."

Reza assumed that the Iraqi motorcade commander had sent the same message to his men because the bodyguard seated in the front passenger seat spoke to the Quds Force driver in Farsi. To Reza's left and right, the lead and follow armored SUVs maneuvered to flank their vehicle in order to shield it from potential incoming enemy fire.

Reza's heart rate increased but he wasn't worried. The Mi-28 attack helicopter was a formidable adversary and would make quick work of any genuine threat.

"What's happening?" Reza's father asked, looking left and right at the flanking SUVs.

Reza told him about the vehicle ahead.

"Even if word of my visit has somehow gotten out, none of the militias operating in Iraq would dare touch me," the general said, brushing off any concerns with a wave of his hand.

"Dragoon-Six from Dragoon-One," Reza called on the radio. "Any updates?"

"I'm in contact with Heaven's Gate, Dragoon-One," Sadough replied. "Stand by."

Reza craned his neck to get a better view of what was going on at the front of the motorcade. What he saw next froze him in place. The Mi-28, which was flying well in front of them at an altitude of two hundred feet, banked sharply right and began to fire flares and chaff decoys. Then, to Reza's right, there was an orange streak of light. A fraction of a second later, the SUV protecting their right flank exploded with a deafening blast, and the world around him became a giant fireball. Reza's right eardrum burst in pain.

The Quds Force driver swerved, battling to keep all four tires on the road, but it was an impossible task. It was as if an unseen force wanted to raise the SUV and snatch it up from underneath its suspension. The SUV tilted up and rolled onto its driver's side before flipping twice, sparks flying each time the metal ground against the asphalt. When the SUV finally skidded to a stop, Reza had already succumbed to the blackness.

CHAPTER FIVE

Washington, DC

Hammond watched helplessly as the missile struck the security vehicle and exploded. The intensity of the blast was enough to cause the general's vehicle to roll on its side, but Hammond doubted its occupants were dead.

Shit.

"What the hell just happened?" Secretary Hughes asked, out of breath, as if he had just climbed ten flights of stairs.

Hammond didn't bother replying. As if the SecDef's question had opened a valve, the small conference room erupted into a cacophony of shouts as everyone started asking questions of their own.

Hammond shut them all out, even the president. He could still salvage this. He grabbed the headset and turned off the speaker. He needed to concentrate. The Reaper had only one Hellfire missile left, and they couldn't afford to miss. He didn't know why the two security vehicles had suddenly flanked General Ashtari's vehicle, but it didn't matter. In combat, unexpected things happened all the time. How rapidly the person in charge was able to adapt to the new situation would determine the outcome of the engagement.

He triggered the headset's microphone and said, "Have the pilot circle back. I want the next missile on target within thirty seconds."

The mission commander's reply was immediate. "Yes, sir. I've already given that order. But it will take the pilot at least two minutes to reposition. Will advise when ready to fire."

Damn. Two minutes was too much time. On the flat screen, Hammond saw what he assumed to be a mix of Iraqi and Iranian security forces climbing out of their vehicles and running toward the flipped SUV. The window for a second missile strike was already closed. A sudden chill ran through Hammond as he felt General Ashtari escaping from his grasp once again. His face turned red, and he took a deep breath to get his anger under control. He wasn't out of the fight just yet.

"Cancel the drone strike," Hammond ordered. "Have the Reaper stay in overwatch."

"I copy your last, sir. Drone will remain in overwatch," the mission commander replied.

"Give me all the assets we have available in and around Baghdad," Hammond said. "Now!"

Hammond sensed the mission commander wasn't too happy about being micromanaged from the White House, but Hammond didn't care. The conference room had quieted down, and all eyes were on him.

"Sir, we have less than two hundred personnel in Iraq," the mission commander said.

Hammond winced inwardly. "How many of them are combat ready?"

"There's a Special Forces team in northern Iraq training with Peshmerga forces, but that's pretty much it, sir. The rest of our forces are mostly logistics."

Hammond dismissed the Special Forces team. Even if he could establish contact with them, they were too far away to be of any use.

"Hang on, sir," the mission commander said. "One of my aides just told me there's a two-man PJ team from the 24th Special Tactics Squadron in Baghdad. They're actually in the air right now aboard two Mi-17s with elements of the Iraqi 1st Commando Battalion."

Hammond's mood brightened. PJs were some of the most polyvalent and resourceful members of the military. He could work with that.

"What are they doing in Baghdad?" Hammond asked.

"Give me a second, sir," the mission commander replied. "We're looking into it."

Hammond felt someone's presence behind him. Without turning around, he knew it was Hughes. Clearly the man wanted to ask him what was going on, but Hammond ignored him. He had to react fast to what was happening on the ground, and he didn't have a single second to waste explaining and justifying his every move to an incompetent politician. To Hammond, it seemed like everyone but Hughes understood the situation. Even the president was silent.

"They've been in theater for less than forty-eight hours," the mission commander said. "Seems like they're running a month-long training exercise with members of the Iraqi military."

Hammond's mind went into overdrive as different scenarios appeared and disappeared in his head. They wouldn't be able to get near the convoy without undue exposure. But there was a good chance either General Ashtari or his son had been injured in the initial explosion. Anything less than a life-threatening injury and his bodyguards would retreat back to the Falcon in order to return to Iran in the most expedient way. But if the security forces directed the general to the nearest hospital . . .

Hammond felt Hughes's hand touch his shoulder, but he refused to acknowledge the gesture. If Hammond didn't act fast, General Ashtari would once again escape, and this time, the price of failure could be war with Iran.

"You said they were in the air, right? Can you be more specific than that?" Hammond asked.

"We're trying to figure that out, sir. Bear with me."

Hammond's jaw tightened as he managed to control his impatience.

Then, the hand that had been touching his shoulder started tapping it to get his attention. This time, and despite his best effort, Hammond stood, spinning his six-foot-four frame toward Hughes so fast that it made the SecDef stumble backward and fall on his ass, knocking over a fresh platter of sandwiches on his way down. A young aide came to the SecDef's side to help him up but backed away when Hammond gave him a death stare.

Hammond was about to say something, but the president raised his hand and said, "Why don't you take a break and go clean yourself up, Isaac?"

Hammond didn't see the SecDef's face turn crimson red in embarrassment; he had already returned to his chair, focusing on what was important.

"The PJs are less than three minutes' flight from General Ashtari's motorcade, sir," the mission commander said in Hammond's headset.

"Okay. What else can you tell me about the two PJs?"

"One NCO and one officer. The NCO is Technical Sergeant Oscar Pérez. He's a decorated combat veteran who's seen action in Iraq and Afghanistan. Same applies for the officer he's with. Captain Clayton White."

Hammond pursed his lips and sucked in a big breath of air. *Clayton White*. Could his luck have finally turned?

"Are you in contact with the Mi-17 pilots?" Hammond asked.

"Negative, but we've figured out a way to track Captain White via his satellite phone."

"Understood. Stand by for further instructions," Hammond said, reaching for the secure landline next to his laptop.

He picked up the receiver and waited for the White House switchboard operator, placing the call on speaker so that the president could hear. "I'm in the Situation Room with the president, and I need you to immediately patch me through to Brigadier General Maxwell White over at JSOC."

"Yessir. Right away."

As he waited, Hammond angled his head toward the president. The president's face was tense, and his eyes had an urgent look, but he gave Hammond a confident smile. There was a series of beeps and clicks, then General White's powerful voice came on the line.

"This is General White, sir."

"Maxwell, this is Alexander," Hammond said. "I'm with the president in the Situation Room. We need your undivided attention. Can you give it to us?"

"Yes, sir. I'm alone in my office."

Hammond took twenty seconds to brief his friend on the situation in Baghdad. When he was done, it was the president who spoke next.

"General White, this is the president. My next question might seem insensible, but I need you to answer it truthfully."

If Maxwell White was intimidated or taken aback to be on a conference call with the president, he didn't show it.

"Shoot, sir," was his reply.

"How would Clayton react if I was to ask him to kill a man?"

General White didn't hesitate, not even for one moment. "My son's tough as nails. If he's convinced his action will save lives, he'll do what you ask of him."

Hammond glanced at the president, who nodded.

"Understood," Hammond replied. "Then here's what I want you to do, Maxwell."

CHAPTER SIX

Five Miles East of Baghdad

Clayton White shielded his eyes from the swirling maelstrom of sand as the two Mi-17 helicopters landed one hundred feet away from where he was standing. The rotors kicked up loose dust and dirt, forming a dense cloud of sand. Within seconds, the well-trained troops were all aboard, and the Mi-17s lifted back into the air.

White put on the intercom-link headphones and signaled Lieutenant Kaddouri and Technical Sergeant Pérez to do the same.

"Load up was smooth and well executed," White said. "And I like the speed at which you and your men left the danger zone. You didn't mess around with the injured men, which was a good call. Getting your unit out was the priority. Damn impressive if you ask me."

"Thank you, sir," Kaddouri replied. "My men are young, but they're eager to learn and get better. They know they'll be called upon if ISIS continues its advance."

The Iraqi officer was right. In recent months, a new kind of disorder had rocked the Middle East. Amid the increased violence and volatility in the aftermath of the Arab Spring uprisings, the United States had transferred to the region significantly more military aid than it had originally intended after its withdrawal from Iraq. With the rise of ISIS, the Middle East appeared to be more unstable now than ever before.

If that's even possible, White thought, looking down at the passing scenery.

Lieutenant Kaddouri pointed a finger toward Baghdad.

"It will flourish again," Kaddouri said without much conviction.

"Yeah, I'm sure it will," Pérez said, matching Kaddouri's tone.

From an altitude of two thousand feet, White saw how Baghdad could have been beautiful some five decades ago. Earlier that day, while enjoying a quick breakfast at the officers' mess, Kaddouri had shared that his great-grandfather, who had lived in Baghdad during the early 1950s, could go for hours-long walks with his wife far away from their home and come back after dark without being harassed by the authorities. At that time Iraqi women went to school and had jobs, and young people played at public pools and partied at nightclubs without fear. The assassination of Iraqi prime minister Nuri al-Said in 1958 had changed all that. Now, after decades of war and civil conflict, White was afraid that Iraq would never regain its former glory. But he was thankful that men like Lieutenant Kaddouri hadn't given up just yet. Baghdad might not be the international emblem it once was, but Iraq was still home to some of the world's most beautiful archeological sites. Veronica had often talked about how much she'd love to travel to Syria and Iraq to explore their secrets. But Syria's civil war and the recent ISIS push had seriously dampened her enthusiasm.

"Apparently, these ISIS pukes consider the preservation of historical ruins a form of idolatry," she'd complained to White. "So they're deliberately destroying hundreds of them. Can you believe this? It's a cultural genocide!"

White certainly could believe it. He had seen pictures and read reports about the destruction of numerous ancient sites and artifacts. White was glad Veronica had chosen to go to Greece instead of spending time in some war-torn country. He chuckled at the realization that he was once again thinking about Veronica. He was on a training mission in what was still considered a hazardous region, yet his brain wouldn't stop ticking over to her. Should he reconsider the trip to Greece? It would be one hell of a vacation. A bit of fun amid a personal life he'd allowed to grow stale lately.

Live a little, Pérez had said.

Maybe the man's right, White thought. Maybe he could show up unannounced and surprise her? He dismissed the idea, shuddering at the thought. She wouldn't like that.

Feeling Pérez's eyes on him, White turned to face him. As if the PJ could read right through him, Pérez smirked and made the "call her" hand gesture, mouthing the words.

White was about to give him the middle finger when the satellite phone on his chest rig rang. There were fewer than fifty people who had his number, and White couldn't imagine any of them calling him for anything other than an emergency. He removed his headset and pressed the sat phone hard against his ear, cupping his hand over his mouth in an effort to block out the rotor noise.

"This is White."

"Clay, it's me."

White's entire body tensed as he recognized his father's voice despite the roar of the helicopter blades chopping up the humid afternoon air.

"Is Mom all right?" he asked, instantly concerned something had happened to her. His father wasn't one to call for chitchat.

"What? No. Your mother's fine, Clay."

White let out a sigh of relief.

"I'll call you back in fifteen," he replied. "I'm in a chopper—"

"Negative, Captain," his father interrupted. "Do not hang up."

White was momentarily shocked by his father's tone. What the hell was going on?

"Are you there, son?"

"I'm listening."

"I just hung up with General Hammond," his father said. "There's something important he needs you to do."

39

"Does he know I'm in Iraq? I'm not in—"

"He knows, Clay. That's why he and the president reached out."

The president? Had he heard his father correctly?

"Okay . . ."

"Minutes ago, we almost took out General Mohsen Ashtari with a drone strike," his father said.

White was stunned. The Iranian general had been at the top of the kill list for years. Rumors had it that the Tier One guys had tried several times to take him out but had never been able to get to the sonofabitch.

"In Iraq?" White asked. "And you said *almost*. Why? Did the attack fail?"

"We're not sure if the missile strike failed or not," his father replied. "Hammond said the missile hit one of the security vehicles but that the blast toppled the SUV carrying the general. It happened only a few miles from your current position."

It didn't take a genius to figure out what Hammond wanted him to do.

"You want me to go take a look? See if the asshole's dead?"

"That's part of it, son," his father said. "But if he isn't, you're to kill him."

Is this for real? White thought. But he knew the answer.

"It's only me and another PJ," he said. "What kind of opposition forces are we looking at?"

"We believe General Ashtari is protected by members of the INIS and by a small contingent of Quds Force commandos. His son Reza, a Quds Force officer, was also in the same vehicle."

White's mind was spinning. It would be tricky to get to the Iranian general. As if his father could read his thoughts, he said, "I know I'm throwing at you a highly complex scenario, son, but you have carte blanche to do what you feel is necessary to accomplish your mission."

White remained silent as he processed the information he'd been given. His father continued, "The president believes that General

Ashtari is about to green-light an attack against American diplomats. If that were to happen, the president's response would be robust, and the whole damn world could find itself on the brink of war if China or Russia were to back the Iranians."

White cleared his throat; it had gone uncharacteristically dry. "I understand."

"Be clever about this, Clay," his father said. "We have eyes in the sky, and we'll back you up as much as we can.

"I'm sending you the mission commander's direct line," he added, "and a link to the drone feed. Reach out to him, and he'll give you an accurate picture of what's waiting for you on the ground."

"Yessir," White replied automatically, even though he had yet to wrap his mind around what he was being asked to do.

"Good luck, my son. And be careful."

The line went dead. To his left, Pérez was staring at him. "What's going on, sir?"

White gestured for him to wait and asked Kaddouri to order the pilots to fly a holding pattern. Kaddouri gave him a strange look but did as he was told. White dug into his rucksack for the military-issued secured tablet he always kept close by. Connecting the tablet to his satellite phone, he pressed his thumb against the thumb pad. A box appeared on screen, asking White for the ten-digit password that would initiate the download. Moments later, a single untitled file materialized on the screen. He opened it, angled the tablet in a way that Pérez could see, and started to watch the drone feed.

"What am I looking at?" Pérez asked.

White shared what his father had told him. If Pérez was wary about the 180-degree alteration of their mission objective, he kept it to himself. White knew it would take much more than that to rattle the hardened combat veteran's cage.

"How do you want to play this?" Pérez asked.

White's mind scrolled through the limited options he had to complete the surreal task he'd just been given.

"The way I see it, we'll need to involve Kaddouri and his men," White said, closing the gap with Pérez so that his mouth was just above the other man's ear.

Pérez nodded in agreement.

"Here's what I propose we do," White said, then started laying out his strategy.

When he was done, Pérez shrugged and said, "Risky, for sure. But why not? It's worth a try."

White was about to reach out to Kaddouri when the helicopter banked sharply to the left.

"Sir, the pilot informed me that he's been notified that a military convoy has just been hit by what seemed to be an IED," Kaddouri said. "There are several critically injured VIPs. We're the closest medevac, so—"

"VIPs, you said?" White asked, playing dumb—and relieved he wouldn't have to fight with Kaddouri to get the helicopters rerouted toward the motorcade. "Who are they?"

"I don't know, sir. But we're headed there now. We're less than two minutes out."

White gave him a thumbs-up. "We'll do our best to help you guys out."

CHAPTER SEVEN

Baghdad, Iraq

Reza opened his eyes, gasping for breath. For several seconds, he was disoriented and wasn't sure what had happened. The left side of his face felt numb, and he was pretty sure his right collarbone had snapped in two.

He blinked twice, and the interior of the SUV came into focus. When his vision cleared, he saw his father resting against the door to his left, moaning and bleeding, his suit jacket coated in blood.

If he's moaning, he's alive.

Reza studied his own predicament. He was dangling from the shoulder harness, and the overpowering stench of burning fuel made his stomach heave. In his ear, Captain Sadough was screaming incoherently over the radio.

I have to get out, he thought. He wanted to reach for his father, but he couldn't. He was too weak and in too much pain to do anything. Then the door opened. Hands tugged at him before a pair of powerful arms grabbed him underneath the armpits. Reza let himself be lifted. He yelled, the pain so intense he almost stopped breathing. Someone carried him away from the vehicle. People were shouting. He was gently dropped onto the grass.

In Reza's mouth, a mix of blood and bile. And a few loose teeth.

Assaulted by the odor of burning flesh, he let his head roll toward the smell. Behind him, less than one hundred feet away, the frame of a half-destroyed SUV was visible. He stared at the charred bodies still trapped inside the burning vehicle.

Then it hit him. *Drone strike.*

Surely the attack hadn't been random.

The Americans. It had to be them. They were the only ones daring enough to try to take out his father on Iraqi soil. Shoving the pain away, Reza forced himself to think. How long had it been since the missile strike? Two minutes? Three? He knew that whoever had attacked them would have eyes on the target. That meant they'd be aware that the first missile had destroyed the wrong SUV. The drone was no doubt already circling back to take another shot.

They needed to get his father out of the disabled SUV. Now.

It took everything he had, but Reza pushed through the excruciating pain in his right shoulder and propped himself up on his elbows. Two Quds Force commandos were sprinting toward the general's SUV, which had thick black smoke spilling out from the edges of its hood. Reza willed them to move faster. He watched the commandos climb onto the toppled vehicle just as two Iraqi Air Force helicopters flew over the motorcade so low that Reza feared the commandos would be hit by the landing gear. The helicopters flared and touched down just north of the convoy, their rotor blades kicking up sand and dust.

Men in Iraqi military uniform jumped out and formed two groups. The first quickly established an outer security perimeter while the second smaller contingent ran to his father's vehicle carrying gurneys and medical kits.

An Iraqi soldier, his shoulder patch identifying him as a member of the 1st Commando Battalion, knelt next to Reza and started to examine him by checking his vital signs. Reza tried to wave him away, but he didn't have the strength. A second later, his eyes opened wide and he stifled a curse when the commando patted down his left leg, a shock wave of pain radiating along its length. Seeing Reza's reaction, the commando used scissors to cut through Reza's trousers from his waist down to his feet. That's when Reza saw the vile bruise that marked where his leg was broken.

A hundred feet away, members of the 1st Commando Battalion were giving a hand to Reza's men in retrieving his father from the crashed SUV.

"How did you get here so fast?" Reza asked in Arabic, grabbing the man's arm.

"The only thing I know was that we were training a few miles away and were suddenly rerouted here," the commando replied. "And don't worry, your leg will be fine."

Reza wasn't concerned about his leg. He was trying to understand what had happened.

Behind the Iraqi commando, Reza observed his father being put on a stretcher and carried away, an oxygen masked strapped to his face. Four Quds Force soldiers tried to follow, but an Iraqi officer and half a dozen commandos blocked their way. His busted eardrum combined with the noise coming from the helicopters didn't allow Reza to hear the argument between the two groups. But it appeared the Iraqis weren't going to let his father's security detail climb into the same chopper.

Why were the Iraqis refusing to let his father's bodyguards accompany him in the helicopter? It didn't make sense. Something wasn't right. As the commando next to him worked on stabilizing his leg, Reza looked into the man's eyes, trying to determine his true intent, but he only saw empathy and determination.

"Where are you taking him?" Reza asked, nodding toward his father.

The commando looked in that direction. "Same place you're going. Medical City," he said, while gesturing to one of his colleagues to join him.

A second commando arrived, and Reza felt himself being rolled to his side as a stretcher was slipped underneath him. For a brief moment, he thought he was going to pass out from the pain in his leg. The commandos secured him to the stretcher before carrying him toward the first chopper, the one in which his father had been loaded.

"Not in this one," someone yelled in Arabic. "He goes with the others."

At first, Reza wasn't sure who the man was referring to, but when the commandos transporting him changed direction and headed to the second helicopter, Reza understood it was him. Trying to catch a glimpse of his father, he rolled his head to his right, incapable of moving the rest of his body. For the briefest moment, he did see his father, and his heart leaped into his throat.

His injured father wasn't alone inside the helicopter.

The Iraqi officer Reza had spotted earlier was there, and so were two other men wearing combat fatigues. But they weren't Iraqis. The American flag on their shoulders told Reza everything he needed to know about their identities.

And then everything clicked into place, and Reza opened his mouth to scream for help.

CHAPTER EIGHT

Baghdad, Iraq

"We need to take off now," White said.

Kaddouri shook his head and pointed toward two commandos carrying a stretcher.

"Not yet," he said. "There's room for one more."

The commandos were steps away from the chopper, and White recognized the injured man from the pictures the mission commander had sent to his tablet.

Reza Ashtari.

The commandos were about to load the stretcher into the chopper when Pérez yelled in Arabic for them to back off. For White's plan to work, he had to make it look like General Ashtari had died from the injuries he'd sustained during the drone strike. It wouldn't take long for the Iraqis to figure out the United States was behind the attack. They probably wouldn't detain White and Pérez since they weren't directly involved in the missile strike, but they wouldn't hesitate to arrest them if they believed they had anything to do with the general's death. That meant they had to be alone with General Ashtari.

White caught only a short glimpse of Reza Ashtari as the two commandos backed away from the chopper, but it was enough to see that the man's eyes were fixated on the American flag on his shoulder. The look of panic on Ashtari's face told White he had to act.

White jumped off the helicopter and rushed to Ashtari's side. He clamped his hand tightly over the man's mouth and nose. Ashtari tried to yell, but White's hand muffled the sound. Ashtari struggled against his restraints and shook his head, his eyes going wild. As easy as it would be for White to plunge his combat knife into Ashtari's neck and cut it open from ear to ear, the Quds Force major wasn't the mission. He was a guest of the Iraqi government. Killing him would guarantee only one thing: mission failure. Nevertheless, when Ashtari attempted to bite his finger off, White didn't hesitate to hammer fist him in the face, crushing his nose and knocking him out cold. The force of the blow caused the two Iraqi commandos to drop the stretcher. They stared at him, confused, but White didn't have the time to enlighten them.

Climbing back into the first helicopter, he signaled a startled Lieutenant Kaddouri that he wanted to take off right away.

"I don't understand," Kaddouri started, baffled by what he had just witnessed. "Why did—"

"Sorry about that," White said. "I wanted to check if his injuries were serious, and the idiot tried to bite me. I reacted without thinking."

"But—"

"Lieutenant Kaddouri, wake the hell up!" White shouted, pointing a finger at the Iranian general. "This man needs immediate medical attention or he's gonna die. We can't wait any longer. Let's go! We'll come back for the others."

Kaddouri nodded and ordered the pilot to get going. The helicopter lifted off.

Notwithstanding the fact that his orders had come from the very top, White wasn't happy about them. He didn't relish what he was about to do. Truth was, if it had been anyone else but Major General Mohsen Ashtari tied to the stretcher in front of him, White would have disobeyed a direct order. White was an officer of the US Air Force, not an assassin. But General Ashtari wasn't anyone else. He was a terrorist who had ordered the murders of many of White's countrymen, and the president of the United States believed he was about to do it again. If killing Ashtari meant saving even one American life, it was White's duty to make sure it was done.

If the roles were reversed, the Quds Force commanding officer would have no qualms about sending his thugs to chat with White using sharp objects like scissors or bone saws as conversation starters.

In White's professional opinion, General Ashtari would have probably died of his wounds if they'd been more than a fifteen-minute helicopter ride from the nearest ICU. But the pilot had estimated the flight time to the hospital at less than eight minutes, which didn't leave White much time to act. The general's breathing was fast and shallow, his pulse weak. That usually meant that unless immediate medical attention was given, one's stint on earth was nearly over. Still, White simply couldn't take the chance that some hotshot Iraqi surgeon might save the general's life, could he?

He grabbed a medical kit and unclipped his seat harness. He then secured himself to one of the safety loops, slid next to the general, and began assessing the man's wounds. Aware that Kaddouri was watching him, he moved his hands around the general's body, pausing when he came to an exposed bone on the right leg.

Compound fracture. White tore the trousers and used saline water to damp a sterile dressing. He then secured it over the open wound. Despite Pérez's best efforts to distract Kaddouri from what he was doing, White could feel the Iraqi officer's eyes flick periodically in his direction, so he had to make it look legit—as if keeping General Ashtari alive was his sacrosanct mission. Taking a pressure bandage from the medical kit, White used it to cover a deep and bloody gash on the general's neck. He used gauze and electrical tape to stanch the blood oozing from multiple wounds on the left leg. His hands sticky with blood, White bound one more pressure bandage in place by tying it off with a square knot over the general's thigh. He had no idea how much blood the general had lost since the missile strike, but with cuts and bruises this bad, the man had to be in agony. Hence the low but constant moan of pain escaping his lips.

Broken bones. Damaged organs. Does he really need my help to die?
White wondered.

It didn't matter that the general was a dirtbag. White didn't intend to torture the man or extend his suffering.

Then Mohsen Ashtari opened his eyes, and White knew his time was up.

———

White followed General Ashtari's eyes from his face to the Stars and Stripes on his shoulder. At first, an expression not so much of fear but of confusion played across the general's features. Then it was replaced by rage. He opened his mouth to speak or scream, but the general succumbed to a coughing fit that sounded as though he had holes in his lungs. White bent over him and fretted over his bandages in case his coughing fit had attracted Lieutenant Kaddouri's attention. Angling his back in a way that shielded his hands from Kaddouri's line of sight, White's face was stone as he drew his combat knife from his chest rig and locked eyes with his victim. White clamped his left hand over the general's mouth as he pushed the tip of the blade past the man's ribs and into his heart. The general gave a choked groan of pain, his entire body going rigid, then limp.

It was a cleaner death than the one Major General Mohsen Ashtari, commanding officer of the Iranian Quds Force, would have offered to his foe.

And nicer than what he truly deserved, White thought, withdrawing the knife. He wiped the blade three times across the dead man's blood-soaked suit jacket and slipped it back in its sheath. After a quick look over his shoulder to confirm that Pérez still had Kaddouri's undivided attention, White loosened the bandages around the general's wounds. He pumped the flesh around the man's injuries until a small pool of blood had formed underneath the stretcher.

"Shit!" he shouted, starting CPR. "We're losing him."

Pérez, who'd been read into the plan, moved quickly. He was by White's side in a flash, his own medical kit in hand.

"Lieutenant Kaddouri," White yelled over the loud whine of the chopper's rotor blades, "tell the pilot to hurry or he won't make it."

Kaddouri replied with a thumbs-up.

Pérez pushed White to the side and started compressing the dead man's chest, and, as he did so, the pool of blood under the stretcher grew larger. White wasn't naive enough to think the charade would last very long. But it didn't have to. He just had to make sure he and Pérez were gone by the time the Iraqi surgeons realized that the general hadn't died from the wounds he had sustained in the crash.

Three minutes later the helicopter landed at the Medical City helipad, where a five-person emergency trauma team was waiting for them. *Kaddouri must have called it in,* White thought.

The moment the weight of the helicopter settled on its wheel, the team moved forward, bringing a rescue litter with them. Kaddouri was the first to disembark and linked up with a member of the medical team. Pérez finished a last compression and moved clear of the general's corpse, leaving the medical personnel the space they needed to do their job. They seemed to know what they were doing, which would have been of grave concern to White if he hadn't already pierced the general's heart with his knife.

"I briefed the doctor on what happened, Captain," Kaddouri said. "We should go now. The other helicopter is two minutes away."

"You go, Lieutenant," White replied. "Go get your men, and let's regroup at base in the morning. Technical Sergeant Pérez and I will stay here to help out with the new arrivals."

"Are you sure?"

"Absolutely. We'll catch a ride back to the barracks. Don't worry."

For a moment, it seemed like Kaddouri wanted to say something, but White didn't let him complete his thought. He and Pérez had to go, and they had to put as much distance as they could between themselves and the incoming chopper that held the general's son. White wasn't pleased about this new course of action. He would have preferred to continue training Kaddouri and his men for the upcoming and inevitable fight against ISIS, but from what he'd seen of the Iraqi officer, White had no doubt Kaddouri would step up. Kaddouri's commandos were in good hands, White was sure of it.

"You did well today," White said, eager to leave the rooftop helipad. He clapped the younger man on the shoulder. "Now go. Your men need you."

Kaddouri's brow furrowed. There was uncertainty in his gaze, but he nodded nonetheless and ran back to the helicopter. Seconds later, the helicopter took off and headed back toward the motorcade.

On cue, White's satellite phone rang.

"Go for White," he said.

"We're tracking you at the Medical City Hospital," the mission commander said. "Can you confirm?"

"Confirmed."

"Command requests a sitrep."

For the next twenty seconds, White explained the events of the last ten minutes.

"We copy your last, Captain," the mission commander said before giving a grid coordinate to White. "Can you make it there?" he asked.

White showed the coordinates to Pérez, who checked his map.

"If we steal a car, we can be at the rendezvous point in fifteen minutes," Pérez told White.

"Yes," White said to the mission commander. "ETA is fifteen to twenty minutes."

"Roger that. A team from the embassy will be waiting for you. They'll take it from there."

PART TWO
PRESENT DAY

CHAPTER NINE

Miami, Florida

Reza Ashtari became aware of the sound first, a babble of noise that made no sense. He tried to focus on it, to determine its origin, but he had a terrible headache, and he was unable to concentrate. He opened his eyes, and his whole body stiffened. A tall, clean-shaven man of at least six feet was staring down at him. The man was wearing the uniform of a US Air Force officer. Reza felt the man's hands wrap themselves around his neck. He tried to breathe, but there was too much pressure around his neck. He tried to bite off one of the American's fingers but only managed to get hammer fisted in the face.

Reza woke with a start, his lean and muscular body covered in sweat. He pushed back the covers and swore out loud, loathing himself for having once again dreamed about the man who had ended his father's life.

Clayton White. One of the three names on his personal kill list.

It was still dark inside the bedroom, and the only hint that anyone was up at this hour was the sporadic sound of traffic from the nearby causeway. Reza closed his eyes again, wishing himself back to sleep, but he soon realized he was up for good, so he swung his legs off the bed. Although he had shut off the air-conditioning before turning in for the night, the tiles of the eleventh-floor condo were cold under his feet, thanks to whoever had cranked down the thermostat in the unit directly below. Of course, the poor insulation of the condo tower was also to blame.

Why Americans loved air-conditioning so much was a mystery to him. Didn't they know that the United States used more electricity for their precious air-conditioning than Africa—a continent with a population of over 1.3 billion people—used for everything? Since he had left the Quds Force to join his brother, Nader, at the Ministry of Intelligence and Security, Reza had spent his time traveling the world recruiting criminals and washed-out spies to do Tehran's bidding. Nowhere else on the planet did he have the sensation of walking into a fridge like he did here in America in every house or building he entered.

Reza padded down the hallway toward the bathroom, walking past the Finnish-built SAKO TRG 42 bolt-action rifle and the sniper nest he had erected deep inside the guest bedroom. Without turning on the lights, he brushed his teeth and used the toilet before heading back to the master bedroom to change into his running gear.

Reza spent five minutes stretching his six-foot-one frame, then moved into a series of push-ups, crunches, and dips using a chair and a coffee table for support. With his skin once again covered in a light film of sweat, he picked up a tablet from the coffee table and stepped onto the treadmill, making sure to secure the tablet on the treadmill's dash. He then pulled a blue phone out of his shorts pocket and unlocked it by entering an eight-digit password. A single app appeared on the screen. He tapped on it, and several thumbnails immediately popped up.

Reza enlarged the first one—a live black-and-white video feed of the mostly deserted marina parking lot taken from across the street. He swiped down the thumbnail and moved to the next one. This time, the video feed came from a camera mounted on top of the marina clubhouse and offered a clear view of the docks. Reza zoomed in on a forty-three-foot Tiara LS, his target's prized possession. There was no activity on or around the boat. Positioning the phone next to the tablet in a way that allowed him to keep an eye on its screen while he ran, Reza turned on the tablet and unlocked a secret app. He plugged a pair of headphones into the tablet and selected his favorite video before powering on the treadmill. In front of him, the tablet came to life, and a warm feeling enveloped Reza as he forwarded the video to his favorite part.

———

A naked Mustafa Kaddouri, formerly of Iraq's 1st Commando Battalion, sat shivering, his hands nailed to the arms of the wooden chair, his ankles tied tightly together with duct tape, his shoes removed. Although you couldn't see it on the video, both of Kaddouri's feet had been hammered to a pulp inside his socks, which were now red and not white like they once were.

"Why are you even protecting these American pigs, Mustafa?" Nader asked.

"Haven't you suffered enough?" Reza added. "It makes no sense to me. The Americans tricked you. Can't you see that?"

"They're the ones who should be here, Mustafa. Not you," Nader said. "Just give us the names of the two Americans who were with you in the helicopter. Give us the names, Mustafa, and I promise my brother will shoot you in the head. Quick. Simple. Clean."

Kaddouri shook his head and lowered his chin to his chest and began to sob.

Nader gently raised Kaddouri's chin with his hand, as if the Iraqi were a difficult child crying over a lost toy.

"Don't be sad, Mustafa. You're in control here, not us," Nader said softly, tapping his index finger against the Iraqi's chest. "You're the one who decides when it stops."

While Nader was talking to Kaddouri, Reza had grabbed a cylindrical device from a metal table at the right corner of the room. He walked toward Kaddouri but stopped a few feet short.

"Do you know what this is?" Reza asked, showing him the device.

When Kaddouri didn't answer, Nader slapped him hard across the face. "Be polite, Mustafa. Answer my brother's question."

"I . . . I don't know," the Iraqi officer said.

"Not a problem," Reza said jovially. "I'm a firm believer that a theory lesson should always be followed by a practical exercise. Don't you agree?

"Anyhow, here's the theory portion of the lecture," Reza continued, this time not waiting for Kaddouri's reply. "This beautiful instrument is called a dermatome. It does only one thing, but it does it well. It cuts thin slices of skin."

Kaddouri lifted his head and started shaking his head. "No, please no."

Nader once again slapped him.

"Silence!" he shouted. "The lesson has started."

Reza nodded his thanks to his brother and continued. "You see, Mustafa, this particular model is manually operated and was developed in the early 1930s. Nowadays they're mostly operated by air pressure or electricity, but I'm kind of old school, so I'm very fond of this one.

"Now let's move to the fun part, shall we? The practical exercise."

Reza moved behind Kaddouri and placed the dermatome on top of the Iraqi's left shoulder. Kaddouri screamed as Reza began slicing his skin.

"Clayton White! Captain Clayton White!"

But Reza continued slicing until he had a four-inch-wide by twelve-inch-long strip of skin. He tossed the skin onto Kaddouri's lap.

"I'm sorry. Did you say something?" Nader asked.

"Please stop," the Iraqi screamed, pleading. "I'll . . . I'll give you the names."

"Then talk," Reza said, placing the dermatome against Kaddouri's left thigh. "Now!"

"United States Air Force Captain Clayton White and Technical Sergeant Oscar Pérez."

Then Kaddouri fell silent, immobile but for the muscular spasms caused by the immense pain he was in.

———

Out of breath, Reza managed to smile. He didn't care how many times he'd seen it; he never tired of viewing his interview with Lieutenant Kaddouri. *Interview.* More like a weeklong enhanced interrogation. He and his brother had broken Kaddouri in just under two hours, but frustrated that the two Americans were out of their reach, they had kept going at him for days—just for the sake of it. Torturing the Iraqi officer had somehow—even if it had only been for a short period of time—dulled the pain and dishonor Reza had felt at failing to protect his father. In the end, they had let Kaddouri die of thirst and blood loss.

Reza powered off the tablet and pushed the up arrow on the treadmill's dash several times. As the treadmill accelerated, he focused on his breathing. For the last five mornings, his routine had been to run until sweat drenched his shirt to below his belly button. He'd gotten used to the monotonous exercising on the treadmill, but he would have much preferred to run outside in the neighborhood's lush tropical setting or on the sun-splashed shores of Miami.

But not enough to risk missing my targets, he thought. Not *these* targets.

He'd been dreaming about this very opportunity for eight years, and never before had he gotten so close to killing one of the persons responsible for his father's death, let alone two at the same time.

It will happen, he thought, willing his phone to send him the notification he so desperately craved. *It has to.*

If his targets didn't show up in the next couple of hours, he would have no choice but to leave. He gritted his teeth at the thought, but he couldn't push his luck. What he was doing in Miami was personal—and well outside the scope of the sanctioned mission in the Florida Keys his brother had tasked him with. He had to be careful. There was only so much he could get away with. It was never a good idea to piss off the

MOIS's deputy director of the Directorate of Foreign Operations, even if you were his brother.

To supervise the sanctioned operation in the Florida Keys—a mission Reza should have been leading in person from Havana—he had hired a former Cuban intelligence officer still well connected with the Cuban regime. It was an easy way to keep the Venezuelan mercenaries who would take part in the operation at arm's length from the real source of their payday, and it had allowed Reza the freedom to mount his own extracurricular wet work.

After his forty-five minutes of hard running, the treadmill's motor breathed a sigh of relief when Reza slackened the pace to walking speed. He looked down at his shirt.

Completely damp.

He grabbed the white towel hanging below the digital console and wiped his face and neck. After a short shower, he dressed and had a breakfast of bread, cold cuts, and fruits, followed by two cups of strong coffee. He was about to pour himself a third when the blue phone next to his coffee mug chirped. It was an update from his Cuban contact. The mother ship had left Havana the previous night without incident and was about to launch the three smaller boats into the Florida Strait. It would then head back toward Cuban waters at full speed.

Good. Traveling at close to thirty knots per hour, the three boats would need less than fifteen minutes to reach their target—an American research vessel presently navigating the Florida Keys. Reza placed the phone on the table and rubbed his temples. His mind reeled with a jumble of mixed emotions. On one hand, his Cuban contact was a pro, and with the help of the powerful Cuban intelligence service, Reza had no doubt his asset had prepared the Venezuelan mercenaries with great care. He was confident that the attack on the research vessel was going to be a success. Tehran would be pleased to have one of its problems taken care of.

Reza would be happy, too, but for a much different reason.

There was someone else aboard the research vessel he wanted dead. A successful attack meant he'd finally be able to scratch the name of one of his father's murderers from his list.

Clayton White.

On the other hand, with the attack on the research vessel now imminent, it meant that his window of opportunity here in Miami was about to close, and there'd been no sign of activity at the marina. It was time for him to pack his things and disappear. He'd have to find another way to kill his father's two remaining assassins. It had taken eight years to get this opportunity. He hoped it wouldn't take eight more to get another, but Reza was ready to spend his entire life chasing and killing the cowards behind the attack if he had to.

His phone buzzed again, shaking him out of his trance. He unlocked the device and stared at the notification on the screen. Reza smiled.

Good things do come in pairs, he thought.

Vice President Alexander Hammond had finally arrived.

At last, the game was about to begin.

CHAPTER TEN

Aboard NOAA Ship **Surveyor**
Florida Keys National Marine Sanctuary

Clayton White closed the cabin door behind him, locked it, and tiptoed to the nightstand, where he set down the two fresh takeaway cups of steaming coffee he had picked up from the ship's galley. Early-morning light peeked through the curtains of the small cabin's single porthole, bathing the double bed in a rose-colored glow. White took off his bathrobe and pulled back the duvet as gently as he could. He took his time slipping between the sheets, not wanting to stir the bed too much, but the old mattress complained loudly as he rolled his six-foot, two-hundred-pound frame toward the woman beside him. They hadn't gone to bed until three in the morning because they'd been up reviewing the data from yesterday's dive, so she needed her sleep. Today was going to be another long day with two more dives on the schedule.

"Hey, baby," Veronica Hammond said, opening her eyes. "Is it morning?"

"We still have a little bit of time to ourselves," White replied, running his hand along the length of her side, her hip, then her thigh.

His fiancée turned toward him and brushed her fingers against the back of his neck. Their faces were close to each other's on the pillow, their voices only a whisper due to the thin walls.

"Yeah? You looked at today's schedule?" she asked with a malicious smile.

"As I said, we have time." He kissed her lips. "Come closer."

Veronica giggled. "I don't think I can get any closer than this."

"I don't think that's entirely true," White said, gently grabbing her by the waist and rolling her on top of him.

She straddled him and buried her face into his neck. He slipped a hand behind her lower back and drew her even closer.

———

"You're something else," White told her a while later, making her laugh.

Veronica collapsed on top of him, her breasts flattened against his chest. She felt his heart pounding on her skin, the deepness of his breath blowing warm air on her ear.

They'd been at sea for three days now, working aboard the NOAA ship *Surveyor* on a seafloor mapping mission for the National Centers for Coastal Ocean Science. Drain2, the revamped mobile application she had built in collaboration with SkyCU Technology, a Silicon Valley start-up, had gone viral. Not only did Drain2 do everything the original Drain app could do, including enabling the general public to use high-resolution satellite imagery to locate still-undiscovered archaeological sites, but it now permitted users to see through up to one thousand feet of water. To gain exclusive access to Drain2, an impressive number of giant tech companies had made offers to purchase SkyCU Technology. Veronica, knowing that her application had the potential to inform and enlighten decision makers about climate change, had convinced the small start-up's board of directors to stay private. Not that she didn't trust the bigger tech corporations to do the right thing, but their interests weren't necessarily aligned with hers.

Through social media, word quickly spread that she was the one who had pushed SkyCU Technology to refuse an $80 million buyout offer from a huge California-based company. Almost overnight, Veronica's popularity, which was already impressive, had soared to unimaginable new heights. With over forty-five million followers across all social media platforms, she was a force to be reckoned with. Not one to waste an opportunity, she'd used her newfound eminence to persuade the same big corporations that had wanted to purchase SkyCU Technology to channel a tiny percentage of their profits toward NOAA, with a promise that the entire amount would be spent toward the blue economy—the main objective of which was to preserve the health of the oceans' ecosystems through the sustainable use of their resources. Despite their initial resistance, the companies quickly came to the conclusion that publicly partnering with her would be an exceptional marketing opportunity, and very good for their bottom lines. Of course, the fact that she was Vice President Hammond's daughter wasn't lost on anyone. Still, the companies that had partnered with her understood that working with her didn't mean access to the White House. In fact, she hadn't been seen at her father's side since Inauguration Day, a little more than one year ago.

Still, not everyone or every corporation was happy with her work and her status as the unofficial blue-economy spokesperson. She knew what their concerns were. She was getting too vocal, too powerful for their liking. Her calls for action in recent months had scared more than one board of directors, and some of them, afraid for the profit margins of their companies, had hired investigative journalists to try to bring her down. These boards' worst nightmare was that the American public would feel inspired by her words and that they would force their elected representatives to enact radical changes in the way their customers used energy. They couldn't allow that to happen, not only for their shareholders but for their employees too. There were a lot of people counting on them to shut her up—one way or the other.

The freelance journalists had done their best to dig up dirt and exploit the void between her and her father. They'd started with the attempt on her life at the Ritz-Carlton San Francisco the year before. Smelling blood, the reporters had turned their attention to her fiancé, the somewhat camera-shy Clayton White, the former special agent in charge of her protective detail at the time. Through research and several Freedom of Information Act requests, they had uncovered that White had been dismissed by the US Secret Service for being involved with Veronica while in the service of the government. For a few days, the reporters thought they had unearthed the Holy Grail, the juicy piece of information that would derail Veronica's rise to the top. Unfortunately for them and for their financial backers, someone had leaked to several traditional media outlets the joint Secret Service–FBI investigation into the Ritz-Carlton attack. In no uncertain terms, the lengthy report painted White as the man who had ultimately saved the day and her life.

Frustrated by this sudden turn of events, the freelancers dug deeper into White's military career. They'd interviewed many of his former colleagues, hoping to find at least one of them ready to piss on him. But they once again hit a wall. The type of men White had served alongside weren't the type to betray their brother-in-arms. It became quickly apparent that White—who had now fully retired from government service—had served with distinction. The final nail in their coffin was when two marine aviators who'd been forced to crash-land their SuperCobra attack helicopter in ISIS-controlled territory in northern Iraq seven years ago signed a significant book deal with a large publisher to write about their heroic rescue—a bold operation led by none other than Captain Clayton White. An operation for which his bravery had been rewarded with a Silver Star—the third-highest military combat decoration that can be awarded to a member of the US Armed Forces.

Veronica smiled, kissed White on his forehead, and rolled off him. But he grabbed her before she could get out of bed, pulling her back toward him.

"I need to get going," she complained without any vigor.

"Just a little longer," he said, spooning her.

Damn, this feels good, Veronica thought. She breathed out a soft sigh and let herself relax. White enveloped her in his arms, one of his hands resting delicately on her belly. Her heart quickened, a crazy idea flashing through her mind. An outrageous idea. A scary idea. She willed it to go away, but it remained there, demanding her attention.

I'm thirty-seven, and soon to be married to the man of my dreams, she thought. *Is wanting a child with him such a crazy idea?* She'd known White since her teenage years and had been involved with him romantically for more than five. Wasn't it time to talk about the next step? If it was, why was she so terrified?

"Hey," White said softly into her ear. "What's going on, Vonnie? You're shaking."

She placed her hand on top of his, interlacing their fingers. Maybe now wasn't the right time. She had a lot on her plate at the moment. The ten-day seafloor-mapping session was only the first phase of the project she was coleading in the Florida Keys National Marine Sanctuary. The sanctuary, established in 1990, protected approximately thirty-eight hundred square miles, encompassing more than fifteen hundred islands, and included the Florida Reef, the only barrier coral reef in North America. Veronica's objective was to use the capabilities of Drain2 to fill the gaps in bathymetry within the sanctuary, improving the seafloor maps' resolution. These enhanced maps would in turn help identify sensitive reef habitats and assist in the management of the coral reef and fisheries resources in the sanctuary. One of the most astonishing things Veronica and her fellow scientists had discovered while analyzing the data collected by Drain2 was that the application was also able to map fish densities in a survey area. What used to take days to do with a multibeam echo sounder could now be accomplished ten times faster, thanks to Drain2. Of course, the results were still preliminary, and a lot of work remained to be done, but Veronica was excited about everything Drain2 could do to help preserve not only the unique ecosystem around the Florida Keys but also all the others around the world.

Was it selfish of her to want children, knowing there was so much to do, so many projects she could take part in?

She twirled around so she could face White. He was looking at her with a smile and a curious, warm light in his eyes.

"What's going on in that beautiful mind of yours?" he asked.

Veronica touched the side of his face, the three-day stubble scratching her fingers. She thought about lying, but what would be the point? Her desire to know if he'd at least considered becoming a dad was just too strong.

"Do you ever think about children?" she asked, taking the plunge and unconsciously biting her lip.

White's eyes twinkled, and his lips curved into the sexy smile she loved so much.

"All the time," he said. "I would love to chase little ones around the house with you."

For a moment, she didn't know what to say. Then his lips moved to hers, tentatively and slowly at first, then with more vigor, which sent her pulse racing. She pressed her body against his, the rush of emotions intoxicating.

Pulling away for just a second, she said, "If this is a dream, I never want to wake up."

"Me neither," he replied.

Then the moment was shattered by three hard knocks on their cabin door.

CHAPTER ELEVEN

Aboard NOAA Ship **Surveyor**
Florida Keys National Marine Sanctuary

White was up, dressed, and at the door in less than twenty seconds, but whoever stood on the other side hadn't stopped banging.

"What's going on?" White growled, swinging the door open.

He was pushed aside by Emily Moss, a small but energetic woman with shoulder-length blonde hair and big blue eyes who happened to be Veronica's best friend.

"Where is she?" Emily asked as she stormed passed White. "Please don't tell me she's still in bed. It's half past six!"

White stepped into the corridor and looked to his right, where US secret service special agent Tim Kennedy was standing. Kennedy was the special agent in charge of Veronica's protective detail these days. He was tall, with the broad shoulders of the champion wrestler he used to be back in college. White had crossed paths several times with Kennedy while he was with the Secret Service and liked the man.

"I tried," Kennedy said sheepishly. "But she threatened to kick me in the nuts if I didn't let her through."

"Don't worry about it," White replied, chuckling.

"Here, it's fully charged," Kennedy said, handing him a walkie-talkie. "It's not linked up to our net, but you can use it to reach me."

White nodded his thanks and took the radio, appreciating the gesture. Even though he was no longer carrying a badge, the Secret Service special agents not only made a point of keeping him in the loop about the security arrangements but often solicited his opinion.

White turned on the radio and said, "Give me a couple of minutes and we'll do a radio check."

Heading back inside the cabin, he saw that Emily was already in discussion with Veronica. White set the walkie-talkie on the nightstand and grabbed the coffees. He gave his fiancée the coffee he had brought for her and offered his own to Emily.

Emily stopped talking and looked at the disposable cup, then at White.

"I had a couple earlier, but okay," she said, snatching the cup from his hands.

"So, Emily," White said, "what was so important that you had to burst into our cabin?"

A sincere expression of confusion crossed her face. "What do you mean?" she asked, taking a sip of coffee. "Tim was very nice. He let me through, didn't he?"

"Never mind," White replied, shaking his head.

Emily was the kind of person who brightened any room she entered with her energy. She was a fidgety, spirited woman who was constantly on the move. A freelance reporter, she had been awarded the prestigious Pulitzer Prize for International Reporting for her revelatory series, often conducted in perilous conditions, detailing America's deepening political challenges in the Middle East. More recently, she had spent three months in Syria and Turkey researching Iran's involvement in Syria's civil war, including the brutal war tactics Tehran had introduced to strangle civilians during long, devastating sieges.

White, along with Veronica, was part of a very small group of people who had read Emily's still unpublished article. White had found it well researched, and pure dynamite. Another Pulitzer wasn't out of the question. But as great as her reporting was, Emily had shared with them how anxious she was about its publication. Emily Moss was no fool. She knew how dangerous publishing a piece like that could be for her. Tehran had a long history of assassinating its dissidents but had only recently started to target foreign activists and reporters hostile to the regime. And there was no doubt about it: Emily's article didn't paint the Iranian government in a good light, although it certainly underlined how Tehran wasn't limiting itself in providing military support to Syria anymore; it was now infiltrating every facet of Syrian society by building or restoring schools and cultural centers, or by providing loans for power-generation projects, strengthening its presence in the Syrian economic system in the process.

"So you think Tehran has a five-year plan for Syria?" White had asked Emily after reading the article.

"No. I think they're operating on a much longer timetable," she'd replied. "More likely a twenty-five- to thirty-five-year plan."

"Iran's turning into a totalitarian and expansionist regime," Veronica had added. "Some high-ranking Iranian officials have even started calling Syria a *province.*"

"Exactly," Emily had agreed. "Everything the Iranian government is doing in Syria is aimed at threatening US and Israeli interests in the region. Left unchecked, the next generation of Syrian youths will be more loyal to Tehran than they are to Damascus."

But what had shaken White and Veronica to their cores was Emily's uncovering of Tehran's active role in the arbitrary executions of over ten thousand prodemocracy civilians in torture chambers.

White had heard rumors about this, but he had never seen any proof. Emily wanted to change that. One of the sources she had recruited in Syria, a former officer in the Syrian military disgusted by how his government was treating its own populace, had brought her the evidence she needed to write a convincing and truthful article. For the best part of an hour, White, Veronica, and Emily had scrolled through hundreds of photos of mutilated bodies, most of them branded like cattle so the executioners could keep track of who they'd killed. As damning as these pictures were, Emily still had to corroborate their validity through a second, unrelated source before even considering publishing the article.

Finding that second source was proving quite difficult. White assumed it was because Tehran was sparing no efforts—or expenses—when it came to permanently silencing anyone who had knowledge of these atrocities.

"What do you think, Clay?" Veronica asked, her voice bringing White back to the here and now.

"He wasn't listening," Emily said, leaving her empty cup of coffee on Veronica's bedside table.

"I'm sorry, I was thinking about something else," he said.

Veronica beamed at him but then seemed to realize that he might not have been thinking what she thought he was thinking, because her radiant smile morphed into a weird grimace.

"It's okay, Clayton," Emily said. "I don't think we really need your input anyway."

White chuckled. Had this come from anyone else, he might have taken offense. But Emily was a different animal. She had no filters and wasn't shy about speaking her mind. Her brain, which White was persuaded operated at a level far superior to his own, had deduced that whatever he might say, it wouldn't change the verdict she and Veronica had reached. So why waste precious time listening to him?

Emily squeezed past him. "See you later."

Once Emily had shut the cabin's door behind her, White took a seat next to Veronica.

"What was that about?" he asked.

"She received an email from her agent late last night," Veronica said.

"Someone made an offer on her article, right?"

Veronica nodded. "She wanted our opinion—"

"Your opinion," White interrupted with a smile. "She wanted your opinion."

"Moving on," Veronica continued, ignoring him. "She's seriously considering accepting the offer, Clay. It's from the *New York Times*, and it's six digit."

White whistled. "I told you, Vonnie. She might get another Pulitzer for it. But what about validating the pictures she showed us?"

"That's the thing. That came through too."

"What? How?" White asked. "Did you reach out to your father like she asked you to?"

Veronica shook her head. "I didn't. I'm not saying I wouldn't have reached out to him at some point, but I was still pondering the pluses and minuses of doing so."

There were two reasons Emily was on the *Surveyor* with them. The first was to cover Veronica's sea-mapping mission for NOAA. Veronica had offered her friend exclusive access, and Emily had wasted no time accepting it. The second reason was to share her article about Iran's involvement in a possible genocide in Syria with White and Veronica, and to ask Veronica if she'd be willing to ask her father for his assistance in validating the pictures, knowing that the vice president had access to databases that weren't readily available to private citizens like her.

"So, who validated these photos, then?" White asked.

"I don't think she knows," Veronica replied, running a hand through her hair. "Her agent told her the *New York Times* editor was very close to doing it through one of her own contacts. Emily's supposed to meet with the editor at the end of next week in New York. She wants me to go with her."

White shot her a perplexed look but shrugged. "Why not?"

"I know what you think," Veronica said. "It sounds strange. But I don't think they would have made her an offer if they hadn't found a reliable source to confirm the veracity of the photos, do you?"

"For a scoop? They might," White said. "That also means it's gonna be the editor's ass on the line, not hers."

"That's true," Veronica said. "And I won't have to involve Dad in this, which is a good thing, right?"

Although Emily was aware that there were some unresolved issues between Veronica and her father, White didn't think his fiancée had shared with her all the details about why they weren't speaking. Truth was, White had only recently shared with Veronica the reason he wasn't on good terms with her dad.

It had taken White months to summon the courage to tell Veronica about her father being implicated in a black-ops joint operation between the United Kingdom and the United States involving a floating prison for ISIS and other enemy combatants deemed to be in possession of information too valuable or time sensitive for the standard prisoner-processing protocol. Once the prisoners had no further value, Hammond had authorized the sinking of the prison ship in the Arabian Peninsula, killing all souls aboard.

But some things were better kept secret, even from one's true love. As evil as Alexander Hammond could be, White knew he loved his daughter. That's why White hadn't told Veronica that Hammond had ordered White's father killed seven years ago when Maxwell White had threatened to expose the atrocities committed during Operation CONQUEST.

White had to tread carefully. The vice president of the United States was a dangerous man. He had betrayed White once before and had even sabotaged his own daughter's professional life to save himself. White knew it was only a question of time before Hammond did it again.

Unless I take him down first, he thought.

"Yeah, baby," White said, holding his fiancée in his arms. "It's a good thing you didn't call him."

CHAPTER TWELVE

Aboard NOAA Ship **Surveyor**
Florida Keys National Marine Sanctuary

The warm breeze of the morning air brushed White's cheek as he reached the *Surveyor's* wheelhouse. Despite the early hour, the sun's heat was already strong. It was going to be a hot one, and White wondered if he had made the right decision to only join Veronica for her afternoon dive.

"Good morning, Captain Shannan," White said to the medium-height, stocky woman in charge of the 124-foot *Surveyor* and its crew.

"Good morning to you, Mr. White. Did you sleep well?" she asked, bringing a large US Coast Guard coffee mug to her lips.

"Hard not to in these beds, right?" White replied.

The captain gave him a knowing smile. "*Surveyor's* due for a full refurbishment," she said. "Once it's done, you'll be hard pressed to see the difference between this ship and a Four Seasons hotel."

White gave her a quizzical look, wondering for the briefest of moments if she was serious.

"Oh yeah, and when is that supposed to happen?" he asked.

"Two, three decades from now," she replied, winking at him. "This beauty was commissioned in 2001. It's almost brand new."

White rolled his eyes, but he had to admit that the *Surveyor* was a nice vessel, even if it was more than twenty years old. *Surveyor's* primary mission was to map coastal waters to update nautical charts. Of course, depending on the needs of NOAA, *Surveyor* had been built to support many other activities, like the testing of autonomous underwater vehicles, buoy deployment and retrieval, and general oceanographic exploration. On White's first day aboard the vessel, Veronica had spent an hour walking him through the entire ship, taking her time explaining its capabilities and technological instruments, especially the ones located in the dry lab space configured for hydrographic data collection. White had been enthusiastic about the grand tour, but it wasn't the ship's multibeam echo sounders or how Veronica had been able to link Drain2 to *Surveyor's* side-scan sonar that excited him.

No, what White wanted to know was what speed *Surveyor* could reach, whether it had a dive locker with compressor and filling station, and what type of secondary vessel it carried—in case they needed to make a quick getaway. He knew the four Secret Service special agents onboard had probably been through all this with Captain Shannan, but White still considered himself Veronica's first and last line of defense. Although the Secret Service's risk assessment for this mission was low, it was important for White to understand the ship's configuration and capabilities in the event of an emergency. Security in and around the boat was tight, and even though the special agents seemed reasonably vigilant, White could tell no one thought anything serious could ever happen.

White himself had made that mistake at the Ritz-Carlton last year, and he'd almost lost Veronica. He intended for it to never happen again.

One deck below, his fiancée, already wearing her wet suit, was helping Emily hoist an oxygen tank onto her back. White scanned the horizon, moving from left to right. Beyond the tiny waves that slapped against the hull of the ship, the ocean was like glass, reflecting the deep blue sky and white clouds on its surface. The pair of eleven-meter rigid-hulled inflatable Zodiacs—call signs Mercury-One and Two—operated by the Secret Service were crisscrossing the water slowly and silently about five hundred meters out.

All in all, it was a great day to be at sea. For White, the ocean had a calming effect on his soul, very similar to what he felt when he spent time in the mountains. He'd have no problem sitting on the deck for hours drinking coffee and watching the sea, letting his mind drift off. That's what he was planning to do—until the ping of an incoming text message startled him.

The message was from Pierre Sarazin. Only a few minutes ago, White had contemplated checking in with his friend, a former French spy, but had opted to wait a little longer. The sun hadn't yet risen in Seattle, and Sarazin was known to like his sleep, so White was a bit alarmed now, knowing the Frenchman very rarely got out of bed before 10:00 a.m. since he had officially retired from the Direction Générale de la Sécurité Extérieure, France's foreign intelligence agency.

White read Sarazin's message:

@CW49234 How's your trip down to the Keys?

@P.Sarazin So far so good. Everything ok?

@CW49234 Couldn't be any better. La vie est belle!

@P.Sarazin You're bored, aren't you?

@CW49234 *Un peu.* A little. We'll need to chat about Kommetjie when you return. Nothing serious. Just some stuff that's bothering me.

White frowned. Kommetjie was a small coastal village located on the western side of the Cape Peninsula and about thirty miles south of Cape Town, South Africa. Kommetjie used to be home to Oxley Vineyards, the winery belonging to the now deceased Roy Oxley—a former SAS officer turned businessman who had run CONQUEST for the British government. It was where White had first met Sarazin, who'd ultimately saved his life. At the time, and without the knowledge of the French government, Sarazin had been working under Alexander Hammond's orders, as had White. In a twisted way, it had finally been through Oxley—the man Hammond had sent White to kill—that White had uncovered Hammond's role in his father's murder. Oxley's proof had shattered White's entire world.

That evidence was so dangerous White kept it under lock in a non-descript security box at a small bank in Washington State. He hadn't shared it with anyone, not even with Veronica.

Especially not with Veronica.

White typed his reply and was about to send it when something twenty-five meters to starboard caught his eye. By the time he turned toward the movement, what had drawn his attention was gone.

Then it reappeared, and White saw a group of dolphins, their dorsal fins arching gracefully in the water. Veronica had seen them, too, because she was pointing her fingers at the ten or so fins cutting through the surface. She looked at White, beaming, and waved at him.

He laughed and waved back. Funny. Smart. Gorgeous. It didn't get much better than that, did it? A stunning woman like Veronica willing to marry a guy like him, and now they were talking about having kids? Was this for real? White took a deep breath, the salty tang of sea air filling his lungs. He figured he was as content as a man could get.

Veronica was in her environment, too, doing what she loved and believed in. He was happy for her. He leaned out so he could get a better view of his fiancée and her team. She gave him a thumbs-up as she stepped into the middle of the dive platform secured on the side of *Surveyor*. Four more wet suit–covered bodies joined her as they checked each other's equipment one last time before being lowered into the water.

As the hydraulic platform gently dropped into the ocean, a flurry of bubbles foamed up next to the five divers. Then they were gone, and White's walkie-talkie crackled to life.

CHAPTER THIRTEEN

Aboard NOAA Ship Surveyor
Florida Keys National Marine Sanctuary

White grabbed the walkie-talkie from his belt. "Say again, Tim," he said, adjusting the volume.

"Mercury-One is reporting three unidentified small craft fast approaching our positions," Special Agent Kennedy said.

"Where are they coming from?" White asked, his eyes moving to Captain Shannan to make sure she was listening to the conversation.

"They're approximately three miles south of our location, heading right at us," Kennedy said.

Shannan, who was staring at the large radar screen, nodded. "I see them now," she said. "Sorry, I wasn't paying attention."

"Try to reach out to them via VHF, and remind them that there's a quarter-mile no-entry radius around *Surveyor*," White told her, making sure to keep his voice cool and composed. The captain wasn't a combat veteran, and he didn't want to alarm her, and frankly, the boats were probably carrying either freelance reporters trying to find a way to mess with Veronica or day boaters who wanted to take a peek at what was going on.

They were in a high-traffic area, and with Veronica's incessant, but well-intended, posting on social media, the Secret Service had to intervene at least a couple of times per day to prevent boaters from getting too close to *Surveyor*.

"Where are you?" White asked Kennedy, using the walkie-talkie.

"Main deck," the special agent replied. "I'm having one of my guys suit up. Just in case."

"I'm on my way," White replied, clipping the walkie-talkie back to his belt.

Two boats traveling in a pair wasn't worrisome, but seeing three of them was somewhat atypical. White was glad Kennedy and his men were on top of things.

White left the wheelhouse and took the stairs down to the main deck to join him.

"Mercury-One is on its way to intercept," Kennedy said, handing the binoculars to White. "I've asked Mercury-Two to cover them from a distance."

White raised the binoculars to his eyes. A mile out, the Secret Service boat was racing toward the three unidentified craft, the two blue strobe lights mounted on its overhead bars flashing.

"Remind me of the weapons they have on board," White said.

"Small arms only," Kennedy replied. "MP-5s and sidearms. The heavier weapons systems are onboard *Surveyor*."

White knew that the large gun safe bolted to the floor of the wheelhouse contained ballistic helmets and goggles, and half a dozen rifles with spare magazines. One level below the main deck, in Kennedy's stateroom, was another safe. This was where the AT4 rocket launchers were kept with the SR-25 sniper rifle.

White panned the binoculars to the right, making a slow sweep until he spotted the three boats. The leading craft was less than half a mile away from Mercury-One, and even though its driver should have spotted the Secret Service boat speeding toward them, it didn't slow down, nor did it make any attempt to change direction. In contrast, the two fast-moving boats behind it diverged from their paths and steered directly toward Mercury-One. The craft were still too far away for White to accurately count how many occupants were aboard, but there were at least three or four people in each vessel. The three incoming boats looked identical. They had the long, sleek design of a cigarette boat, but they had been heavily modified. They seemed heavier, sitting lower in the water than they should.

"What are they doing?" White wondered out loud, not liking what he was watching.

These weren't regular boaters driving pleasure craft. White was sure of it. Moments later, his dread was confirmed.

He sighted one person carrying what looked like a rocket-propelled grenade launcher—followed quickly by a multitude of rifle barrels as more men exited the boat's cabin.

Shit.

"I see weapons," White shouted. "RPG!"

"What?" Kennedy said, looking at him in disbelief.

"Advise Mercury-One and Two, and for Chrissake, get Veronica out of the water!" White roared, slamming the binoculars into the special agent's chest. "Move!"

Not waiting for Kennedy to reply, he sprinted up the stairs and burst into the wheelhouse. If he had read the situation correctly, they had less than two minutes before the attack began.

Captain Shannan was on the VHF radio, still trying to reach the approaching boats.

"I'm not able to—" she started but was cut short by White.

"Send a distress signal to the coast guard. They should have a direct-action team on standby. Tell them we're under attack by three vessels loaded with an unknown number of men equipped with RPGs and small arms. I want all nonessential crew to go to the safe room and the engineers in the engine room. Did you—"

White was interrupted by the crack of rifles in the distance, followed by the heavier chatter of a crew-served machine gun. Seems that he hadn't read the situation accurately after all.

The attack had already begun.

CHAPTER FOURTEEN

Miami, Florida

The three-car motorcade stopped in the nearly empty marina parking lot. Vice President Alexander Hammond squeezed his wife's hand. They hadn't shared a word since they'd left their vacation home in Aventura, both of them too busy working on their laptops.

"We're here, honey," he said. "You ready?"

Heather Hammond closed her laptop and sighed.

"Hey, what's wrong?" Hammond asked. "I thought you wanted to come."

"It's not that I don't want to be here, Alex," she replied, stretching her neck. "But there's so much to do, and I'm exhausted. Seems like we're always on the move. I wish we could slow down a little, you know?"

Hammond knew what she meant. The working schedule since he had become vice president was almost nonstop. That was why they'd decided to purchase a vacation home in the south of Florida. The two-story, 3,500-square-foot house was supposed to be a place where they could disconnect and spend some time together away from the controlled chaos that was Washington, DC. For the last three months, they'd been able to escape for a couple of nights every ten days or so. It had been a real treat, especially when they were able to make good use of his new forty-three-foot Tiara LS to catch fish.

With the exception of these quick getaways to Florida, they'd had very little time for themselves since he'd become vice president. And, by the look of it, the hard tempo would continue not only for him, but for his wife too. Heather, a strong advocate for the economic empowerment of women, had just returned from a ten-day trip to Africa visiting refugee camps. And she was now preparing the launch of her brainchild, Together, a nationwide initiative to ensure that former service members of all branches of the military had the necessary tools to succeed in their postmilitary lives. They were doing important work; both of them knew that.

It wasn't as if they'd had a ton of free time on their hands when he was the commanding officer of JSOC either. And as always, Heather had been very supportive of him during the presidential campaign and had embraced her role as the Second Lady of the United States. Hammond knew she would have preferred it if he'd simply retired, though. Maybe she hoped that after the initial four-year term he would step down, let someone else lead the country. But Hammond was far from done. In fact, if he was honest with himself, he didn't think he'd ever be done. Internal polls had revealed that having his name on the ticket had won the White House for the current administration. Political pundits even predicted that if the president were to yield his place to him in time for the next election, Hammond would win in a landslide. When he'd shared these results with Heather, she hadn't been impressed.

"Haven't you done your part, darling?" she'd asked. "Isn't it time to sit back, relax, and enjoy the good years we have left? Or have we bought this house in Florida for nothing?"

Why Heather wasn't thrilled about the possibility of becoming the First Lady of the United States escaped him. Sipping rosé was fine and good, but after a couple of days of sunbathing, Hammond had usually had enough and itched to go back to work—unless he was fishing, of course. That he could do weeks at a time. Especially with his new toy. *Titus.* God did he love this boat. It had been a crazy purchase, that was for sure. Almost a million bucks. But damn if that thing didn't make him smile. And they had the money, right? Even after purchasing the boat and the Florida house, they had more than enough set aside to live comfortably for the rest of their lives. His generous pension and the significant amount Heather had received in inheritance from her parents had seen to that.

Hammond considered himself a man of action, and to him, the White House was the natural next step. Deep down, though, he knew he wouldn't enter the biggest race of his life without his wife's support. He owed her that much. But that didn't mean he wouldn't do his best to change her mind.

"Guys, can you give us a minute?" he asked the two special agents seated in the front of the armored Suburban.

"Of course, sir," the driver replied.

When both men had exited the vehicle, Hammond turned to face his wife, still holding her hand.

"C'mon, Heather, cheer up. It's gonna be fun. How long has it been since our last day on the water together?"

She looked back at him with her big green eyes. "We were here ten days ago, Alex."

Hammond scowled. "That doesn't count. We didn't catch any fish that day."

A light chuckle escaped Heather's lips. She kissed the back of his hand and said, "As long as we don't come back too late, okay?"

"I know, I know—you're going out for dinner tonight," he said. "Did your friends change their mind about me going?"

"Absolutely not," Heather said, slapping him on the shoulder. "Women only."

"What am I supposed to do all by myself?" he asked, knowing he'd made a mistake the moment the words had come out of his mouth.

"I have an idea," his wife replied. "Why don't you try to make amends with our only daughter? She's in Florida, as I'm sure you know."

It was Hammond's turn to sigh.

Of course he knew she was in Florida. For months Tim Kennedy had been sending him short but daily reports about Veronica's activities. Not that his wife needed to know that. Mercifully for all involved, Heather's relationship with their daughter hadn't changed. They still talked at least three times a week. As far as Hammond knew, Veronica hadn't shared with her mom the reasons she wasn't speaking to him any longer. Because if she had, he doubted Heather would have stayed quiet about it.

"She won't return my calls," he finally said, signaling to the Secret Service special agent outside the vehicle that he needed a bit more time. "It's not that I'm not trying, because I am."

"I know you are," she hastened to say, full of her usual kindness. "And I wish I could help, but you're both refusing to let me in. I don't like to be left outside of the conversation, Alex."

"I'm not even sure what it's all about," he lied, managing to keep a straight face. "I wish I did."

For a brief moment, a mix of sadness and resignation crossed his wife's features, and Hammond knew she didn't believe him. But she once again proved that she was the better person by not calling him on it.

"You're her father; the ball is in your court. Be an adult, for God's sake, Alexander, and reach out to her, will you?"

And with that, Heather climbed out of the vehicle and headed for the boat, leaving him alone in the Suburban.

Damn.

He didn't like disappointing his wife. It pained him. It truly did. But it wasn't as if he could share everything with her either. Was it because he loved her too much, or was it because he was being selfish, afraid she'd leave him if she knew about the terrible things he had done? How would she react if his involvement with CONQUEST came to light, his direct involvement in the death of the detainees? Heather had never seen his darker side. She had no idea what he was truly capable of. And what about Maxwell White? She would be disgusted at how quickly he had turned against his friend. Maybe, just maybe, she would understand his actions with CONQUEST, but she would never in a thousand years forgive him for his betrayal of Maxwell White.

She could never learn of his treachery. Whatever he had to do to protect her, he would. Nothing was off limits.

Nothing.

CHAPTER FIFTEEN

Aboard NOAA Ship Surveyor
Florida Keys National Marine Sanctuary

White moved to the starboard side of the wheelhouse where the large
gun safe was located. He entered his eight-digit code and pressed his left
index finger against the biometric reader. The safe opened, and White
grabbed a ballistic helmet, two of the six suppressed M4 rifles—all
equipped with red-dot sights and infrared lasers—and four thirty-round
magazines. He closed the safe and ran down the stairs to the main deck
two at a time.

Kennedy was on the radio, giving instructions to his men. Judging
from the panicked voices of the special agents aboard Mercury-One,
the Secret Service boat was engaged in a firefight with two of the enemy
vessels and was taking effective fire. Next to Kennedy, another special
agent wearing a wet suit, dive mask, and fins was getting ready to enter
the water. He jumped into the ocean just as a third agent showed up
carrying two AT4 rocket launchers and an SR-25, the lone sniper rifle
they had on board.

White handed Kennedy the helmet and one of the M4s with two
loaded magazines in exchange for the binoculars. To White's dismay,
Mercury-One was dead in the water. One of its two outboard motors
had caught fire, and one Secret Service agent was sprawled on the starboard gunwale. A long burst of machine-gun fire erupted from one

of the unidentified boats, and the remaining special agent stumbled backward, then fell into the ocean.

The lead unidentified vessel was now less than a mile away from *Surveyor's* port side. With Mercury-One now out of play, the other enemy vessels were converging on Mercury-Two, whose driver, despite seeing his two Secret Service colleagues cut down by machine-gun fire, charged ahead. White knew exactly what was going through the special agents' minds. If they were going to die, they were going to do it bravely and boldly, carrying out their sacred duty to the very end.

A stream of red tracer rounds from an enemy boat arched toward Mercury-Two, but the special agent at the helm evaded by sharply turning to starboard, almost ejecting his passenger from the rigid-hull inflatable boat.

"A coast guard helicopter is on the way with a direct-action team aboard," Captain Shannan shouted from the top of the stairs. "What do you want me to do?"

"Is it coming from the north?" White asked, handing the binoculars to Kennedy.

"Yes, and they're about three minutes out," Shannan replied.

At least a bit of good news, White thought.

"All right, as soon as Veronica is back aboard, I want you to start the engines and head due north. In the meantime, keep an eye on the radar and make sure we're not being flanked."

"You got it," Shannan said, retreating inside the wheelhouse.

Kennedy, his eyes glued to the binoculars, said, "The closest boat is now three-quarters of a mile away, and it ain't stopping, Clay."

White turned his attention to the special agent to Kennedy's right, who was prepping the SR-25 sniper rifle.

"How comfortable are you with it?" White asked. "And now isn't the time for a bullshit answer."

"Our sniper was Mercury-One's driver," the special agent said. "I've fired this kind of rifle a few times at the range."

There was a whole world of difference between firing at paper targets in a safe, controlled environment and shooting to kill at someone who was firing back.

"What about you?" White asked Kennedy.

Kennedy shrugged and snatched one of the two AT4s. "I've used these in Iraq a few times," he said, expertly prepping the rocket launcher.

The AT4—a wordplay on the 84 mm caliber of the weapon—was an unguided, man-portable, single-shot, and recoilless light antitank weapon system. Although ineffective against most modern-day battle tanks, the AT4 was great at disabling lightly armored vehicles and damaging fortifications. White hoped a direct hit on the incoming enemy vessel would do the trick or, in case of a miss, scare the boat's driver enough for him to reassess his plan of action.

The only problem was that the AT4's maximum effective range of three hundred meters wouldn't give Kennedy much time to reengage with the second AT4 in case of a miss.

"I'll take the SR-25," White said, taking the special agent's place behind the rifle.

The special agent didn't argue and took White's M4 with an extra magazine. White didn't like firing a precision rifle he hadn't zeroed in himself, but he couldn't afford to be picky. He took a second to check the ten-round magazine before inserting it. He deployed the bipod and balanced it on the large gunwale of the main deck. It wasn't the most comfortable or stable firing position, but he had to start sending rounds down range.

White gauged the wind. *Five knots, moving diagonally from left to right.* He adjusted the SR-25's scope, then aligned the sight on the upcoming boat's driver, his cheek resting on the rifle's butt. The boat was about eight hundred meters away and closing fast. It wasn't going to be an easy shot. White laid the scope's crosshair on the man's center mass and placed his finger on the trigger. He took a breath, paused, and let it out. He pulled the trigger.

The SR-25 gave a muted cough. Seven hundred and fifty meters away, the driver was still standing behind the helm, but the head of a man seated to his immediate left exploded. White fine-tuned his aim and squeezed the trigger again. Another muted *pop*. This time, the round punched through the driver's chest, shoving him backward. The boat veered sharply right and almost capsized. White continued to fire, sending round after round at the vessel.

"Good shooting," Kennedy said, the AT4 resting on his shoulder.

White lifted his head from the scope, got his bearings, and sighted on the two enemy boats fighting it out with Mercury-Two one mile out. The three boats were circling each other like hungry scavengers, firing bullets at one another. One of the hostile vessels had been hit. Thick black smoke was pouring out of its starboard motor. Even better, the two special agents aboard Mercury-Two were still in the fight and continued to buy Veronica and the rest of the civilian divers precious time.

White wished he could help them, but they were out of range.

"No shot," he said, inserting a fresh magazine into the SR-25. "They're too far off."

A few meters away, to the left of White and the two special agents, the dive platform began to rise. Soon, White was able to make out Veronica and the rest of her team.

"Go to the wheelhouse and advise Captain Shannan we're good to go," White said to the special agent holding the M4, relieved they would soon get underway.

"Shit!" Kennedy said, tamping White's enthusiasm. "They're circling around."

White rotated the SR-25 so he could aim at the nearest boat, which was now traveling at full speed and heading toward the *Surveyor's* bow. To White's horror, two of the men aboard were setting up a crew-served machine gun. They wouldn't be able to aim properly, but they only needed to get lucky. White zeroed in on the two men and started squeezing the trigger, knowing it would be a fluke if any of his rounds hit their intended targets. He'd quickly emptied the ten-round magazine and was about to reload when bullets started pinging off *Surveyor's* superstructure. The bad guys were firing up at an angle, so White was aware that the only way he and the special agents next to him would get hit was if they were standing up above the gunwale. Veronica and the divers, though, weren't protected. The dive platform wasn't shielded.

White let go of the sniper rifle and ran toward the team of divers, his eyes fixed on the opening leading to the dive platform. He spotted Veronica—her pink-colored dive mask making her easy to pick up—and was only feet away from her when a hail of bullets raked through the exposed group.

CHAPTER SIXTEEN

Miami, Florida

Reza Ashtari opened the sliding doors of the bedroom and got belly down behind the SAKO TRG 42 bolt-action rifle. He peered through the scope. The angle and elevations to the target area were perfect. Two hundred and fifty meters away, four Secret Service agents had set up a security perimeter around the three-car motorcade and were waiting for the vice president to climb out. Among them was Special Agent Oscar Pérez. Reza's heart skipped a beat as the excitement of what was to come next continued to mount. He had known all along that Pérez might be a no-show. Hammond's protective detail was large, and not all agents assigned to it worked the same shift.

What about Hammond's wife? Was she there too? Reza had no intention of killing her, but wouldn't it be lovely if she were to witness the death of her husband?

C'mon, old man, he thought. *What's taking you so long?*

For some reason, the vice president wasn't exiting the SUV. Reza turned his attention to a black Ford pickup truck that had just pulled into the parking lot. The pickup was towing a large rigid-hull inflatable boat with two big outboard motors hanging on the back. The driver brought the truck in front of the boat ramp and started backing up. During the last few days, Reza had laughed out loud more than a dozen times watching boaters do the silliest of things while launching their boats. One particularly stupid American had almost sunk his Dodge Ram trying to launch a pair of wave runners. But that wasn't about to happen now. The driver backed the Ford pickup straight and true without the need to pull up even once. When the driver opened the door, Reza followed her with his scope.

She was of medium height with a narrow waist and thick blonde hair she kept in a bun. She wore a black polo shirt with a pair of tactical pants. A badge was clipped to her belt in front of her pistol.

Secret Service, Reza thought.

There was a man in the passenger seat, but he didn't get out. The woman walked to the rear of the truck, climbed on the trailer, and reached into the boat. She pulled a line from somewhere inside the boat and tied it to the trailer before releasing the crank. She climbed back into the Ford driver's seat and backed the trailer down the ramp expertly, stopping just at the right moment. The boat slid off the trailer easily and floated behind it. The passenger climbed out and grabbed the line attached to the boat and tied it to a cleat on the dock. Two more armed men climbed out the rear doors of the pickup and joined the others.

Movement at the three-car motorcade had Reza switching back to his initial position. The driver of Hammond's armored SUV and another man had climbed out. But not the vice president. Reza wondered why. He could easily kill Pérez now, but it would be counterproductive.

Reza pondered whether he should engage both Pérez and Hammond the moment the vice president exited the SUV.

Better not, he thought. He could probably make the kill, but why risk it? In the unlikely event that he missed, the bodyguards would have Hammond back into the armored SUV before he could take another shot. It would be preferable to shoot Hammond once he was sufficiently down the long dock leading to his fishing boat. Once on the dock, Reza doubted there would be more than one or two bodyguards accompanying him aboard the Tiara. The others would wait with the motorcade or follow behind aboard the rigid-hull inflatable boat. Once Hammond was down, Reza would then be free to focus on Pérez.

Reza was aiming directly at the rear driver's side door when it opened. His finger moved to the trigger. A tall silver-haired woman climbed out.

Heather Hammond. For some reason, she made Reza think of his own mother and how little he'd seen of her in recent years. Once a dignified woman not unlike Heather Hammond, his mother's world had imploded when Reza's father was assassinated. For months she had accused Reza of not doing enough and had claimed—to whoever was willing to listen to her—that her husband's death was directly attributed to Reza's incompetence and that she wished it was him, not her beloved Mohsen, who had died that day.

Reza understood. He didn't hate her for saying that. In a weird way, she was right. His father's death had been a terrible blow. Not only for him; his brother, Nader; and their mother but for the entire nation. The actions he was about to take weren't only to satiate his thirst of revenge; he was doing this to make his mother proud.

Focusing his attention back to Heather Hammond, Reza thought she seemed upset as she walked hurriedly toward the dock where the vice president's boat was moored. Her sudden exit from the Suburban had surprised the Secret Service agents, and they had momentarily stood in place, not sure what to do. Then Oscar Pérez jogged after her. The rear passenger door opened, and, although Reza didn't have a clear view of that side of the SUV, he knew Alexander Hammond had finally stepped out into the open.

The man was tall. His file said six foot four inches, but Reza wouldn't be surprised to learn Hammond was even taller. Hammond opened the trunk of the Suburban and pulled out a large cooler bag. He swung it over his shoulder and said something to one of his bodyguards.

The four men headed toward the dock. Two bodyguards positioned themselves behind Hammond and another led the way. Hammond walked ramrod straight, his head held high. It was as if the man had been cut from a piece of stone. He had a thick torso and long legs and arms, and there was an air of authority about him.

We'll see how authoritative he looks with a bullet in his heart, Reza thought.

Hammond's wife was the first to reach the boat slip. She removed her shoes and climbed aboard the Tiara. She fished a set of keys from her purse and unlocked the cabin door. Reza watched her take the stairs down into the cabin through his scope. Pérez hadn't followed her and had remained on the dock. Hammond had almost reached his boat slip when his lead bodyguard suddenly gyrated toward him, looking agitated. One second later, Pérez jumped into the boat. While too far away to hear what Hammond's lead agent was saying, Reza did know why the agents had spun into action.

The attack on *Surveyor* had begun, and the Secret Service had just gotten word of it. The timing couldn't have been more perfect. Reza snugged the SAKO TRG 42 stock tighter into his shoulder. To make his shot count, even at this range, Reza required a certain amount of information. The breeze funneled through the spaces between buildings would blow his bullet slightly off its path. The fact that Hammond was moving also added a degree of difficulty to his shot. Reza needed to aim not where Hammond stood when he pressed the trigger but where he'd be when the bullet arrived. Reza made a last-minute adjustment to his rifle.

There seemed to be confusion at the boat slip. Hammond, who had dropped the cooler bag on the dock, had almost pushed one of his bodyguards into the water when the special agent had tried to stop him from jumping into the boat. The two agents behind Hammond tried unsuccessfully to grip the vice president's dark green polo shirt as he rushed ahead. Clearly, Hammond wasn't going to cooperate with his security detail until he got to his wife.

Reza centered the crosshairs on Hammond's upper back just as Oscar Pérez came out of the cabin, a pistol in his hand. Following him two steps behind was Hammond's wife, her head popping out from behind Pérez's large shoulders.

Reza exhaled slowly, steadied his aim, and pressed the trigger.

CHAPTER SEVENTEEN

Miami, Florida

Alexander Hammond almost ran into his lead bodyguard, so quickly had the man pivoted toward him. The special agent had a look of grave concern on his face as he pressed a finger to his ear. He then brought his right wrist to his mouth to speak into the small microphone concealed in his sleeve.

"What is it?" Hammond asked.

"We need to bring you to safety, sir," the agent replied, putting his right hand on Hammond's chest. "*Surveyor*'s under attack. Come with me."

Hammond didn't move. "Is my daughter okay?" he asked, dropping the cooler bag he'd been carrying onto the deck.

"I don't know, sir," the agent replied, trying to push Hammond back toward the armored Suburban. "But we need to go, sir. Now."

Hammond's heart sank. *Please, God. Not again.*

He had immediately recognized the name. *Surveyor* was the NOAA vessel his daughter used as her base of operations to conduct whatever project she was currently working on. Images from last year's assassination attempt in San Francisco flashed through his mind. His one saving grace now was knowing that Clayton White was aboard *Surveyor* with Veronica. White had saved the day in San Francisco, and despite the open hostility between him and his daughter's fiancé, there was nobody in the world he trusted more to protect his daughter.

Looking around and realizing Heather was still in the boat, Hammond acted more on instinct than anything else. He grabbed the special agent's wrist and twisted it, shoving the man aside and almost off the dock and into the water. There was no way he was going to get into the Suburban before his wife.

"Heather!" Hammond shouted as he boarded the Tiara, feeling the outstretched hands of his bodyguards on his back.

Special Agent Oscar Pérez came out of the cabin first. He had drawn his service pistol, and his eyes were scanning the immediate area for potential threats. Heather was next, and Hammond saw that panic had spread across her features.

"Oh my God, Alex," she said, her voice breaking. "What's going on? Is Vonnie all right?"

Hammond grabbed her hand and pulled her in close to him, but she suddenly leaped back, as if pushed away from him by an unseen hand.

Their eyes met and held for a moment, then Heather collapsed and fell backward into the cabin.

"Heather!" Hammond screamed, rushing toward the open door. "Heather!"

He heard commotion behind him but paid no attention to it. At the bottom of the stairs, his wife's motionless body sprawled on the galley floor, her pink summer dress turning crimson around the edge of the fabric where the bullet had dug a hole to get to her heart. Before Hammond's brain could process what it was seeing, something slammed into his back with such tremendous force that he was thrown forward and headfirst down the stairs.

CHAPTER EIGHTEEN

Miami, Florida

The sniper rifle bucked against Reza's shoulders.

"Damn," he swore. Hammond had moved at the last second when he had tugged his wife toward him. The only thing Reza knew for sure was that Hammond's wife had been thrown backward into the cabin. Surely she'd been hit. But was the wound fatal, or had the bullet only grazed her?

Reza cycled the bolt and chambered another round. Hammond had moved to the cabin door. Reza readjusted his aim and fired just as Oscar Pérez moved behind Hammond, making himself as big as he could. Had Pérez seen from where Reza was firing? In the end, it didn't matter. The bullet connected with Pérez's torso, the impact thrusting him hard against Hammond.

"No!" Reza exclaimed as both men disappeared into the cabin.

On the dock next to the boat slip, the remaining bodyguards had also drawn their firearms. Reza didn't think they had pinpointed where the shots had come from yet, but the clap of the bullet cracking the sound barrier on its way to the target had revealed enough that they were all looking up in his direction. It didn't matter. For the next couple of seconds, while they wondered what to do, Reza was going to kill them all.

For his third shot, Reza aimed at the lead bodyguard, the one Hammond had shoved aside. Reza squeezed the trigger.

A direct hit to the man's chest.

The special agent was pitched backward and fell into the water between the dock and a large American-built center console berthed in the slip. Reza pulled back the rifle's bolt, which automatically ejected the spent casing, and rammed it forward to advance the next round. He had only a minor adjustment to make before he pulled the trigger for the fourth time in less than ten seconds. His shot went higher than he wanted it to, but the end result was the same. Instead of hitting his target center mass, Reza had sent his round into the man's face, pulverizing the left side of his head. Before the man's body had hit the ground, Reza had chambered another round.

Another bodyguard, realizing that he was a sitting duck, ran toward Hammond's boat. Reza fired. A miss. He cycled the bolt, aimed, and fired again. The special agent fell face first onto the dock, his left knee shattered by Reza's bullet. The agent's pistol skidded off the deck and dropped into the water. The agent tried to roll to safety, but Reza's next shot drilled him in the back.

Reza looked back through the scope at Hammond's boat. Still no sign of the vice president. Was it possible that the bullet had traveled straight through Hammond's bodyguard and hit him?

Movement at the boat ramp caught his attention. Reza swung the rifle around, but he was too late. The female special agent he had observed driving the Ford pickup had jumped over the tailgate and into the truck's bed. Reza didn't have a clear shot at her—the angle wasn't right—so he searched for a target of opportunity.

The seconds ticked by.

He had fired his first shot thirty seconds ago. This whole scenario had always been based on his firing two shots, one in each target, before making his exit. He hated leaving without being sure that Hammond was dead, but he had to go. Every additional second he stayed in the apartment skyrocketed his odds of being captured.

The sliding doors suddenly shattered as rounds were fired into the apartment. Peering through his scope, Reza concluded that he was being fired upon by the female agent who'd positioned herself in the bed of the pickup truck. If Reza couldn't get a bead on her, that meant she couldn't either.

So why is she firing? Reza wondered. His first thought was that she wanted to keep his head down to cover the advance of an assault team. Then he realized that there was no way an assault team was already in position. He had caught Hammond and his security detail by surprise less than sixty seconds ago. It was madness to think that the four remaining agents were already coordinating some sort of counterattack. No, the Secret Service's top priority wouldn't be to kill or capture him; their duty was to protect the vice president.

Reza swore out loud as he rolled away from the sniper rifle. More rounds tore the air above his head, and he heard them thump into the wall behind him. He grabbed the rifle and hurried toward the living room, where he had a direct line of sight to Hammond's boat slip. Careful not to get too close to the window, Reza chanced a look at the marina down below. What he saw pissed him off.

Three Secret Service agents were sprinting toward Hammond's boat. Reza was tempted to shoot at them but feared the female agent would spot him first. If he was to fire the SAKO again, it would only be for Hammond. But was it worth the risk? His gut told him that if he didn't exfiltrate now, he wouldn't get another chance to do so.

"Damn you!" Reza screamed at the female special agent. "Damn you!"

With one last look at Hammond's boat, Reza threw the rifle onto the sofa next to him and grabbed his blue cell phone. He unlocked it and opened a special app that had been installed by the tech gurus back in Tehran. He typed a twelve-digit password and pressed the send button. Reza closed his eyes and started counting. When he reached ten, the Nissan Altima he had rented using an alias and parked half a block away from the marina exploded. The blast rocked the entire neighborhood.

That should keep you busy, he thought.

Satisfied at the useless destruction he had caused, Reza exited the apartment and followed to the letter the escape plan he had set up for himself.

CHAPTER NINETEEN

Aboard NOAA Ship Surveyor
Florida Keys National Marine Sanctuary

White watched in shock as Veronica and another diver collapsed on the hydraulic platform as he ran toward them. To his right, someone returned fire at the speeding enemy vessel with an M4. The platform finally stopped, having reached the correct elevation, and three of the remaining divers jumped onto *Surveyor's* main deck and took cover behind the gunwale.

Emily Moss stayed put, crouched next to Veronica—who was pinned to the dive platform under the weight of another diver. Emily, eyes wild, screamed for White, then began tugging with all her might at the heavyset diver on top of her friend. The four bullet holes in the back of the diver's wet suit told White the man wasn't going to be able to roll off Veronica without help. He recognized the diver as the special agent who had gone into the water after Veronica. The moment he had heard incoming gunfire, the bodyguard had reacted on instinct and had positioned himself between the threat and Veronica. It had cost him his life, but his courage had saved hers. Before White could lift the diver's body, Mercury-Two exploded in a ball of fire, spewing water, oil, and body parts into the air and sea.

A cold sense of dread enveloped White, his mind refusing to accept what he had just witnessed. Goose bumps spread along his arms. Very few people were ready to lay down their life for a friend; even fewer were prepared to do so for someone unrelated to them. Yet five Secret Service special agents had done just that in the last three minutes. They had made the ultimate sacrifice to save Veronica.

Expecting more bullets to be fired in their direction, White wrapped his arms around Emily and lifted her up so that her feet were dangling in the air. She tried to wriggle free, her legs and arms flailing wildly, but White didn't let go. He dropped her on the main deck, then grabbed the dead special agent under his armpits.

As White lifted the special agent's body, Veronica got to her knees and staggered off the dive platform, holding her right leg.

"You hit?" White asked, dragging the special agent's body to the main deck.

"Just a graze, I think. I'll be fine," Veronica replied after she had pulled the regulator from her mouth. "What the hell is going on?"

"Make sure everyone stays low and behind the gunwale," White replied, scurrying away. He didn't have time to explain more than that. "Stay there, Vonnie, and stay safe. That's your job."

Kennedy, who had moved farther up the boat toward the bow, was sitting on the main deck, his back against the gunwale. The blood oozing from a wound between Kennedy's left shoulder and neck had stained his white shirt crimson.

"I nailed a couple of them, I think," Kennedy said, reloading his M4. "But I couldn't get a shot with the AT4. Anyone get hit? Is Veronica okay?"

"She's fine, but Mercury-Two's no more, Tim," White said.

"Yeah," Kennedy said, slowly getting up. "I heard the explosion. Who the fuck are these guys?"

"No clue," White replied, taking a moment to check Kennedy's injury. It was worse than he had originally believed. The gash was deep enough that White could see bone.

"Get a medical kit, Tim," White said. "You need to put pressure—"

"What I need to do is stop these assholes," Kennedy replied, picking up the M4. "I'm still in the fight, Clay."

White nodded, then picked up one of the two rocket launchers off the floor and sprinted to the opposite side of the boat. A special agent was firing at the lead enemy boat with the SR-25, successfully keeping it at bay. With everything going on, White hadn't noticed that *Surveyor* wasn't at anchor anymore. It was traveling north, at about five nautical miles, and accelerating.

"They want to ram us," the special agent said as more rounds flew overhead.

"Agreed," White replied. "I asked Captain Shannan to get moving as soon as the divers were safely aboard. It's gonna make it more difficult for them to hit us."

"You think they're loaded with explosives?"

"Yeah. That's why they're strafing us from a quarter mile away. They want us to keep our heads down," White replied, removing the safety pin at the rear of the rocket launcher. "That means they're about to make another run at it."

White couldn't help but think about the rubber dinghy loaded with explosives that had rammed the USS *Cole*, a US Navy destroyer, in October 2000. The explosion had blown a forty-by-forty-foot hole in the port side of the ship. The attack had killed seventeen sailors and injured thirty-eight more. He couldn't let that happen here.

White peeked above the gunwale and confirmed the location of the enemy vessel. He moved back the front and rear sight covers, and the sights popped up into their firing positions. White moved the firing rod, cocking the lever forward, and took aim at the enemy vessel, which was now about three hundred meters away and zigzagging toward them. White held down the safety lever and placed his thumb on the red firing button. He thought about checking the backblast area but remembered that this version of the AT4 was the CS, the one specifically designed for urban warfare.

The disadvantage of the AT4 recoilless design was that it had originally created a dangerous backblast area behind the launcher, which could cause severe injuries to friendly personnel in the vicinity. The AT4-CS had a saltwater countermass installed at the rear of the launcher to absorb most of the backblast, so the weapon could now be fired from enclosed areas.

Another hail of bullets raked the side of the ship, their impact making a huge and intimidating racket, but White stayed still, keeping his aim true as the special agent beside him continued to fire rounds at the boat.

"Two hundred and fifty meters," the special agent called out. "Two hundred meters."

The boat was well within range now, but if the driver's intent was really to ram a boat filled with explosives into *Surveyor*, White couldn't miss. He only had one shot. It would have been nice if Kennedy could have joined him, but White knew the injured special agent in charge was busy fighting off the other enemy vessel.

"One hundred and fifty meters," the special agent shouted. "Reloading!"

Just a few more seconds, thought White.

Now that *Surveyor* was traveling at almost ten knots, the closing speed between the enemy vessel and *Surveyor* wasn't as fast as before, which made the bad guys' job a tad more difficult. It also allowed White the extra second he needed to confirm his aim.

Sighting in on the helm, White gave it just enough lead. He pressed the red firing button with his thumb and sent the projectile downward. The rocket hit the front of the boat and exploded, sending flaming metal shrapnel and shards of plastic composites flying. White and the special agent next to him ducked behind the gunwale just as an enormous secondary explosion shuddered the *Surveyor* from bow to stern. The shock wave knocked White off his feet, and intense heat enveloped him, robbing him of his breath and making his skin feel as if it were melting. The heat dispersed quickly, but his ears and the inside of his brain vibrated with a high-pitched ringing that was threatening his sanity. He clamped the heels of his hands against his ears in a desperate attempt to ease the debilitating sensation. Next to him, the special agent who'd been operating the sniper rifle was doing the same.

Remembering that there was another enemy boat to take care of, White managed to get to his feet, as shaky as his legs were, and limp toward the last place he'd seen Kennedy. As his brain started to regain its focus, White realized that *Surveyor* was still steaming ahead, which was very good news indeed. The fact that the vessel didn't seem to be taking on water was also not lost on him. If he had missed his shot with the AT4, chances were that *Surveyor* wouldn't be afloat anymore—not with the extraordinary strength of the secondary explosion.

White found Kennedy at the bow, part of his head blown off by a large-caliber round. Next to him was a discarded AT4 rocket launcher and an M4. It wasn't difficult to understand what had happened. Kennedy had left the relative safety offered by the gunwale in order to fire the AT4 and had been hit by one of the strafes coming from the final attacking boat.

White dropped to the deck as tracer rounds stitched a line across the *Surveyor*, cutting through the windows of the wheelhouse.

Shit. Captain Shannan.

White jumped back to his feet and headed toward the stairs leading to the wheelhouse. But he never made it. An RPG slammed into *Surveyor*'s superstructure just below the wheelhouse, its impact rocking the entire ship. White was thrown against a bulkhead with such force that he was momentarily winded by the impact. Every inch of his body hurt. When he looked up, the ceiling of the wheelhouse had been peeled off as if someone had used a giant can opener.

Stunning White, who didn't believe anyone inside the wheelhouse could have survived the impact, Captain Shannan descended from the bridge, looking disoriented. The captain's face was bloody, gashed by shrapnel. There was a large piece of twisted metal embedded in her left thigh, but she managed to climb down the stairs on her own.

White made his way to her, shouting for her to stay low.

"I'm fine, goddamn it," Captain Shannan said. "What are you doing standing here looking at me? Go do your job, Mr. White!"

White's assessment of Captain Shannan was that she was in shock and needed immediate care, and that wasn't counting the piece of metal in her leg. That said, he couldn't treat her before he dealt with the last boat filled with bad guys. Another well-placed hit could sink the *Surveyor*. If White wasn't mistaken, the vessel's two big diesel engines had stopped. He couldn't feel or hear their rumbling anymore. That wasn't a good sign. Had *Surveyor* already started taking on water? Had there been more than one rocket hit? One thing was clear—*Surveyor* was now a sitting duck.

White needed a weapon. He hurried to where Kennedy had fallen to pick up his M4, but Veronica beat him to the punch.

"For God's sake, Vonnie," White roared. "I told you to stay put."

Veronica ignored him, as she often did when she didn't agree with him. White watched as she checked that the magazine was seated correctly. She then pulled the charging handle and brought the butt of the M4 to her shoulder. White peeked over the gunwale at the same time that Veronica started firing. The enemy vessel was less than 150 meters away. He identified two immediate threats. The first was a man reloading an RPG, and the second was a two-man team inserting a new belt of ammunition into what looked like an M240 machine gun. They had to be taken out. Now.

Veronica must have determined the same because White saw one of her rounds hit the man with the launcher. The impact spun him around, and Veronica's next two rounds propelled him forward. Veronica was in the process of adjusting her aim when the crew-served M240 began sending rounds in her direction. White crashed into his fiancée, knocking her to the deck as bullets pinged against the gunwale and drilled the bulkhead behind them. He covered her with his body, afraid a bullet would ricochet down and hit her.

The barrage of fire continued for another five seconds; then there was a lull, and White rolled off Veronica, snatching the M4 she had let go of. But before he could do anything else, a coast guard Sikorsky MH-60T Jayhawk thundered past, not more than fifty feet above his head. White blamed his impaired hearing for not hearing it come in. He caught a glimpse of the coast guard petty officer manning the Dillon M134D electrically driven Gatling gun in the open door behind the chopper's cockpit. An instant later, the gunner opened up with the M134D, and 7.62 mm rounds began slicing through the air at a rate of three thousand per minute.

The next ten seconds was a one-sided encounter, the carnage unimaginable. White had witnessed firsthand what the M134D was capable of in Iraq and Afghanistan, but he was nonetheless mesmerized and unable to look away. The bullets ripped through the enemy boat and its occupants. The two outboard motors caught fire, and a single soul, a man wearing black jeans and a black T-shirt, dove into the water to escape the shower of 7.62 mm rounds raining down from above. When the coast guard petty officer let go of the trigger, the enemy vessel had been turned into an amalgam of blood, plastic composite, metal, and bone.

Two rappelling lines were thrown out of the helicopter and landed on Surveyor's main deck. Next to the chopper gunner, two men appeared. Each had a large medical kit attached to a rucksack frame on their backs. They stood in the open door of the chopper facing inside, their boots on the bottom edge of the doorframe. In unison, they bent their knees and leaped backward, descending the lines.

As soon as their feet touched the main deck, the two coast guards-men signaled that they were cleared, and the rappelling lines were brought up. The chopper gained altitude and started a holding pattern above Surveyor.

Unlike the US Navy, the US Coast Guard didn't have its own corpsmen, so White assumed both men were health-service technicians.

"I'm Clayton," he said. "Captain Shannan needs immediate medical attention."

White led the guardsmen to the captain. Shannan was slumped against the bulkhead. Emily Moss knelt next to her, holding a bottle of water to the captain's lips. Shannan slowly looked up at the guardsmen. Her eyes were open but blank, and her skin was pale. Her hands were shaking badly.

"She needs help," Emily said as one of the guardsmen began assessing Shannan's wounds.

"Where's Veronica Hammond?" the second guardsman asked.

"I'm right here," Veronica replied from behind him. "Follow me. There are more injured people this way."

"No, ma'am," the guardsman said, grabbing her arm. "You're coming with us to Jackson Memorial Hospital—"

"I'm fine. My leg's okay. It was just a—"

"This isn't about you, ma'am," the guardsman said. "Your mother and father have been shot."

Veronica spun around and looked at White in complete disbelief. White was too shocked to say anything, but if it was true, the guardsman was right. Veronica had to go.

"There's two more choppers waiting for us to clear the boat. Once we're off station, more health technicians and a couple of navy doctors will board the vessel," the guardsman said. "You understand what I'm saying? We need to get moving."

"Let's go, Vonnie," White said. "I'm coming with you."

CHAPTER TWENTY

Jackson Memorial Hospital
Miami, Florida

Veronica felt the chopper bank slightly to the left as they flew over Fisher Island—a small but very wealthy 216-acre private island off the coast of Miami only accessible by ferry and helicopter. At the front, the pilot gave the two-minute warning. Veronica looked at her watch. They'd been in the air for just over fifty minutes.

Clayton had explained to her that with a range of eight hundred miles, the US Coast Guard Sikorsky MH-60T Jayhawk would have no problem reaching Jackson Memorial Hospital without the need to refuel. She'd asked the flight crew numerous times for updates on her parents, but no one seemed to know, which made her even more anxious than she already was.

It was like San Francisco all over again. It made her sick. At first, Clayton hadn't wanted to tell her how many members of her protective detail had lost their lives, but she had insisted.

Six.

In the span of no more than five minutes, six brave men had died protecting her, including Tim Kennedy, a man she had learned to appreciate very much over the last few months. Kennedy had spoken to her about her father's request to keep him in the loop about her whereabouts and activities. Kennedy hadn't been comfortable with the request. He'd even shared with her that he was considering asking for a reassignment, which Veronica knew would have sunk his career. She had told Kennedy to go ahead and write the daily reports her father wanted so much. In retrospect, Kennedy would have been better off with a lateral move to another position within the Secret Service.

He'd still be alive, she thought, closing her eyes. A profound sadness washed over her, but there were no tears, only a dry rage and a wish to kill the people responsible. When she opened her eyes, Clayton was looking at her. He gave her a weak smile from across the cabin, but she could tell he was angry. And when her fiancé was pissed, it usually didn't end well for whoever he was pissed at.

A guardsman had cleaned and bandaged her wound, but her leg was still throbbing where the bullet had grazed her. A medical team would be waiting for her at Jackson Memorial, but she'd whoosh them away. Her wound could wait. She wanted to see her parents. She prayed that they were okay.

The chopper pilot brought the Sikorsky in for landing hard and fast, as if someone's life depended on it. The helicopter flared and touched down on the concrete helipad, next to two more identical rescue helicopters already on the ground. The pilot shut down the two General Electric gas turbines, and the rotor blades slowly came to a stop.

Veronica saw men in tactical gear around the parked helicopters. That told her these were the helicopters that had transported her parents to the hospital. The guardsman that had bandaged her wound opened the heavy door of the Sikorsky and hopped out of the chopper. Two men in tactical gear approached the guardsman, who in turn nodded toward Veronica. She unbuckled her seat harness and climbed out with Clay right behind her.

One of them introduced himself to her. "Miss Hammond, I'm Special Agent Albanese, Secret Service."

"Where's my mother?" Veronica asked, grabbing Albanese's arm. "Take me to her."

"Follow my colleague, Miss Hammond. He'll take you right inside," the agent replied.

CHAPTER TWENTY-ONE

Jackson Memorial Hospital
Miami, Florida

White watched Veronica follow Special Agent Albanese's colleague under the covered walkway leading to the trauma center. She stopped and looked behind her when she realized he wasn't following. White gestured for her to keep going and that he'd be right there.

"You okay, Clay?" Albanese asked.

White had known Albanese for years. In fact, Albanese had been his first boss when White had been sent directly to the Protective Intelligence Division after his graduation from the Secret Service Academy.

"I don't know, brother. I'm still processing what the hell happened. How are Angler and Tangerine?" White asked, using the Secret Service's code names for Hammond and his wife.

"The VP's injured, but he'll pull through."

"And Vonnie's mom?" White pressed. "She's okay too, right?"

Albanese sighed and diverted his eyes for an instant. "She's gone, Clay," he said. "I'm sorry, man. I really am."

White felt an enormous pressure in the center of his chest as immense guilt wrapped itself around him. It was as if he'd received a spikelike thrust deep into his side. His knees buckled involuntarily, and his throat turned dry. As justified as his quarrel with Hammond was,

White was conscious of the fact that Veronica hadn't seen her parents in a very long time because of what he'd told her about CONQUEST. Veronica wouldn't blame him, but he did.

White had once considered Hammond a mentor, someone he could trust and count on implicitly. It wasn't his father who had taught White how to throw a curveball; it had been Hammond. And when White had thrown a baseball through the window of his father's new car, it was Hammond who had fixed it before his father had come home. Like most Americans, White had seen Hammond as the embodiment of everything that was good about America. His drive, courage, loyalty, and utter devotion to his family, friends, and country . . .

A smokescreen. All of it. Absolute bullshit.

Somewhere along the road, Hammond had lost his way and had become the very evil he'd sworn to protect his nation against. Seven years ago, he'd had a choice to make. Either he accepted responsibility for the mistakes that were made during CONQUEST, including the sinking of the vessel containing dozens of captured terrorists, or sacrifice his morality, integrity, and honor to bury the truth. In the end, Hammond had decided that covering up his action was the best course of action—even if it meant facilitating the murder of White's father, then steering White away from the truth and even taking him under his wing.

White caught himself wishing it had been Hammond who had died today, not Veronica's mother. Heather Hammond was one of the most caring, loving, and giving people he'd ever met. After his father's death, it had been Heather who'd first traveled across state lines to comfort White's mother. And Heather Hammond was the only person White knew who still sent Christmas cards every year to all her friends.

He forced all the images of Heather out of his mind and took several deep breaths to steady himself.

"What happened?" he murmured, staring at Albanese. "Tell me."

Albanese winced. "C'mon, Clay, you know I can't—"

115

White cut him off. "What. The fuck. Happened." His voice sounded like the devil himself.

Albanese took a step back and raised a hand in surrender. "They were going for a boat ride," he said. "A sniper was waiting for them across the street."

"Single shooter?" White asked, surprised.

Albanese nodded. "And a good one at that. He took out Tangerine and four agents in less than thirty seconds."

"Who knew about this outing?"

"Except for us, not many people. Angler is different from his daughter—you know that, Clay. He and Tangerine aren't active on social media, except for their official accounts handled by White House staffers. I can tell you right now that this day trip on the water wasn't public knowledge."

"Well, someone found out," White said.

"Listen, give us a few days to figure out what happened," Albanese said. "I promise I'll keep you in the loop, okay?"

White nodded. "I'm sorry, brother. It's a fucking tragedy."

"It hasn't sunk in yet. Tomorrow's gonna be rough," Albanese confessed. "But I promise you we'll catch whoever is behind these attacks."

White had no doubt the Secret Service and the FBI would do their best, but he wasn't going to wait on the sidelines for their report. Someone had tried to kill Veronica and succeeded at killing her mother; it was his job to see them dead.

CHAPTER TWENTY-TWO

Jackson Memorial Hospital
Miami, Florida

Alexander Hammond's gut tightened. He'd never liked hospitals. That his tall frame barely fit in the railed bed did nothing to change his mind. The pillowcase felt coarse against the wounds on the side of his face. As always, the odor of antiseptics was awful, and it made his head pound. He had long ago decided that the scent of the disinfectants used to clean and cover up the catastrophes that brought people into a hospital embodied the smell of death.

Death.

His heart lurched, and he gulped for air as he tried to contain the emotions swirling inside him. The agony inside his chest consumed everything. There was nothing but pain, and rage. Lots of rage. It took all his willpower not to scream out his misery.

The doctors said he'd be okay but had ordered a CT scan to rule out internal bleeding or other serious brain injury. He had knocked his head pretty hard when he fell into the cabin of the Tiara. He'd woken on the shoulders of Special Agent Albanese, a member of his protective detail who had been tasked to drive the Secret Service rigid-hull inflatable boat. Seconds later, a medevac helicopter had landed in the marina parking lot. Then he'd passed out again. The brain surgeon who had just left the room had told him he'd gotten a grade III concussion, meaning that Hammond could expect to have some difficulty keeping his balance, among other things.

"What other things, Doctor?" Hammond had asked with a thick tongue.

"Well, Mr. Vice President, for the next few days, in addition to mental fogginess and a greater sensitivity to light and noise, you might find yourself incapable of focusing or even recalling things or events you'd usually remember. Again, it will only last a week or so. Maybe less."

A week or so.

His wife hadn't been so lucky. The doctors swore to him his Heather hadn't suffered, but Hammond knew they were only saying that for his benefit. He'd seen the disbelief in her eyes just before she fell. She knew and understood what had happened. She knew she'd been shot, and her last conscious thought had been to blame him. He was sure of it.

Before he had left Hammond alone to requisition the CT scan, the doctor had told him that his wife's body hadn't been moved yet, that it was still inside the trauma center.

Hammond simply couldn't stand the idea of not seeing her one last time. It was maddening. He couldn't believe he would never hear her laugh again.

He shifted his weight in the bed but immediately felt light headed. He forced himself to control his breathing until the feeling passed. He swung his legs out of the bed and disconnected the sensors attached to the adhesive pads on his torso. He did the same with the finger sensor, and the machines instantly beeped for attention. He didn't care.

He got up, took two steps, and stumbled, his legs buckling beneath him. Grasping at air as the room spun around him, he knocked down a medical cart, sending a bunch of medicine vials flying. Hammond hit the tiled floor of the private hospital room with a thud and was hardly aware of the sound of breaking glass as the vials shattered, their contents spilling into a grisly, sticky sludge. His left shoulder took the brunt of his fall, but his forehead still bounced once off the tiles. Pain shot through his neck, and Hammond yelped in pain. For the very first time in his life, he felt useless, inadequate. He'd failed to protect his wife, and his daughter had once again been the victim of an attack. As he lay on the floor, dazed and hurting, he had to keep himself in check when he felt tears spilling from his eyes.

"Get a grip. You're a goddamn embarrassment," he muttered to himself.

He wiped his eyes with the back of his hand and blinked hard to clear the fog in his brain. It wasn't like him to wallow in self-pity. People were counting on him to take charge. What would the American people think if they saw him like this?

They'd think you're a pathetic idiot. That's what they'd think.

Hammond mustered his strength, and with what seemed to him like a superhuman effort, he managed to sit, but not without cutting the palm of his right hand on a broken piece of glass. A surprising amount of blood poured from the wound and began to pool around him.

"Dad?"

Hammond's heart almost stopped. He blinked again. As his vision cleared, he saw Veronica standing in the doorway. An instant later, a nurse rushed past her but stopped midstride when she saw Hammond sitting on the floor.

"Mr. Vice President. What the hell?"

CHAPTER TWENTY-THREE

Jackson Memorial Hospital
Miami, Florida

Veronica had never seen her confident, self-assured dad like this before. Never had she seen him look so weak, so broken. The cotton waddings rammed up his nostrils and the bandages swathing the left side of his head didn't help, nor did the enormous swelling on his left eye—its eyelid looking as if it were covering a golf ball. What startled her most, though, weren't the medical dressings or the pads attached to his chest; it was the tears on her father's cheeks. She averted her eyes, incapable of looking at him anymore.

The bank of medical monitors next to his bed was blinking and beeping. A nurse helped her dad up and took him back to his bed. Two more nurses entered the room and were quickly followed by a physician. The nurses turned off the monitors and patched the cut on his hand.

"Sir, we told you not to get up," the doctor said, not bothering to hide the angry edge in her voice. "Were my instructions unclear in any way?"

Her dad looked at the doctor, an angry scowl on his face. Veronica approached the physician from behind and gently touched her shoulder.

The doctor turned to face her, her eyes lighting up in recognition. She was dressed in blue surgical scrubs, and a mask dangled from her neck. She had light brown hair and large, intelligent blue eyes.

"Miss Hammond, I'm Dr. McWatters," she said. "I'm so sorry for your loss. We did what we could but—"

"This isn't on you, Doctor," Veronica said, tears biting at the corner of her eyes. "Thank you for everything."

"Your dad will be fine," McWatters said. "But he needs to rest for the next couple of days. In the meantime, we'll get him a CT scan to clear any doubts."

"Is it okay for me to spend some time with him?" Veronica asked.

"Of course, Miss Hammond. Please let me know if you need anything."

Dr. McWatters signaled for the nurses to follow her. Once Veronica and her father were alone and she had closed the door, she approached his bed. For a long moment, neither of them spoke. Then she slid her hand into his. He gave it a gentle squeeze. Her dad looked up at her, his eyes moist, and for a brief moment, Veronica felt like his little girl again.

"She's gone, Vonnie," he said, his voice breaking.

"I know," she said in an unsteady whisper.

She felt her bottom lip tremble, then let the tears she'd been holding back fall freely down her cheeks. She scolded herself for appearing so weak in front of him, but part of her longed for her dad and the way things used to be between them. They used to be two peas in a pod. When she was a child, he'd made her feel like she was his entire world, that he'd always be there for her, supporting her no matter what.

Then he'd lied to her.

How could she ever forgive him? Her own father had tried to sabotage everything she'd worked so hard for. Of course, once she had confronted him with irrefutable facts, he'd claimed his effort to discredit her and SkyCU Technology had been to protect the national interests of the United States. A bit of that might have been true, but his ultimate objective had always been to cover up the terrible mistakes he'd made with CONQUEST, no matter the consequences. When she looked at him now, she couldn't see the loving father she hoped might still be hidden deep behind his carapace; the only thing she saw was the face of a manipulative sonofabitch.

She removed her hands from his grip. Her father's lips parted as if he would protest, but the words turned into another breath instead. She wiped her tears with the sleeve of the wet suit she was still wearing.

"You're injured," he said, his gaze on the dressing on her leg.

"I'll be fine," she replied curtly. "But I can't say the same about the six agents who lost their lives protecting me, can I? And what about your protective detail? How many brave souls gave up everything for you today?"

"Vonnie . . . please. I—"

But Veronica wasn't done. The sadness and grief she'd felt only moments ago were being replaced by an unusual and intense anger—most of it directed at her father.

"And where the hell were you when my mom got shot? Huh? What did you do to protect her, you goddamn coward?"

Her dad cringed, her words stabbing him. Deeply. Maybe she shouldn't have said that, but damn if it didn't feel good. In her eyes, it was the man in front of her who had robbed her of precious time she could have spent with her mother. It was because of his actions, his bad decisions, that her mom was forever gone.

"You can think what you—" her father started, but she shut him up with a wave of her hand.

"Don't waste your breath," she said as she stormed out of the room, "because I won't believe anything you'll say anyway."

———

White didn't want to intrude, so he stayed outside the room, waiting for Veronica to come out. The door to Hammond's room swung open, and White looked up. The reunion hadn't lasted nearly as long as he'd figured it would. His fiancée left the room, and she seemed to want to slam the door shut before changing her mind. Special Agent Albanese, who was waiting right outside the door, exchanged a few words with her before heading into Hammond's room.

Veronica sat next to him.

"How did it go?" he asked.

"I hate him," she replied, shaking her head. "With all my heart."

White remained silent. If Veronica needed to vent, he was there for her. He wasn't about to pass judgment or add anything that could further fuel the divisiveness between her and her father. As much as he distrusted Hammond, White would never prevent Veronica from spending time with him, or making peace with what he had done. White had said his piece months ago. He had shared what he thought Veronica had to know. Now it was up to her to make up her mind.

"I can't believe she's gone, Clay," she said. "Shit."

He put an arm around her and pulled her close. She pressed her face into his neck. If there had been a way—any way—for him to take away her pain, he would have. But there wasn't, and she began to cry, her warm tears falling unchecked down her cheeks and onto the base of his neck. White just held her tight. He didn't say a word, but his mind was racing ahead, trying to figure out who was responsible for the two-pronged attack. Was it someone from Hammond's past—again? Or had it been state sponsored? If it was indeed state sponsored, whichever state was behind it had just declared war on the United States.

"I'm sorry, Miss Hammond," Agent Albanese said, interrupting White's reflections. "But Vice President Hammond wants to speak with Mr. White."

Veronica sniffled once, then raised her head. "Why?"

"He didn't say, ma'am."

"You don't have to talk to him if you don't want to, Clay," she said.

White looked at his beautiful fiancée. Her eyes were red and puffy, her face flushed. It hurt him to see her in this condition. She didn't deserve this. Unfortunately, he knew whatever *this* was wasn't over, not by a long shot. For months, even years, the media would talk about the day's events. The fallout would only get worse, especially if they were to fail to identify the people responsible. The American public had loved Heather Hammond, and they wouldn't soon forget, or forgive, her assassination. They would want results and accountability.

For the time being, and until everybody involved in today's massacre was dead, White was happy to put his differences with Hammond aside. There wasn't a thing he wasn't prepared to do to bring peace to Veronica. But first, he had to make sure that Hammond wasn't in on it, that he'd had no knowledge of the attacks. The fact that it was even a possibility would have been absurd a year ago.

Not so much anymore.

White kissed Veronica on the forehead. "No, it's okay, baby. I'll talk to him."

CHAPTER TWENTY-FOUR

Jackson Memorial Hospital
Miami, Florida

White entered Hammond's room and closed the door behind him. Special Agent Albanese made no attempt to follow and remained at his post outside the room. The last time White and Hammond had spoken was at the congressional inaugural committee luncheon twelve months ago, right after the vice president's swearing-in ceremony. White had been blunt, but while he hadn't disclosed everything he knew about CONQUEST to Hammond, he'd revealed enough to make the vice president understand that despite his and Roy Oxley's best efforts to cover up the atrocities that were committed under their watch, the underwater graveyard off the coast of the Arabian Peninsula was still there. White had made it abundantly clear to Hammond that the sunken vessel, with the corpses of the tortured terrorists locked in its cargo area, could still represent a menace to him if he didn't stop interfering with Veronica's work.

White approached the bed where Hammond lay, taking in the bandages, the swollen eye, and the medical monitors.

"You look awful," White said, not bothering with any form of greeting.

Hammond snorted and threw White a wry smile. "It's been a while since we last talked, Clayton."

"Not long enough for my liking," White said, grabbing the railings of the bed.

Hammond seemed genuinely offended. "What have I done to you so that you would turn my own daughter against me and my wife the way you did?" he asked, almost with a straight face.

White stared at Hammond in disbelief, all his anger and grief welling up again. He wanted to tell Hammond that it was he who had turned his back on his daughter and on his friend Maxwell, not the other way around. Then again, Hammond had no idea that White was aware of his involvement in his father's murder, though he must have suspected Oxley had told him. White was certain it was killing Hammond on the inside not to know for certain, so he kept his temper in check.

"I'm sorry for your loss, Alexander," he said. "I can't even imagine how you must feel, you being there and all."

Hammond's eyes darkened. "What the hell do you mean by that?"

"It's always the good people who bite the dust, right, Mr. Vice President?" White said. "We both know it shouldn't have been her getting killed at the marina."

Hammond's face reddened, and the veins in his neck popped, like worms crawling out. He raised a hand into a fist and cocked it toward White.

"You sonofabitch," he hissed. "You think I wouldn't give my life in exchange for my wife's? You think I'd hesitate even one instant to take a bullet for her?"

"Yeah, I do," White said matter-of-factly. "You tried to sabotage your own daughter, for Chrissake. That tells me loud and clear that your family isn't top of your priority list."

His words had the desired effect on Hammond. The vice president gasped, and his good eye flashed with livid anger.

"How dare you challenge me like this?" Hammond shouted. "I'd eat my own gun if it meant getting Heather back!"

White studied his face for tells that he was lying. How to detect microexpressions had been part of his advanced training, and White was pretty good at it. Not only did that skill set often come in handy when he played poker; it was also a great asset to have in his toolbox when interviewing suspects.

For the moment, Hammond was being honest, and his tears genuine.

"All right," White said, once he was satisfied that Hammond wasn't putting up an act. "What do you want to talk about?"

"You told Vonnie about CONQUEST," Hammond muttered. "That's why she won't talk to me, isn't it?"

"She's disgusted with you," White admitted. "She looked up to you all of her life, believed everything you said to her. In her eyes, you could do no wrong."

Hammond closed his good eye and let out a long breath through his mouth. "I had no choice. That damn mobile app was going to—"

"You could have told her the truth," White snapped, his voice cracking like a whip. "You could have told *me* the truth. Instead you went behind both our backs and sabotaged Veronica's lifework."

Hammond pointed a shaking finger at White. "You're missing the point. Vonnie was so eager to use the mobile app to explore the waters around the Arabian Peninsula that it left me with no other option. I had to intervene."

"No, you didn't," White cut in, appalled that Hammond couldn't even see the obvious alternative. "You could have taken responsibility. Come clean."

Hammond straightened in his bed, the disappointment evident in his features.

"I never imagined you'd be so naive! What's so freaking hard to understand? It could have brought hell on earth for the United States if someone had found the underwater graveyard. Can't you see that?"

"What I see is that your actions could have gotten you arrested and sent to Leavenworth," White said.

Hammond's face turned bright red, and his rage was like nothing White had seen before.

"It's not about me! It would have bogged down our country in congressional and senatorial hearings and investigations for years."

"Bullshit," White spat back. "Don't tell me it isn't about you."

"I did nothing wrong!" Hammond shouted, his eyes wide and wild. "Oxley sank the boat, not me!"

White stayed silent, his body stiff as steel. For almost a minute, the only sound in the room was the methodic beeping of a monitor by Hammond's bed.

"I know it wasn't you who sank the ship," White finally said. "Oxley told me that much."

His answer seemed to puzzle Hammond. "Then what's your problem?"

"My problem? Your poor leadership and your lies almost got Veronica killed, you idiot. Twice."

"Don't you think I know that? There isn't a single day I haven't thought about San Francisco. Not one. And now—" Hammond's voice cracked. He sniffled, licked his lips, and cleared his throat before he continued. "And now, I'll have to live with Heather's death on my conscience. For the rest of my life."

With some regret, White realized his questions had made Hammond relive his wife's murder. Silent sobs shook the vice president's entire body, almost prompting White to reach out with a sympathetic hand on his shoulder.

Almost.

"Believe it or not, I'm not a monster, Clayton," Hammond said after a while. "Think what you want, but CONQUEST was a necessary evil."

The muscles in White's jaw tightened again. Had his father's murder been a necessary evil too? White resisted the urge to wrap his hands around Hammond's throat and squeeze the truth out of him.

"Did I make some terrible decisions? Were there choices I made I wish I hadn't? Would I change anything if I could go back in time?

"Of course," Hammond conceded, answering his own questions. "There are a lot of things I'm not proud of. And yes, some of these bad decisions I made were to protect my own ass. I'll admit that. But the ship isn't a worry anymore, so that case is closed."

"You cleaned up the underwater graveyard?" White asked. "When?"

"The British did it. Took them three months using small civilian vessels not to attract attention. Even I didn't know they were doing it until they were halfway done.

"The point is that you have to trust me when I say that I never intentionally did anything to jeopardize Veronica's safety. Never. Same goes for Heather."

"Okay," White said, glad to know that Hammond no longer had any reason to mess with Veronica's work at SkyCU.

"Okay? That's all you have to say? So you're done with your accusations?" Hammond shook his head as little beads of sweat began to trickle down his forehead. "No more? Aren't there any more insults you want to throw my way?"

Hammond was clearly in pain, both physically and emotionally. White had no pity for him, but what had happened to his wife was downright unfair. He took no pleasure in Hammond's suffering. He might have hated the man, but he was still Veronica's father.

"Know this, Alexander," White said. "If there was a way that would see me not talking to you ever again, I'd take it. But right now, I'm afraid I'll need to put aside my personal feelings for you if I'm to get what I want."

Hammond cocked his head to one side and raised an eyebrow as he gave White a puzzled look. "And what would that be?"

"Hopefully the same thing you want," White said, locking eyes with Hammond. "Veronica's safety."

Hammond leaned back in his bed and let out a loud sigh. "You're right, there's that," he said. "But there's something else I want almost as much."

"I don't do revenge," White said, anticipating what Hammond was about to say next.

"Call it justice if it makes you feel better," Hammond said impatiently. "It's all the same to me."

White paced the end of the bed and rubbed a hand over his face. The FBI and the Secret Service were about to launch a massive investigation into the attacks. The media would join in, and the whole thing would become a circus. Leads would run cold, and whoever was behind this would slip away in the confusion.

"Have you pissed off anyone lately?" White asked. "Because I've read the latest threat assessment the Secret Service prepared, and other than the usual lunatics, I didn't see any red flags."

"Right," Hammond replied. "Well-organized and well-funded operations like these aren't run by your average nutcase."

"Keeping in mind the resources needed to pull off this kind of operation, do you have any idea who would want you and Veronica dead?"

Hammond pinched the bridge of his nose between his thumb and forefinger.

"Not off the top of my head," he said. "But—"

A knock at the door interrupted Hammond. The door eased open, and Special Agent Albanese stepped inside the room.

"I apologize for the intrusion, Mr. Vice President. I just wanted to let you know that the agents that boarded the enemy vessel that Mercury-One disabled seized equipment and material left aboard by the assailants."

"I assume investigators from the Forensic Services Division will have first look?" Hammond asked.

"Yes, sir," Albanese replied. "The FBI wasn't even there when our agents seized the material. This is definitely our case."

"What kind of material did you seize?" White asked.

Albanese looked at Hammond, who nodded, giving him permission to share the intel with White. White knew Albanese would have done so anyway, but now that the vice president had officially sanctioned the deal, Albanese was off the hook.

"It wasn't much, but in addition to the weapons, we got two flip phones," Albanese said.

"And where are the flip phones now?"

"Still on *Surveyor*, with the agents that seized them."

"Thank you, Chris," Hammond said.

Understanding he'd been dismissed by the vice president, Albanese closed the door.

"You think there's something of value on these flip phones?" Hammond asked.

"I have no idea," White replied. "What I do know is that we need a starting point."

Hammond narrowed his cold, calculating gaze on White. "We?"

"I might need you to unlock some doors for me," White said.

For the first time, the hint of an authentic smile flickered across Hammond's face.

"Oh, Clayton, I can do much better than that."

CHAPTER TWENTY-FIVE

Miami, Florida

Reza took one more glance into the rearview mirror before turning his new rental car—a Toyota Camry—through the open gates of a large parking structure. He'd checked the traffic behind him numerous times during his circuitous drive through the streets of Miami. Reza told himself he was clean; he hadn't seen a single hint of a tail during his two-hour-long surveillance-detection route. There had been plenty of police cars, but none had paid his Camry any attention. Reza cruised up to the top floor of the parking garage, then down, looking for a last-minute tail he might have missed. He left the parking structure through the same entrance he'd used and backtracked three blocks. His eyes moved constantly, cautiously probing faces and vehicles from behind his dark sunglasses. Over the years, this sort of tradecraft had become second nature for him.

Satisfied, he turned into the parking lot of a large shopping mall and backed the Camry into a spot facing an exit, ready for a fast escape if it became necessary. He unbuckled his seat belt and climbed out of the car, taking a moment to adjust the holster on his belt. Inside the mall, he bought three prepaid cell phones, then crossed the street to a coffee shop. The busy streets, packed with people of different ethnicities going about their business, made it particularly easy for him to get lost in the crowd. That was the good thing about Miami: there was always something going on.

Reza entered the café at the same time a group of elderly women was leaving, each of them carrying a hot beverage. He held the door for them, and one of them even winked as she passed him. Reza stepped inside and was welcomed by the scent of fresh pastries. There were patrons inside, but the morning rush was over. He made his way to the heavily tattooed kid behind the cash register.

"A small coffee and a croissant," Reza said. "And two creams with the coffee." He peeled two five-dollar bills from the small wad of money he kept in his pocket.

"Will that be for here or to go?" the kid asked.

"Give it to me in a to-go cup, please. You have Wi-Fi?"

The kid slid a piece of paper across the counter, printed with the name of the Wi-Fi network and its password. Reza took his coffee and croissant to a table next to a window. From where he sat, he had a direct view of the Camry. He'd be able to confirm soon enough if he was indeed in the clear or not. He ate his croissant and spent the next fifteen minutes sipping the coffee while keeping an eye on the Toyota and activating the first of the prepaid cell phones.

He texted the preestablished code to his contact in Havana, letting him know that he was now available for an update. The response was immediate and came in the form of a video. Reza glanced around. Seeing no one in his vicinity, he pressed the play button.

Video footage of the assault on the NOAA ship *Surveyor* began to play. Each of the three attacking vessels had been equipped with a high-resolution video camera. The feeds were linked via a Russian satellite to a secret military facility a few miles away from Havana. As per Reza's instructions, the crews of the vessels had only started recording once they were less than two miles from the target.

Reza felt the blood pulsing in his temples, so anxious was he to see the results of his carefully planned operation. He fast-forwarded the feed to the first gunfight and was pleased to see how quickly the first Secret Service boat was dispatched. As the crew pushed the throttles and guided the boat toward *Surveyor*, Reza spotted the second Secret Service boat heading straight at his men. Seconds later, the Secret Service boat opened up with small arms fire. Even worse, the lead boat, the one filled with explosives and tasked with ramming *Surveyor*, suddenly veered right. Had it been hit? Had the Secret Service managed to return fire? It was hard to tell as the camera was no longer pointing in the direction of the NOAA vessel.

Reza let out a curse as the boat carrying the camera stopped in the water. The footage had no sound, so it was impossible for him to confirm what was happening. Thankfully, the current swung the craft back toward the action, allowing Reza to witness the destruction of the second Secret Service boat. The intelligence he had collected had confirmed that the Secret Service had only two rigid-hull inflatable boats protecting *Surveyor*.

The hard stuff is done, he thought. *Come on, now. Go finish the job.*

Reza paused the video and opened the message app again. It was strange that there was only one video. In theory, there should have been three. He resumed the video, but the boat had swayed too far left, and the only thing Reza saw was the ocean. He moved the video forward a few frames with his finger, hoping that the camera had caught what happened next.

There. Surveyor. He pressed the play button again.

The NOAA vessel was at least one mile out, so Reza had a hard time understanding what he was seeing on the small screen of his phone. *Surveyor* was no longer still; it was moving. The lead craft was in pursuit and was quickly closing the gap. Quivers of excitement ran through him as he anticipated the massive explosion about to occur. Then, from *Surveyor's* main deck, there was a flash of light. Reza knew instantly what it was. He watched in horror as a rocket hit the lead boat, sending a towering fireball into the sky. Although he couldn't hear it, the secondary explosion was worse. The eight hundred pounds of C4 the boat was carrying detonated, and a flash of white light occupied the whole screen for an entire second. When the image cleared, *Surveyor* was sailing away, thick black smoke billowing from its mangled wheelhouse.

Cold sweat broke out on the back of Reza's neck as a white-hot anger began coursing in his veins.

For the next two minutes, the camera lost sight of *Surveyor* as the bow of the boat continued to sway under the current. Reza scrubbed his hands over his face, his heart banging against his chest. When the camera finally pointed toward *Surveyor* again, a US Coast Guard helicopter was hovering above it.

The sanctioned operation had failed. His brother would be pissed. Still, although Hammond's fate was unknown, Reza had at least managed to scratch Oscar Pérez's name off his kill list. He picked up his empty coffee cup and threw it in the trash with the paper bag from his croissant. He exited the coffee shop and headed back to the Camry, his mind preoccupied with everything that had gone wrong. He was only a few steps away from the Camry when his burner phone vibrated in his pocket. Reza looked at the screen as he opened the Camry's door. It was an unlisted number, so he didn't pick up. He sat behind the wheel and closed the door. It took less than half a second for his instincts to scream at him that something was wrong. But it was too late.

There was a cold spot at the back of his neck where the tip of a pistol pressed against his flesh. He thought about drawing his own gun, but it would take way too long from his seated position. He was doomed—unless he could open the door of the Camry and throw himself on the ground. He could then draw and . . .

"You've made enough mistakes today, Reza," his brother, Nader, said, interrupting his thought process. "Please don't make another."

CHAPTER TWENTY-SIX

Miami, Florida

Nader Ashtari replaced his pistol in his shoulder holster. "Have you lost your edge, Reza?"

"What are you doing here?" his brother shot back. "Shouldn't you be in Tehran? I thought you'd have enough on your plate with Afghanistan."

"My office can handle it for a couple days. But thanks for your concern."

The sudden departure of the Americans from Afghanistan had created a fantastic opportunity for the MOIS to embed its spies within the new Taliban government. The supreme leader claimed to whoever cared to listen that he had orchestrated all of it almost singlehandedly, but Nader knew otherwise. The Americans' precipitous retreat had caught everyone by surprise, except for Nader Ashtari. For the last two years, and with the significant power and autonomy he'd acquired since becoming the deputy director of the MOIS Directorate of Foreign Operations, he'd been quite busy arming and financing the Taliban.

His rise within the MOIS had been nothing if not meteoric. He was the architect behind Iran's success in building loyal proxy forces. It was Nader's network that Tehran had activated and used to help defeat the Islamic State. But what had made him a star within the Iranian intelligence community was how effective he had been at using major international crime organizations—including drug cartels—to advance the MOIS's objectives overseas, including the capture or assassination of dissidents of the regime. The supreme leader himself had taken notice. Thankfully, Nader's notoriety hadn't extended beyond the Iranian borders, which allowed him—with the right backstop—to still operate on foreign soil once in a while.

"You're taking a big risk being here," Reza said. "You shouldn't have come."

"And you've taken an even bigger risk going after that pig Hammond," Nader replied, biting his lip in an effort to control the anger welling up in his gut. "What were you thinking, Reza? Killing Hammond serves no purpose. None whatsoever."

"You're wrong," Reza roared. "It does for me."

Nader sighed, frustrated by his brother's inability to see the big picture. With China's help, Iran was finally getting back on its feet economically. On the Syrian front, the supreme leader's agenda was also progressing well, and it wasn't foolish to think that within a decade or two, Syria would become one of Iran's provinces. All of this was a balancing act, and one tiny misstep could potentially crumble Iran's recovery.

"Can't you see that what you've—" Nader started but was immediately cut short.

"It is you who can't see," his brother hissed. "My honor, our honor, won't be restored until Alexander Hammond and Clayton White die by my hands, just like Oscar Pérez did."

Nader was momentarily stunned. "What? How?" he babbled.

"Do you really think you're the only one capable of collecting and analyzing intelligence reports?" Reza growled. "For years, while you were concentrating on your career and busy climbing the ranks of the MOIS, I was in the field, scrutinizing and investigating every bit of intel I could find on the three people that killed our father."

Nader wasn't sure how to respond. If any MOIS agent other than Reza had strayed so far from his assignment, Nader would have had him killed. But part of him understood what Reza was going through. Their father had died on Reza's watch. It had been Reza's responsibility to protect him. And he had failed.

Seeing how badly this had impacted his brother, Nader had used all the resources at his disposal to track down their father's killers. So when two months after his father's murder, Nader learned that Lieutenant Mustafa Kaddouri—the Iraqi officer who had helped the Americans—would be leading an exercise along the Iraq-Iran border, Nader had developed a plan to capture him. But as shrewd as he was, Nader was no shooter. Convincing Reza to leave the Quds Force and join him at the MOIS had been even easier than he had anticipated—especially after he'd promised his brother that he'd be leading the operation to kidnap and interrogate Kaddouri.

But after the initial thrill of the Kaddouri operation, it quickly became apparent to Nader that his brother wasn't at his best working behind a desk in Tehran. Not that he wasn't doing a great job, because he was, but Nader could see there was something missing in his brother's life.

Combat. His brother was a skilled operator, and keeping him inside an air-conditioned office was akin to keeping a bird of prey in a gilded cage. So, when a young French investigative journalist from Reuters had somehow managed to collect raw evidence of Nader's involvement with the Taliban, Nader had opened the door of the cage and let Reza free. The French journalist had been Reza's first contracted assassination for the MOIS. And many more would come.

Weeks later, Nader hadn't hesitated to call on Reza again when several Afghan parliament members had accused Iran of setting up Taliban bases in Iranian cities. It took Reza less than two months to silence them all—and right under the nose of the Americans. Word quickly spread within the MOIS that Reza Ashtari, son of the famed general Mohsen Ashtari and brother to the new deputy director of the Foreign Operations Directorate, was the go-to in-house operator for black missions on foreign soil. What followed were years of perfectly executed assassinations of Iranians or foreign nationals brave enough to openly criticize the Islamic Republic. Poets, novelists, university professors, and Kurdish leaders, among others, died as direct results of Reza Ashtari's operations.

But Nader wasn't so sure anymore that he'd understood his brother. Maybe Reza's sole motivation all along had been avenging their father's death.

He met his brother's eyes in the rearview mirror and said, "Tell me more."

"Four years ago, Oscar Pérez joined the Secret Service, and last year, he was assigned to the vice president's protective detail. The target package you sent me about Emily Moss mentioned she was a friend of Veronica Hammond, who's . . ."

"Who's engaged to Clayton White," Nader said, finishing his brother's sentence.

"This is why I wanted to blow up the entire ship. I knew that if Veronica Hammond was there, Clayton White would be too."

Nader had to admit that his brother had thought this through. "And since you never intended on being aboard one of the three assault boats anyway, you decided to go to Florida to kill Hammond and Pérez."

"You're the one who taught me to use proxy forces whenever I can," Reza said, his tone lighter than it had been a minute ago.

"How did you know Hammond would be in Miami?" Nader asked.

"I wasn't sure, but the American media had mentioned several times that Hammond had purchased a vacation home in Florida. There was even a picture of his new fishing boat. It wasn't difficult to figure out at which marina it was docked."

Nader remained silent for a long moment. Oscar Pérez was dead. That was something positive, wasn't it? At least at the personal level. The problem was that Emily Moss hadn't been eliminated.

"Your actions have put me in a very difficult position, Reza," Nader said. "The journalist is still alive."

Reza nodded. "And for that I'm sorry."

"A Quds Force special action team is on its way to Emily Moss's apartment in New York and will finish the job when she gets home," Nader said. "As for you, I want you out of the United States by tomorrow. I'll have a new exfil strategy ready for you by the end of the day. We'll talk again when you're back in Tehran. Don't think you're off the hook."

Nader had his hand on the door handle and was about to get out when his brother turned around.

"I'll leave the United States, but I'm not going back to Tehran."

His words had a chilling effect on Nader. "What did you say?"

"You heard me. I can't go back to Tehran. Not yet. I'm not done."

"I don't care how good you think you are," Nader growled, waving a finger. "The Americans will eventually find something to connect you to your ill-conceived and unauthorized Miami operation."

"Not if I give them a big bone to chew on," Reza replied.

"What do you mean?"

A devious smile appeared on Reza's lips. "Whether you accept it or not, failure is always an option. So I made sure that certain bread crumbs were left behind. Trust me, brother. The Americans won't look in our direction."

Nader weighed his options. If Reza had found a way to point the American intelligence and law enforcement apparatus away from Iran, he'd be a fool not to at least hear out his brother's proposition.

"Okay, I'm listening," he said.

"It's all about manipulation and misdirection. Because of the attempt on Hammond's life, the Americans will have to assume that the attack on the *Surveyor* was intended for his daughter, Veronica. They'll never suspect that the objective was to kill Emily Moss."

Nader thought about it for a moment. Reza had a point. His brother's reckless Miami operation now acted as a smokescreen for the primary mission. But the diversion wouldn't last long if the Americans weren't given a target, or at least a potential suspect, to go after.

"What about the bread crumbs you mentioned?" Nader asked.

"As I said, they'll lead the Americans far away from us. I got the idea from an interesting report written by a MOIS intelligence asset within the South African Police Service. It was about a married couple named Roy and Adaliya Oxley."

"Tell me more."

And Reza did. When he was done, Nader nodded, giving his brother the authorization to proceed. It seemed that Reza wasn't just a blunt instrument after all. He had become quite a good spy. By all accounts, Clayton White would be dead by week's end.

CHAPTER TWENTY-SEVEN

US Secret Service Field Office
Miami, Florida

White had never visited the Secret Service Miami field office before. The large three-story white-and-yellow building was located just off the Ronald Reagan Turnpike and less than a mile from the East Coast Buffer Water Preserve Area.

Veronica had wanted to come with him, but Special Agent Albanese had convinced her to stay at the hospital and to get checked out by a physician. After using the hospital facilities to clean up, White was driven to the field office to meet with Benjamin Foster, the special agent in charge. Foster was a tall man in his late forties with the deeply tanned features of someone who enjoyed the outdoors.

"Glad to finally meet you," Foster said, shaking White's hand.

"Thanks for seeing me on such short notice," White said. "I know you guys must be busy."

"You know how it is, right? Even though the agents killed today weren't from our office, we all feel like we've lost family members. We'll do whatever we can to catch the motherfuckers who did this."

White understood exactly what Foster meant. As a combat rescue officer, he'd lost men in combat. He'd been unfortunate enough to repeat the experience when he had led Veronica's protective detail.

Special agents had fallen on his watch, and there wasn't a day their deaths didn't tear at his mind.

"I guess you knew one of them, too, right?"

"Yeah," White replied. "Tim Kennedy was a good agent, and I got along well with the other guys too."

"Oh, yes, of course. But . . . that's not what I meant," Foster said, hesitant. "I was talking about Oscar Pérez. I read his résumé. You guys served together in the air force, didn't you?"

White felt a wave of nausea first, then guilt. With everything that had happened in the last few hours, he hadn't had the time to check the casualty list. He knew the former PJ had joined the Secret Service and had been assigned to Hammond's detail, but it had happened a couple of months after White had retired, and he had only spoken to his former colleague once since then.

"Oscar was among the men killed at the marina?" he asked quietly, steeling himself for the answer.

"Shit. I thought you knew," Foster said. "I'm sorry."

"Not your fault," White said, shaking his head.

"For what it's worth, he took a bullet for the VP. If it wasn't for Pérez, Hammond wouldn't be at the hospital; he'd be at the morgue."

White swallowed hard, angry at the unfairness of it all. Hammond for Pérez—that was a bad deal all around.

Both men were silent for a moment. And then, acknowledging that there were things they needed to discuss, Foster said, "Can I offer you something to drink?"

White declined, but he took a seat in one of the two armchairs facing Foster's massive oak desk while the special agent in charge slid into a well-worn swivel chair. A large single window behind Foster gave White an unimpeded view of the parking lot.

"I've been told to assist you in any way I can, but I haven't been given the specifics," Foster said. "Mind helping me figure out what I'm supposed to do?"

"I'd like access to the two flip phones the guys have seized from one of the boats," White said. "I'm told they were brought here."

"Right. We've got them at our forensic lab downstairs. We were told not to touch them before the FBI got here."

"Are they bagged and tagged?" White asked, wondering if they'd been officially entered in the evidence log.

"I can't say for sure," Foster said, lifting the handset from the phone on his desk. "But I'll check with my technician."

"Do you know the ETA for the FBI?" White asked.

"I'm not even sure they've left Quantico yet," Foster said, dialing a number.

"Probably a team from the Operational Technology Division," White thought out loud.

"That's what I assumed too."

If the FBI had decided to send a team from Quantico, that meant they were sending the very best digital forensic examiners in the country. These scientists, based at the FBI Laboratory in Quantico, Virginia, were unsung heroes. Their work rarely made the news since they weren't the ones making the arrests, but the world-class capabilities deployed by the OTD had not only been instrumental in averting more than one terrorist plot but had also helped identify a number of adversaries involved in assassination attempts and espionage activities.

"Olivia, it's Benjamin," Foster said into the handset. "I'm with Clayton White. Have the two flip phones been entered into evidence yet?"

"Shit," he said a moment later. "Ah, okay. Good. Wait for us to get down. We'll be there shortly."

Foster replaced the handset in its cradle.

"So?" White asked.

Foster got to his feet. "Follow me, my friend. I'm afraid the phones have already been entered into evidence, but it seems that my forensic technician got some intel out of them before locking them away."

Given the small size of the Secret Service office in Miami, White hadn't expected to see a state-of-the-art crime lab. It was spacious, well equipped, and professionally staffed. He remembered that when he had joined the Secret Service, some of the labs were staffed by an ever-changing rotation of special agents who cycled through the positions and left as soon as they had learned the ropes. That wasn't the case here, and White thought that having a lab staffed entirely with civilian experts was a significant improvement.

Foster introduced White to Olivia, a slim-built woman in her late thirties with leaf green eyes whom he recognized from the photo in Foster's office.

"Clayton's been given access," Foster said. "Tell him what you've found."

Olivia looked at White. "First, I'm so glad Veronica Hammond is fine," she said, placing a hand on her heart. "I've been using her mobile app since its launch. She's a formidable role model for our daughter."

"Thank you," White said, thinking that Veronica was indeed a formidable role model, even to him. "I'll make sure to pass along your kind words."

They followed Olivia to a circular room filled with monitors and computer stations. Two other forensic specialists were typing away on their keyboards. One of them briefly looked up before focusing once more on her monitor.

Olivia sat down behind a computer and began to type in commands. White stood silently behind her, watching over her shoulder.

"You have to understand that I had only spent a few minutes with the phones before Benjamin told me I needed to wait for the FBI team to arrive before proceeding any further," Olivia said.

"Were you able to hack the phones or not?" White asked.

Olivia replied with a question of her own. "Did you know flip phones are making a comeback, especially among celebrities?"

"I don't follow these kinds of trends," White replied, wondering where this was going.

"Well, they are," she replied. "Care to guess why?"

"They're less expensive?" White hazarded.

Olivia stopped typing and looked over her shoulder. He could almost see the *Are you serious?* question mark hovering above her head.

"No, Clayton, I don't think celebrities care how much their data plan costs per month," Olivia said with a light chuckle. "They're making the switch because in the age of cloud accounts being hacked and confidential emails being leaked, having a flip phone gives its user much more security."

"But you did find something, yes?"

"I did, and, in all honesty, I don't think the FBI will get much more out of it."

"Why?"

"These particular flip phones are simplistic devices," she explained. "They do offer heightened security against hackers who operate online, but they're very easy to break into when you actually have them in your possession."

"Does that mean you were able to download pretty much everything the users have done with these phones?"

"Yes." She grinned. "That's why I'd be shocked if the FBI can squeeze anything more out of them."

Olivia rolled her chair to the side to give White some space.

"Here are the numbers and text messages I was able to download. But I wouldn't pay too much attention to the text messages," Olivia warned. "All of them were exchanged exclusively between the two phones we seized."

White stared at the screen, scanning the two dozen or so text messages and numbers. The messages were all in Spanish, which was interesting. None of the phone numbers rang any bells, but White noticed that the area codes didn't originate from the United States.

"Did you cross-reference them with any federal databases?" he asked.

"I was just about to do that when Benjamin called."

For the next few minutes, Olivia entered each phone number into a special search engine reserved for federal law enforcement agencies.

"It's gonna take a while for the numbers to grind through all the public data files," Foster said. "The algorithm will first try local, state, and federal databases; then it will move on to the records made available to us by our international partners."

"You don't have to go through Interpol for those?" White asked. "I wasn't aware we had access to other countries' files."

"If you want a full research and analysis, then, yes, Interpol remains the way to do it," Foster explained. "This new direct initiative started six months ago, but most countries aren't yet online. It's a reciprocity project, really. You need to share intel to get intel. So far, the Canadians, Australians, and the Brits have joined. And it only allows for a quick preview of the files. But it's better than nothing."

"We've had some luck no later than last week," Olivia said. "So we know it's working."

"There seem to be a whole lot of numbers from overseas," White said, still looking at the call records. "4-4-2-0. Where's that?"

"London, UK," Olivia replied without hesitation. "I have an aunt who lives there."

"Six calls originated from this number in the last seventy-two hours," White said. "The latest was this morning, approximately twenty minutes prior to the attack. I want to know who it belongs to."

Olivia let her fingers loose on the keyboard, and strings of texts appeared and disappeared from the screen, too fast and too many for White to read. He heard her grunt a few times. She even cursed once, which caused Benjamin to frown at her.

"I can't find anything on this number on open sources," Olivia said, staring at Foster as if she was waiting for his authorization to do something else.

Foster nodded, then said, "Cover your traces, Olivia. Now isn't the time to piss off the wrong people."

Olivia reached for a bag under the computer station. From the bag she retrieved a laptop and a thumb drive. She powered up the laptop and inserted the drive.

"What are you doing?" White asked.

"You want to find out who that London number belongs to, right?" she said.

"Can you?"

"You'll know soon enough," Olivia replied, clicking on the icon that had popped up on screen. The computer hummed to life.

"The USB drive will wipe all traces of her search as soon as she powers off the laptop," Foster said. "And while she's online, the internet protocol address she's using is bouncing around the globe every thirty seconds to discourage anyone from monitoring or tracking her activities."

"That's nice," White said. He knew these things existed, but he'd never understood or learned how they worked.

"It is, as long as you're not using whatever info you acquire in front of a judge," Foster said.

"I'm not looking to win a criminal case," White said.

"I didn't think you were."

Olivia's laptop beeped twice. A block of plain, unformatted text appeared. She grabbed a pen and a piece of paper and wrote something on it, then gave it to White.

"There you go," she said. "The phone's registered to a holding company in the Bahamas."

"That's the company's name?" White asked, looking at the string of numbers Olivia had written.

"No, it's not. I have no idea what the company calls itself," Olivia said. "The numbers I've written down are associated with the law firm that set up the holding company. But I'll have to check that 2-7-2-1 code. I have no idea where it's from."

"No need," White said. "It's a Cape Town number."

"Cape Town? Like in South Africa?" Foster asked. "Does that mean anything to you?"

"Yes," White said, thinking about that talk Pierre Sarazin had wanted to have about Kommetjie. "It certainly does."

CHAPTER TWENTY-EIGHT

Miami, Florida

Since the news media had reported the attack on *Surveyor*, Veronica's phone, email, and social media accounts had gone crazy. As much as she wanted to reply, even if only to reassure her followers, Special Agent Albanese had strongly recommended against it.

"Please, Miss Hammond," Albanese had pleaded. "Let the White House press secretary handle this."

While she'd so far resisted posting anything, she'd called her associates at SkyCU Technology to let them know she was okay. Her friend Emily had texted her five minutes ago to say she was done giving her statement and was now on her way to the hospital with a change of clothes and some food. Clay was on his way, too, and her fiancé had sounded a little bit more pissed off than when he'd left a couple of hours ago. White had preferred not to discuss on the phone what he'd found out at the Secret Service Miami field office, but he'd promised to share everything with her once he was back at the hospital.

A nurse had applied a generous amount of antibiotic ointment to her injury before bandaging it once more. The wound on her leg had been deep enough to require thirteen stitches, and the surgeon had confirmed it would leave a permanent mark, but that wasn't why her hands were shaking. The loss of her mother was.

Today's events were hard to digest. Her mother's assassination by an unknown sniper weighed heavily on her. She had a tough time coming to terms with the reality that the person she admired the most was no more. It was her mom, through her own charitable work, who had inspired her to better herself in all aspects of her life, to become a pioneer in her field, and to never compromise her principles. She knew that the overwhelming feelings of sadness would eventually lessen, but for now they were crushing her.

Veronica took several long, deep breaths. She looked down at her hands. They had stopped shaking.

For now.

She wasn't sure if she was angry, sad, or afraid. She guessed it was a mix of everything. She looked around the hospital room, which was located two doors down from her dad's, and the scene around her looked all too familiar.

White walls. A hospital bed. Blue curtains. Two stiff, ugly chairs in one corner and a wastebasket in the other. It reminded her of all the hours she'd spent with Clay at Pierre Sarazin's bedside while the former French spy was recuperating from the gunshot wounds he'd sustained in South Africa. Thinking about Sarazin, she grabbed her phone, unlocked it, and then proceeded to scroll through the gigantic number of emails she'd received since this morning.

There. Pierre's message was almost at the very top.

Vonnie—

I'm worried sick about you and Clay. Saw the news about what happened. Please let me know you're okay and if there's anything—and I truly mean any-thing—I can do to help.

Love,
P.

Veronica typed a reply, reassuring Sarazin she and Clay were fine and promising to call him before the end of the day. Sarazin was a good, loyal friend. He didn't deserve to be kept in the dark. There was no way she would make him wait until the White House's official statement to let him know she was okay.

Her phone pinged. Sarazin had sent his reply. She opened it.

Thanks for your response. I spoke with Clay a few minutes ago. I'm on the next flight to Miami. See you soon.

Veronica put down her phone and rested her head on the pillow. She closed her eyes and regretted it immediately. Images of the man she'd shot and the special agents who'd fallen to protect her burst forth in her mind's eye. She fought the images, but they refused to go away, and with each passing moment, another wave of angst roared through her being. Her guilt was becoming overwhelming, its viselike grip snaking its way around her chest, making it difficult to breathe. Then, as if they were blown away by an unseen gust of wind, the images were replaced by her mother's voice.

I'm still here, Vonnie. I'll never leave you, my dear. Be strong. I love you.

The tears she'd been fighting to keep back began to flow down her cheeks, bringing some sort of relief to the choking sensation she'd been experiencing since she'd spoken to her dad.

———

"Hey, girl," Emily said, entering the room with bags in her hands.

Startled, Veronica sat bolt upright in her bed, gasping for air, and realized she'd fallen asleep.

"You okay?" Emily asked, rushing to her side.

Veronica stifled a sob and got out of bed. She hugged her best friend tightly, blinking back the tears she once again felt coming.

152

"Holy shit, Vonnie, you're shaking," Emily said, pulling away. "Let me call the doctor."

"No, I'm fine," Veronica said, grabbing Emily's arm.

Emily stood next to her, looking at her eyes, examining her face. "All right, then."

"How are you feeling?" Veronica asked.

"I'm the one who should be asking *you* that," Emily replied. "I didn't lose my mom today, nor did I get shot in the leg."

"The leg's fine. I swear. The doctor stitched me up. I'm as good as new."

"Maybe, but what about what's going on in there?" Emily asked, tapping a finger on the side of her head.

"It's tough, I won't lie, but I can feel her, you know?" Veronica said, placing her right hand on her heart. "She's in here. With me."

Emily gave her a long, heartfelt hug. "I'm here if you need to talk, okay?"

Veronica nodded, then said, "Listen, Emily, I'm so sorry you had to go through this, being shot at and all. I'm so sorry for everything—"

"Stop it, Vonnie," her friend snapped back. "How's this your fault? Tell me, please. Because I can't seem to figure it out."

Veronica rubbed her eyes with the back of her hands and said, "I know. I know it's not my fault. It's just, I feel terrible. I . . . I don't know what to think anymore."

"Well, Vonnie, I'll tell you one thing. You're one tough chick."

"Come again?" Veronica asked, surprised.

"There's a couple of guardsmen who told me you shot one of the terrorists. Is that true?"

Veronica swallowed hard, but this time no images of the bad guy appeared. "He was about to fire an RPG," she said, shaking her head. "So yeah, I shot him. Twice, I think."

"I wish I'd been at your side when you killed that man, but I wasn't. I froze when bullets started flying over my head. You didn't. You saved my life. Thank you."

"Please, Emily, don't thank me. I still have no freaking idea why all of this happened."

"Did your dad tell you anything? Do you think he knows?" Emily asked, always the journalist.

"He hasn't shared anything with me."

"And what about Clayton? Where's he?"

"He's already on the hunt," Veronica said, leaning against the bed. "I think Clay and my dad have reached some sort of truce."

Emily raised an eyebrow. "I get that Clay wants to go after whoever is responsible, but there's no way he's already figured out who's behind the attacks. Do I have this wrong?"

"Who's asking? The Pulitzer-winning journalist or my best friend?"

"Can it be both?"

"I'm afraid not," Veronica said. "But the answer would be the same. I don't know."

Emily shrugged as if it didn't matter anyway and handed Veronica one of the bags she'd brought with her. "There you go. Fresh clothes, a bottle of shampoo, and some shower gel. I even found your makeup bag."

"You're the best," Veronica said.

"Now, let's get some food into you. I can hear your stomach growling and it's freaking me out," Emily said, opening the second bag. "Then I have a flight to catch."

"What? To New York?" Veronica asked, a bit shocked that her best friend was able to glide through the day's events so calmly.

"I'll meet up with you in New York next week for my meeting with the *Times* editor," Emily replied. "But I'm not going home just yet."

Veronica gave her a quizzical look. "Where, then?"

"You remember Angus?" Emily asked.

"Yeah, how could I not? This guy was perfect for you. But didn't you leave him before you took off for Turkey and Syria?"

"I did, but I'm back now, ain't I?"

Veronica smiled. A near-death experience like the one they'd gone through aboard *Surveyor* was a profound personal phenomenon. Everyone dealt with traumatic events in different ways, and it seemed that Emily's method was to reunite with the only man Veronica knew her friend had truly loved.

"He knows you're coming?" she asked.

"No," Emily replied, grinning. "What would be the fun in that?"

———

Veronica was halfway through her second egg-and-swiss-cheese sandwich when her fiancé returned. He was dressed in a pair of blue jeans and a plain white T-shirt that showcased his hard, defined arms. His eyes lit up when he saw her.

"Hey, baby," White said.

"Hey," she said, her mouth full.

She set the sandwich down and stood, and he wrapped his arms around her. They pressed their foreheads together for several seconds, their eyes closed.

"Tell me what you learned," Veronica said, pulling away.

White looked around the room. "Where's Emily?"

"On her way to the airport to catch a flight to Chicago."

"To see Angus?" he said. "Good for her."

"How did you know?" Veronica asked, frowning.

"She lives in New York," White said. "There's only one reason for her to go to Chicago. Love."

Veronica studied him for a moment, running a finger along his jaw. She rose on her toes and kissed him.

"Now," she said a moment later. "Tell me what you learned."

"Okay, but that stays between you and me," White said, looking inside the grocery bag Emily had brought with her.

"Of course," Veronica replied.

White pulled out an apple from the bag and sat down in one of the chairs. "There's a possibility that the attacks came from someone inside Roy Oxley's former organization."

Veronica hadn't expected this. She rubbed a hand over the back of her neck.

"Are you sure?"

"No, I'm not," White replied, reaching into one of his pockets. "But with your help, maybe I can get a better idea."

He took a bite of the apple and handed her a piece of paper with a Cape Town phone number on it.

"What am I supposed to do with this?" she asked. "Call it?"

"You've told me before that SkyCU Technologies is more than a one-trick pony," White said while chewing. "You even suggested that they had the bandwidth to access or break into pretty much any databases that aren't protected by military-grade software."

"Not sure where you're going with this, but yes, they can do that." Veronica scrunched up her face. "But it's illegal."

"I know," White said, taking another bite.

"And isn't it something the FBI or the Secret Service could do?"

"Yes, but they'd need a warrant from a judge, which I doubt they could get since I didn't get this number by following protocols. But even with a warrant, their search would leave traces because the agents executing the warrants would need to document their actions."

"And that's a bad thing how?"

"I want this inquiry to remain low key, Vonnie," White said.

"What do you need exactly?" she said, examining the phone number.

"I want to know when this phone was first activated, where it has been, and—"

"And you want to see if we can track it," Veronica finished his sentence for him.

"Will you do it? I wouldn't ask if I didn't think it was important."

"I'll give the number to Brad, SkyCU's chief technology officer," she said, reaching for her phone. "He's a straight shooter, and I trust him. He'll let us know if he's willing to help or not."

"All right. Thanks," White said. He kissed her on the cheek and headed for the door.

"Where are you going?"

"I'm gonna talk to Special Agent Albanese," White said. "I figure you'd like to leave this place before dinnertime, yes?"

"Not sure," she replied, pretending to think about it. "The nurse promised me I was going to travel the world through my dinner tray tonight."

White laughed. "Then I guess you're going to Russia," he said. "I hope you fancy bland cabbage soup and overcooked, dry pastry dumplings."

She shooed him away with a flick of her wrist.

CHAPTER TWENTY-NINE

Pompano Beach, Florida

Apparently, arranging for a safe house was more difficult than White had told her it would be. In the end, it was Benjamin Foster—the special agent in charge of the Secret Service Miami field office—who had come through for them. At 10:30 p.m. a new contingent of special agents had arrived to replace the exhausted team who'd been there since the early morning. Albanese had asked to stay on to ensure continuity and cohesion. Foster had approved the request, but Veronica hoped the man would soon get some well-deserved rest.

The one-story safe house was less than a quarter mile south of the Pompano Beach Airpark and had three bedrooms, two full bathrooms, and a large combined kitchen and living area that opened to a wooden deck that overlooked an immense grass lawn at the back of the house. The attached garage was big enough to park two of the three black SUVs inside it, which helped keep the Secret Service presence low key. The third SUV was in the driveway with two special agents aboard, ready to go at a moment's notice.

White and two other special agents had cleared the house as soon as they'd arrived, making sure all the doors and windows showed no signs of forced entry. The house wasn't luxurious by any means, but it would do just fine.

She and White had just started digging into the Thai food Albanese had picked up from a nearby restaurant when Pierre Sarazin knocked on the wall, startling her.

"You've ordered enough for me?" the Frenchman asked, approaching the table.

Veronica jumped to her feet, almost knocking her chair over. "Pierre!" she squealed, delighted to see him.

"Je suis tellement heureux de vous voir, mes amis!" Sarazin said, his arms open wide, a big grin on his face.

He hugged her for a long time before letting her go. He kissed her on both cheeks.

"I'm so sorry for your mom, Vonnie." Sarazin's voice was filled with honest, heartfelt compassion. "She was a great woman, and I can only imagine how much you must be hurting."

"Thank you," she said, feeling her heart squeeze as she spoke the words.

"I'm sure the next few days and weeks will be extremely busy. If there's anything I can do, please let me know, all right? I really mean it."

"You're a good friend, and thanks for being here. I promise I won't hesitate to ask."

Her answer seemed to satisfy him. Her mom's death had been so unexpected that she'd caught herself wondering more than once whether it had really happened. She still couldn't believe she'd never hear her mom's soft voice ever again. She was having a hard time processing the murder, but she hadn't shed a single tear since she had left the hospital. In fact, her sadness had mutated into a righteous anger.

What had her mother done to deserve such a tragic end? And what about her? Who wanted her dead? And why? She might not know the *who* just yet, but the *why* was easier to satisfy. In this case, the most obvious answer was probably the correct one.

Her father.

Her dad's actions had triggered the assault at the Ritz-Carlton in San Francisco last year. It would make sense if they had also precipitated today's attacks. Clay was right: her father was toxic.

Sarazin took two strides toward White and offered him his hand. "I almost had a heart attack when I watched the news."

White ignored Sarazin's outstretched hand and pulled him in for a manly hug.

"We appreciate you being here, Pierre, but you didn't have to fly to Florida," White said.

"Nonsense! And like you suggested in your text message, I was bored out of my mind. So here I am, ready to help in any way I can."

"You mentioned Kommetjie in your message," White said. "What is it you wanted to talk about?"

Sarazin chuckled. "Nothing. Just my head playing tricks on me," he said, taking a seat at the table.

Veronica noticed that the small Frenchman—as usual—was impeccably dressed. He wore a tailored sport jacket over a white collared shirt and light blue designer jeans. It certainly didn't look as if he had spent the last five hours cramped into the economy seat he'd purchased at the last minute. For years he had operated undercover as a sommelier in two Michelin-star restaurants in California, conducting industrial espionage for the French Republic by targeting visiting foreign officials and American business leaders dining at the high-end establishments. There had been almost no risk involved, and the quality of the intelligence he had provided to his superiors at the DGSE had made him a rising star within the spy agency. All of it had come to an abrupt end when he'd tried to hack into her dad's phone—at the time, her father had been the commanding officer of JSOC. The hack had backfired. Coerced to work as a double agent for her father, Sarazin was sent to Kommetjie, South Africa, to manage Roy Oxley's vineyard. Sarazin's real mission, though, had nothing to do with wine. His job had been to report Oxley's activities directly to her dad. In the end, Sarazin's actions at the winery had saved White's life, and for that she'd always be grateful.

"I hope you're hungry, Pierre," White said, gesturing toward the paper plates and half dozen take-out containers on the dining table. "There's more than enough food to feed the three of us."

They sat down at the table, and Sarazin ceremoniously placed the cheap paper towel on his lap as if it were made of linen.

"Bon appétit," he said.

Veronica was glad to see Sarazin. Less than a year ago, Roy Oxley had shot him twice in the chest. Sarazin had nearly died. Now he looked healthy, and Veronica thought her friend had even gained a bit of weight since she'd last seen him, which wasn't surprising given the speed at which Sarazin was shoving pad thai into his mouth.

"Emily's gone, I see," Sarazin said. "That's too bad. I love that girl."

"She left this afternoon," Veronica replied, taking a bite of her spicy green papaya salad. "She went to seek comfort and support in Angus's arms, it seems."

"Understandable," Sarazin said. "I'm sure she's shaken."

"She surprised me on that boat today," White said, using his thumb to push some coconut rice onto his fork. "She didn't seem at all fazed when the shit hit the fan."

"She's a tough cookie," Veronica said. "I'm wondering if she'll write a piece on what happened."

"I'd be surprised if she didn't," White said. "I wouldn't hesitate if I was in her shoes—"

Veronica's vibrating phone interrupted him. She leaned over to look at the number.

"It's Brad," she said. "I'm gonna put the call on speaker so you guys can hear what he has to say." She did so, her expression keen.

"Hey," she said to Brad. "I'm with Clayton and another friend. You can speak freely. Did you find anything?"

"I did, but I'm not sure how much of it will be useful—"

"Let me be the judge of that. What you got?" Veronica asked, her impatience showing.

"The number belongs to Gehardus van Schoor," the SkyCU's chief technology officer said. "He's—"

"I know who he is," Sarazin said, cutting him off. "He was Roy Oxley's attorney in South Africa. He's based out of Cape Town. He also represented Oxley Winery and Roy's wife, Adaliya, in all legal matters. Not a bad guy, actually."

"Hi, Brad. Clayton speaking. Do you have a home or office address for Mr. Van Schoor? I'd love to speak with him."

"I have an address, but I don't think it will help you out much."

"How so?"

"It's all over the local Cape Town news," Brad replied. "Van Schoor was mugged a few hours ago by a bunch of angry teenagers. Witnesses are saying he resisted and was stabbed to death. They haven't caught any of the culprits."

Veronica thanked Brad and disconnected the call. She turned to White. A frown marred her fiancé's face.

"Someone's busy covering their tracks," he said. "Van Schoor's fingerprints are all over this morning's attack. Whoever's behind this didn't want him to talk."

"Cape Town is a dangerous city," Veronica pointed out, playing the devil's advocate. "You guys have to remember that it was only a couple years ago that they averaged eight murders a day."

"I remember this vividly," Sarazin said. "The government even deployed the South African Army to help stop the violence. A sommelier friend of mine, who at the time worked at one of the wineries, told me that forty-three people were killed in one single weekend in July of that year."

"Listen," White said, putting his fork down. "I'm not denying that it's possible Van Schoor was killed by a bunch of kids for no other reason than that he was at the wrong place at the wrong time. But most of the violent crimes committed in Cape Town happen between rival gang members. I think Van Schoor was targeted. This wasn't random."

Veronica agreed. "What do you want to do? I hope you're not thinking about going back to South Africa."

White waved his hand. "No, but I'm seriously considering paying a visit to someone in London."

It didn't take long for Veronica to make the connection. "Adaliya Oxley," she said through clenched teeth. "You're right, this isn't a coincidence."

"I had a hunch this lady wasn't done causing problems," Sarazin said.

"What do you mean?" Veronica asked.

"That's what I wanted to talk to you about," Sarazin said, pointing his fork toward White. "I've been thinking about my time in Kommetjie a lot recently, and knowing how close and connected Adaliya was to her husband's businesses, I couldn't believe she had simply retired quietly to London. Now I see I was right."

"She wants revenge," White said levelly, pouring himself a glass of sparkling water. "It's as simple as that. She feels she was wronged, and now she wants payback."

"So do I," Veronica hissed, clenching her fists in anger. "You think she ordered the hits on me and my father?"

Her fiancé met her gaze. White seemed to consider his next words.

"Who said her intent was to kill your father? Your mother could have been the target all along," he said. "Think about it, Vonnie. Adaliya knows your father is at least somewhat responsible for her husband's death. Maybe for her, getting payback doesn't mean killing your dad."

Veronica's throat tightened. "She wants him to suffer by seeing my mom and me die."

"I think that's something we should consider," White replied.

"As I said, the lady was fully involved in all of her husband's schemes. She isn't the victim the media portrayed her to be. I can guarantee you that," Sarazin said, stabbing a shrimp with his fork. "The only thing the South African media talked about was how great the Oxleys were, and how much their financial contributions helped the country's poorest residents."

"The real question we should ask ourselves is if Adaliya Oxley actually has the means and contacts to mount such precise and concurrent operations," White said. "Maybe we're wrong about this, and the ops were state sponsored."

"You're right," Sarazin said.

"There's only one way to find out," White said.

Veronica looked at her fiancé, guessing where this was going. "No," she said, wagging a finger at him, then at Sarazin. "Pass on the intel to the Secret Service or the FBI and let them deal with this, Clayton. You guys aren't going to London. No freaking way."

"I think we are," White said, grinning. "And you're going to California."

PART THREE
FOUR DAYS LATER

CHAPTER THIRTY

SkyCU Technology
Palo Alto, California

Veronica entered her ten-digit code and opened the door to the computer lab. There were only three people inside the lab. Two nerdy-looking guys were seated behind desks, focused on the computer screens in front of them. Veronica recognized them as two of the newly hired software engineers SkyCU had recently brought in. Noticing the headsets over their ears, and the fact that their eyes hadn't moved from their screens, she didn't bother trying to greet them. Seated one row farther down was Brad, who was enthusiastically waving at her to join him.

The computer lab was located in the middle of SkyCU Technology's newly built headquarters in Palo Alto. The lab had no windows, and it was soundproof. Although there were ten workstations, there was enough space left for a coffee bar and two plush white-leather sofas. Each workstation was equipped with two thirty-seven-inch monitors, an ergonomic keyboard, and a large but modern desk. The floors were white marble and matched the wall color of the brightly lit room.

The new headquarters wasn't large. It was a two-story building of approximately four thousand square feet, but it was theirs, and it had been built to their specifications. Physical security of the building was top notch, but Veronica's main concern was their servers and cloud operations. Personal data was the most sought-after currency of the digital age. The safeguarding of that data was on everyone's mind and had become a priority for every technology company, big or small. Veronica felt the same way. She wanted Drain2 users to feel confident that their data was secure. To that end, and following last year's breach, the SkyCU board of directors had approved the financing of its own cybersecurity division. The company had poured millions of dollars into building a solid and nearly impenetrable structure. So far, it seemed to be working.

As she made her way to Brad, Veronica shivered in the room's airconditioning. The temperature was ideal for computers, but it certainly was not for human beings.

"What's up?" she asked, taking a seat next to him.

"We got in," he said, clearly excited. "You were right, Vonnie."

Brad tapped the center of the monitor with his index finger. "Take a look at this," he continued. "How did you know?"

Veronica leaned toward the screen. There it was. Mary, Adaliya Oxley's oldest daughter, had reactivated her old Instagram account.

"She's a teenage girl," Veronica said. "They can't function without social media. That's the way this generation connects with friends."

Despite this terrific break, Veronica had to give it to whoever was in charge of Adaliya Oxley's digital security. They were running a tight ship. It had taken much longer than anticipated to track down someone in Adaliya's close circle. Not wanting to waste any time, Clayton and Sarazin had traveled to London two days ago and were now waiting for her to come up with intel they could act on.

Adaliya had been part of the elite in South Africa. She and her husband had mingled with Cape Town's top politicians and business leaders and had wielded considerable power that reached out across the South African borders. Veronica had wrongly assumed it would be the same in London. Her rationale had been that Adaliya would want to acquire similar influence in England. Clearly, that wasn't the case. Adaliya had shut down all her social media accounts and resigned from the boards of directors she'd sat on for years—both in England, where her children had long attended private boarding schools, and in South Africa. The folks running digital security for the family had been thorough. Internet search engines hadn't revealed any personal or business details. Adaliya and her children had almost vanished without a trace.

Almost.

"What do we do now?" Brad asked.

Veronica angled the keyboard toward her and started typing. "I want to know when she last logged on."

It didn't take long for Veronica to figure out Mary's pattern. She opened a new tab and enlarged what she found on the screen. She looked at her watch.

"If she logs in today, it's gonna happen soon. You see this?" she asked, her finger tapping the chart she'd downloaded. "Mary logs in every day after school. Usually between four and four fifteen in the afternoon. She doesn't browse, but she checks her direct messages. And she never does it from home."

"That's because she's afraid her phone will automatically connect to the residence's Wi-Fi," Brad said. "She feels safer using the school's network."

"Right," Veronica agreed. "Connecting from the house could potentially lead to her mom finding out she's kept her IG account."

"She seems to be talking to only one person," Brad said, writing down the name.

"Yep," Veronica said, reading Mary's messages. "She clearly wants to see that person again, but that person isn't interested in meeting before Mary explains why she left without even saying goodbye. A boyfriend maybe?" she thought out loud.

Brad shrugged. "Could be. Whoever it is, he hasn't replied to any of her new messages."

That gave Veronica an idea. She pushed her rolling chair with one foot and slid to the next workstation. She quickly logged on and booted up special software that would allow her to surf the internet incognito.

"How do you spell the username of the person she's been messaging with?" she asked.

Brad told her. Veronica entered the name in the in-house search engine and let the program do its job.

"Okay," she said moments later, her eyes going through all the data that had appeared on her screen. "I've got numerous social media accounts for him. Name's Nick Bishop. He's a seventeen-year-old soccer player. Good looking. Likes video games and goes to the same school Mary used to go to in Knightsbridge. Lives in Chelsea. His dad is the cofounder of an online insurance start-up, and his mom's a well-known pastry chef and cookbook author."

"Do you have a date of birth for him?" Brad asked.

Veronica scanned the messages Nick had received on social media. "Got it," she said. "November tenth. Do you need the—"

"Nope," Brad said, raising his arms in the air. "I'm in his IG account. What next?"

Veronica took a moment to carefully consider her next move. She reread the messages between Mary and Nick. When she was through, she looked at Brad and said, "I'm gonna use Nick's account to start a conversation with Mary."

Brad looked at her, startled. "What? You can't do that, Vonnie. They're minors."

"You don't have to be here if you don't want to, Brad. You've already done more than enough," she said, already thinking about what she was going to say to Mary.

"I can't let you do that," Brad said. "That's not right. This isn't what I agreed to help you with, and you know it."

"Then get out," she said, motioning to the door. "Please."

Brad looked taken aback. "That's not fair."

Not fair? The words were like a resounding slap across her face.

"Not fair? Really?" She stood, sending her desk chair rolling backward. Tears welled up in her eyes. "There's a strong possibility that this girl's mom is the person responsible for my mother's death. You get that, right? And if you don't care about my mom, remember that these assholes came after me too, Brad. They wanted to—"

"I . . . I didn't mean—" Brad mumbled, raising his hands in surrender.

"Goddamn it! Let me finish!" she shouted.

This time, her voice carried through the headsets the two software engineers were wearing. For the first time since she'd opened the door of the computer lab, they glanced up from their screens and turned in her direction. They seemed surprised to see her there. She locked eyes with them and pointed toward the door. They hurriedly grabbed their things and left the lab.

In all the years she'd known Brad, Veronica had never raised her voice at him. He'd helped her get this far. Had she been too harsh with him?

She sat back down in her chair and took a deep breath. "I'm sorry. I shouldn't have yelled at you. But I need to do this. Clay's in London waiting for me to give him something he can act on. And unless you have a better idea, I'm gonna message Mary using Nick's account."

Brad scratched his head and sighed. He wrote something on a piece of paper, then shook his head. "I hear what you're saying, but I can't be part of this. I'm sorry."

He got to his feet and headed toward the door. As his hand reached the doorknob, he looked over his shoulder and said, "I hope you won't regret this, Veronica."

CHAPTER THIRTY-ONE

SkyCU Technology
Palo Alto, California

Veronica stretched her fingers over the computer's keyboard. She was taking no pleasure in breaking the law or messing with a teenage girl's life, but if Adaliya Oxley was indeed behind her mom's murder, then Veronica would be a fool not to throw out the rule book—even if it meant getting her hands dirty.

Although Brad had made it clear he didn't want to be part of her little—but illegal—hacking operation, he had nevertheless left Nick's log-in and password information on a piece of paper. Veronica typed the password in and accessed Mary's former boyfriend's IG account. The first thing she did was to reroute Mary's replies to an IP address different than Nick's phone. It was paramount that Nick wasn't notified every time there was a new message from Mary. Once she was done, she loaded a program that would collect packets of information from the phone Mary used to reply—if she replied.

Satisfied with the steps she'd taken so far, Veronica clicked on Nick's in-box and began to read through the direct messages he'd sent Mary in the past. Veronica had never impersonated a seventeen-year-old boy before, so wasn't sure what kind of language teenage boys and girls used to communicate with each other. She didn't want to commit a fatal sin that would in any way clue Mary in that she wasn't really talking to Nick.

Scrolling through Nick's messages, she noticed that he always called Mary "M," never her actual name. That was good to know. While Nick clearly liked typing the number *2* instead of spelling *to*, *u* instead of *you*, and *ur* instead of *your*, Veronica didn't see anything else of interest. In fact, Nick's vocabulary was quite normal, and he kept the acronyms to a minimum, preferring to use emojis.

Confident in her ability to fool Mary—at least for a short period of time—Veronica typed her first message.

@Mary2830TNT: Hey M. Sorry I didn't reply 2 ur previous messages. I'm here now. We can chat. If u want 2. K if not.

Here we go, she thought, pressing the send button. Seconds later, the word *seen*—all in small caps—appeared under her message. Mary's reply came in seconds later.

@NickFoot4Ever: Why didn't you answer??? You always answer!!!!!

@Mary2830TNT: I can't believe u left me without saying goodbye. Rude!!!

@NickFoot4Ever: I know. Sorry. Had no choice.

@Mary2830TNT: Someone kidnapped you???? LOL

@NickFoot4Ever: LOL!!!! LMAO!!! No. But close.

Veronica wondered if she should continue to push. *What would a seventeen-year-old guy do?* she asked herself. *Definitely push.* But before Veronica could type her reply, Mary sent another message.

@NickFoot4Ever: I'm not supposed to say anything, but my mom forced us to move out of Knightsbridge. It sucks!!! Like big time!!!!

@Mary2830TNT: What??!? OMG!! Why??

@NickFoot4Ever: IDK

IDK. Veronica had to think for a second for this one. She hadn't seen Nick or Mary use that acronym during their previous chat session. Then it came to her. *I don't know.*

@Mary2830TNT: I miss you M. Where r u?

@NickFoot4Ever: Can't tell u. But I tried to get away. Please believe me. I wanted to. Still do. But one of my mom bodyguards caught me. I almost made it to the Tube station. Mom was so pissed she sliced my PS4 in two with a chainsaw.

@Mary2830TNT: WOW!!

@NickFoot4Ever: I'm fucking miserable. I hate my life.

@Mary2830TNT: Don't say that M. Please let me see u. I'll come to your house.

@NickFoot4Ever: U really want 2 C me?

@Mary2830TNT: Can't stop thinking bout U.

When Mary hadn't replied after a full minute had passed, Veronica began to worry. Had she said something wrong? Had she scared Mary away? She stared at the screen, willing Mary to write something. Anything.

Shit. Shit. Shit.

Veronica was about to send another message when Mary replied.

@NickFoot4Ever: Me too. Like every second of every day. My mom is SO cruel. You have no idea. We had to change our names!! CRAZY BITCH. Can u help me escape?

Isn't that a bit extreme? Veronica thought. But this was getting interesting and going in the right direction.

@Mary2830TNT: I would do ANYTHING for U, M.

@NickFoot4Ever: R U serious? Don't lie. Please.

Veronica hesitated, uncomfortable about the next step. Now that she had successfully cornered Mary, she wasn't sure she had the guts to go further. The poor girl was desperate, and it felt wrong to play with her emotions. Veronica was playing a dangerous game and she knew it. But then her thoughts moved to her mom and the dead Secret Service agents, and the doubts instantly disappeared.

@Mary2830TNT: Im 100% serious.

@Mary2830TNT: I luv U.

@NickFoot4Ever: OMG OMG OMG IM SHAKING!!!

@NickFoot4Ever: We should get married and run away together.

@Mary2830TNT: YES!!

@NickFoot4Ever: Ok. U can't come to the house. Too dangerous with bodyguards. And they have guns. Always a minimum 3 of them inside house. Only 1 when my mom drives us 2 school. Can we meet at my school?

@Mary2830TNT: Yes. Where is it?

Veronica stretched her neck. This was the moment of truth. Then Mary's next message came in, and there it was. The name of her new school in London.

Perfect. Clay's gonna love that, she thought.

@NickFoot4Ever: You have to come after the long midday break cause I can't miss lunch. The 2 bodyguards who keep an eye on us would know. There's a side entrance they never watch. I can unlock it for u. Can u come tomorrow??? Do you have money?? My mom keeps like 10K inside the house. I know where it is.

@Mary2830TNT: I know where my dad $$$ is too. But tomorrow is no good. Let's chat later to figure everything out. K?

@NickFoot4Ever: OMG I CANT WAIT. I LUV U SO MUCH!! Got 2 Go. My mom is here.

Veronica buried her face in her hands. She had done it. She had found a way in. Remembering the packets of information her program should have downloaded from Mary's phone, she navigated to the app interface and clicked on the link.

"Oh my God!" Veronica said out loud. "Jackpot."

CHAPTER THIRTY-TWO

London, England

White shifted his weight around the back seat of the car and slowly rotated his neck to relieve the tension. He massaged his eyes with his thumb and forefinger, hoping it would ease his headache. He usually didn't mind surveillance details, but the constant broken sleep since the attacks had started to take a toll.

There's a reason why sleep deprivation is considered a form of torture, he thought.

To suit the elegant neighborhood, White had rented a Mercedes S-Class. Not exotic enough to warrant unwanted attention, but classy enough to fit right in. Sarazin had opted for a full-size dark-colored Range Rover, which seemed to be the SUV preferred by London's wealthiest residents. White couldn't believe the exorbitant price he'd paid for the two rentals. The Range Rover's weekly rate alone cost more than White's monthly salary back when he was with the Secret Service. It was a good thing he had paid using the SkyCU Technology credit card Veronica had given him.

After two days in London chasing their tails, it had been Veronica who'd discovered the tiny bit of information that had allowed White and Sarazin to get things rolling in London.

White smiled at how resourceful Veronica was. His fiancée always seemed to find new ways to impress him. From all the information she'd been able to download from Mary's phone, Veronica had been able to access all of Mary's siblings' school email accounts. Adaliya's accounts had been another story. In fact, it had been impossible to identify them. It was as if Adaliya no longer had an online presence.

What they had found out was this: Following her husband's death, Adaliya Oxley had legally changed her name and the last names of her five kids. She'd sold her grand Victorian home in Knightsbridge and, using her new name, had moved across the river Thames to West Greenwich, where she'd purchased a magnificent six-bedroom Georgian home with direct views of Greenwich Park.

Armed with the address of the oldest children's school, White and Sarazin had set up surveillance and quickly identified the two body-guards Mary had mentioned. Alternately every half hour or so, one of them had climbed out of the SUV and walked the perimeter of the school. In White's professional opinion, the two bodyguards looked bored and not too switched on.

White had branded them the "B Team."

Just after 4:00 p.m., two identical Cadillac Escalade ESVs had pulled into the circular driveway of the school. With the help of his monocular, White had watched the scene and confirmed that Adaliya Oxley was behind the wheel of the first Escalade with one of her preteen boys riding next to her in the passenger seat. Just like Veronica's chat with Mary had suggested, Adaliya hadn't come alone. From the second Escalade, a massive man dressed in business attire had exited the front passenger door. White had estimated the man's height at approximately six and a half feet and his weight to be well north of 350 pounds. The man's head was completely shaved, and his neck was as thick as a tele-phone pole. It was possible that under all that flab was some muscle, but the man was no doubt employed for his ability to stop bullets and not for his ability to run. The man looked like he could stop an artillery shell with his stomach.

Another bodyguard had exited the rear passenger door, but the driver remained inside the vehicle. The bodyguards were quickly joined by the B Team White had earlier identified. Seconds later, three of Adaliya's five children had come out of the school's main entrance and down the stairs toward the Escalade their mother was driving. White estimated that the whole process had taken just under sixty seconds. Although he hadn't been able to confirm that Adaliya's fifth child was also in the vehicle, White assumed the kid had taken a seat at the back of the classy SUV. With the children secured in the lead Escalade, the big bodyguard had closed the door and climbed back into the second SUV. The B Team had made no attempt to return to their vehicle and had stayed behind while the two other SUVs had departed the school's premises.

White and Sarazin had taken turns following the two-car motorcade to Adaliya's new residence in Greenwich. White had kept an eye out for the B Team in case they were running countersurveillance, but he hadn't spotted their vehicle. Adaliya's two-car convoy had driven into the attached garage precisely twenty-one minutes after departing the older children's school.

With the address confirmed, White had immediately conducted a reconnaissance of the adjoining streets. He had then established a surveillance plan and shared it with Sarazin for his observations.

"Hard to pull off when it's only the two of us, but I think we'll manage," Sarazin had said.

Adaliya's new house was in one of the poshest neighborhoods in London. Sprinkled in among the surrounding streets were the mansions of business leaders and celebrities. Most of them were outfitted with CCTV. White and Sarazin had parked their vehicles in a way that would prevent anyone from leaving the house without being picked up by one of them. White's objective was to build a pattern of life that would facilitate his entry into the residence. He wanted to confirm the information Mary had shared with "Nick" during their chat. White had no beef with anyone except Adaliya Oxley. Under no circumstances should the kids be placed in danger. Although the bodyguards were fair game, White's first choice was to slip through the residence unnoticed—preferably when security was at its lowest level.

So far, White had identified five different bodyguards. Since they'd returned from school almost seven hours ago, none of the children had come out of the house, and the Cadillac Escalades hadn't left the garage. Neither had Adaliya. The moon had found a way to break through the clouds and was now casting the streets in a milky gray light.

"Lights off in the upstairs bedrooms," Sarazin said, his voice coming through White's earpiece.

"The upstairs lights are all out on my side too," White replied from the back seat of the Mercedes, his hand reaching for the half-full piss bottle on the floor behind the front passenger's seat. "But the basement's lights are still turned on."

"You think the security team members live on site?" Sarazin asked.

"Something like that," White replied. "I think they work long shifts like some firefighters do back home. This means they rotate in and out every twenty-four or thirty-six hours."

"That's not necessarily a bad thing for what you had in mind," Sarazin suggested. "What do you think?"

As White relieved himself into the bottle, he wasn't sure what to think. As much as he wanted to rush inside the house and put a bullet between Adaliya Oxley's eyes, he had to tread carefully. A little voice in his head told him not to jump to conclusions. Sarazin had said that Adaliya was nearly as bad as her husband, but White had never met the woman. The evidence against Adaliya was damning, but it was all circumstantial. If White was to find hard evidence that it had indeed been Adaliya who had contracted killers to eliminate Veronica, he would dispatch Roy Oxley's widow without any hesitation.

Wanting to stay off the radar, White had decided not to call upon the US Secret Service attaché working out of the embassy on 9 Elms

Lane in London to provide him with a firearm. Instead, White had relied on Sarazin to come up with the goods, and the Frenchman hadn't disappointed. Within six hours of touching down in England, Sarazin had managed to get his hands on two PAMAS G1 semiautomatic pistols—the French version of the Beretta 92—with two extra fifteen-round magazines for each pistol and a couple of suppressors.

"Clay? Are you there?" Sarazin asked, bringing White out of his trance.

"I'm gonna get one shot at this," White said, squirting a large dollop of alcohol-based sanitizer in his palm. "I can't move in until I know she's in there. And I'd like it better if the kids were at school."

"Understood," Sarazin replied. "Good thing I brought my caffeine tablets."

White rubbed his hands together and stretched his stiff legs. Mercedes S-Class or not, it was going to be a long night. At least it wasn't too cold outside. He had almost given up on seeing Adaliya before the next morning, but then the double-garage door of her residence opened. A single white Escalade slowly came out.

White felt an instant rush of adrenaline. "You're seeing this, Pierre?" he asked. "There's a white Cadillac Escalade about to exit the driveway."

"Just to clarify, this is one vehicle, not two. Correct?" Sarazin asked. "Ten-four."

White had a decision to make. Should they tail the white SUV or stay put at the residence? There was a big chance that at this hour the Escalade was carrying security personnel off the property for a shift change. But it was also possible that Adaliya was aboard the vehicle, having waited until all her kids were in bed to leave the house. If they went after the Escalade, they might have a hard time finding parking spots with a direct view of Adaliya's house again. They'd been lucky the first time around, but White doubted they'd be so fortunate the second time. But the opportunity was hard to pass up. If it was indeed Adaliya, and she was traveling alone or with a single bodyguard, White would have his chance for the one-on-one with her he so much coveted.

Damn. It wasn't like him to hesitate like this. He would have to ask Sarazin for some of his caffeine tablets.

"Get ready, Pierre. We're going after it," White said, having made his decision. "Wait for my word before leaving your spot."

"Bien compris," Sarazin said, letting White know he'd copied his last.

White observed the Escalade turning right and away from the Mercedes.

"The driver has made a right turn out of the driveway, and the Escalade will pass your position in a few seconds," White said.

"Copy that."

"Stay put," White said. "Don't start your engine and don't make a U-turn. Let me take the lead."

"Of course," Sarazin grunted back.

White knew Sarazin had received surveillance training at the DGSE academy, but it had been decades ago. It was normal that the former spy didn't remember the tactics, but it wasn't a fact he enjoyed being reminded about.

White slipped into the driver's seat and started the Mercedes's engine. He slowly pulled out of his spot and accelerated toward the stop sign. He made a right turn just in time to see the Escalade's taillights disappear behind a belt of trees around a bend two hundred meters away.

White sped up past Sarazin's Range Rover, but he couldn't shake the feeling that he'd made a strategic mistake by following the Escalade.

CHAPTER THIRTY-THREE

London, England

Reza Ashtari leaned in closer to the monitor. Then his eyes went wild, and his heart rate spiked.

Is this it? Are the Americans finally here? More importantly, was Clayton White among them?

Reza and his five-man team had been in position for three days, and doubts about the whole operation had started creeping in. His brother's constant oversight didn't help. Reza loathed being micromanaged. Nader might be his boss, but he didn't have Reza's field experience. Nader's job was to provide Reza with the resources he needed to accomplish his mission, not to nitpick his every decision. Still, Reza had begun to wonder if he hadn't overestimated the Americans.

Reza couldn't stay in London forever. The British government had just heightened the terrorist threat level to critical—which meant a terrorist attack in London was very likely in the near future—so Reza expected to see additional police and intelligence resources dispatched in the area momentarily. The MOIS had given him and his men decent covers, but still thinner than he would have liked considering the current threat analysis.

He'd assured Nader he would be able to wrap up the operation in less than five days, but until now it had seemed as if Reza would break that pledge, which would have been disastrous. If the Americans had somehow missed the bread crumbs he had left behind for them to find, it was possible they would have at some point realized Iran's involvement in the two Florida operations. And on a more personal level, it would have meant that he wouldn't get to kill Clayton White—the man who had physically pushed a blade into his father's heart.

But now they were here. White was here. He was sure of it. He could feel it in his gut.

Reza keyed his tactical radio and said, "This is Domino-One. Does anyone know how long that Mercedes has been there? It must have been just outside the scope of our video feed. I saw its lights switch on less than twenty seconds after the Escalade left the residence."

"Domino-One, this is Domino-Six," came the reply. "Stand by. I'll check my notes."

It could be a coincidence, but Reza's gut said otherwise. There was barely any traffic at this time of night, and it had been more than twenty minutes since he'd last seen a car drive by that intersection. It was worth checking out.

For this operation, Reza had subrented two small apartments strategically located less than half a mile away from Adaliya's house. His men worked in two-man teams, each with its own nondescript sedan. His last man—Domino-Six—was a floater, meaning that he could augment any team at a moment's notice. Like the other teams, Domino-Six drove a four-door sedan, but he also had access to a motor scooter, which made it easy for him to weave in and out of London's traffic.

"Domino-One from Six, I observed the Mercedes for the first time this evening at six fifteen. Windows are heavily tinted, but there wasn't anyone seated in the driver's seat when I drove by. The vehicle was still there when I made another pass at nine oh three."

"Message received, Six," Reza said, then continued. "To all call signs, be on the lookout for additional vehicles to follow suit."

When there's one, there's two, he thought, staring at the monitor that collected the feed from the six high-definition cameras his team had discreetly set up over the course of the last three days. All but one of the cameras had infrared capability, and all were positioned strategically around the periphery of Adaliya's property. They were far enough away not to get noticed, but sufficiently close to provide a clear understanding of the tactical situation.

For the last three nights in a row, Reza had spotted the white Escalade leaving Adaliya's residence at about the same hour. On the second night, he'd sent his two teams after it and learned that the Escalade was transporting members of Adaliya's security team back to an address in Stratford, a borough five miles north of Greenwich, where the headquarters of the private military firm she'd retained to take care of her family's safety was located. From there, and with the help of several MOIS analysts, it hadn't been much of a challenge to discover that the company was actually owned entirely by Adaliya through an offshore trust based in Luxembourg.

In approximately forty minutes, the Escalade would return with a fresh contingent of security professionals. By visiting the company's website, Reza had learned that most of the firm's employees were former members of the South African or Pakistani armed forces. Hard men for sure, not the typical run-of-the-mill part-time security guards usually found working protection gigs around town. Reza was curious to know what method White and his team would be using to get to Adaliya. If they were smart, they'd try to interrogate her instead of putting her down. But Clayton White was a killer. Reza knew that for a fact.

On the top left corner of Reza's monitor, a large SUV had turned on its headlights. Reza had been staring right at the screen, and he hadn't seen anyone climbing into the vehicle.

Someone's been inside for quite some time, he thought, his excitement growing.

Reza called out the vehicle to his team but once again advised them to stay put.

Patience is a hard virtue to acquire, my son, his father had once told him. *But in our line of work, it is indispensable.*

Although he was yet to master it, Reza sensed his father would appreciate the effort. Reza's prediction was that the Americans would realize the purpose of the Escalade and would wait until the next shift change to covertly assault Adaliya's house. All Reza had to do was to wait for the Americans to make their move, then send his own forces to storm the residence and kill everyone inside. Children and Clayton White included.

CHAPTER THIRTY-FOUR

London, England

White watched as two hundred meters ahead the white Escalade turned into a driveway leading up to a large electric gate. White kept driving, but glanced at the big SUV as it accelerated through the opening gate. He pursed his lips and swore under his breath. *Damn.*

"Pierre, take your next right or left, and let's get out of here," White said, looking at his phone, on which he was tracking Sarazin's position.

"Understood," Sarazin replied. "I'm on a parallel street heading toward you and about three hundred behind your current position. What happened?"

"The Escalade turned into a private entryway," White replied, calling out the address. They were in the industrial area of Stratford, a suburban town in East London.

"You want to return to Greenwich or regroup?" Sarazin asked.

White gave Sarazin an address in Canary Wharf. "Let's meet there in ten minutes."

White needed to clear his head. And he needed coffee. He drove through London's streets wondering what to do next. He was yet to come up with a good option when he spotted Sarazin's Range Rover parked in front of the address he'd given him. White pulled up behind him and turned off the Mercedes's engine. Sarazin climbed out of the SUV and leaned his back against it, crossing his arms over his chest.

"The address you gave me came back to a private military company," Sarazin said once White had joined him.

"You googled it?"

Sarazin nodded. "Didn't need my friends over at DGSE to figure this one out."

"My guess is that this was a shift change," White said, peering down the street for a coffee shop. To his delight, he spotted one that seemed open across the street next to an alley. White headed toward it, Sarazin in tow.

"If they do the same tomorrow night, it could be our best time to go in," the Frenchman suggested. "Less resistance."

White had no intention of bringing Sarazin along for the last part of the operation, but he hadn't told him yet. The former French spy wasn't a trained shooter like White. He'd proved himself capable of handling a firearm in South Africa, but White knew the man was still living with the effects of what he had done. Killing a man, even in self-defense, wasn't something one's mind could easily get over.

"There's only one thing I'm sure about, Pierre," White said, crossing the street.

"What's that?"

"We can't stay outside Adaliya's residence indefinitely, waiting for her to go out. At some point, neighbors will become suspicious, or her security team will spot us. Someone will call the police, and it will be game over. We're both carrying unlicensed firearms, which is never a good idea in the UK."

"Agreed," Sarazin said.

"We need to make a move," White said as both men stepped onto the sidewalk.

"Again, I agree. That's why I'm suggesting we try to gain access to the house tomorrow night during the shift change."

White shook his head and opened the door to the coffee shop. "I thought about it on my way here, but I'm not comfortable going in while the kids are in the house."

"I understand. I wouldn't either, now that I think about it. What, then?"

The beginning of an idea was starting to take shape in White's mind. "I think I might have something that will work," he said. "Care to hear me out?"

CHAPTER THIRTY-FIVE

London, England

Standing in a small grove of trees two hundred feet deep inside Greenwich Park, White adjusted his black baseball cap lower on his head before tucking his hands in his pockets. From the corner of his eye he watched the two white Escalades carrying Adaliya and her children disappear from view. White wore a pair of light brown coveralls with black soft-sole athletic shoes. Hung over his left shoulder was a small black backpack in which he carried his radio, a PAMAS G1 pistol, the two spare magazines, and a suppressor, among other things. White, like many of the other people walking in the park at this hour, looked like a construction worker who had just climbed out of the Tube from one of the poorer boroughs of London to work on one of the major exterior home-renovation projects in well-to-do Greenwich. In addition, a crew of workers wearing city uniforms had started drilling the asphalt two blocks away from Adaliya's residence for some kind of public-funded roadway rehabilitation.

White took a deep breath of fresh air and looked up. The morning clouds he'd seen earlier when he'd checked out of the hotel had moved on. The sky was bright and blue, but the meteorologist he'd absently listened to while getting dressed had said a thunderstorm was in the cards for later in the day. White glanced at his watch and noted the time. It was 8:09 a.m. At best, he had forty minutes before the return of

Adaliya and her security detail. To play it safe, White had set his timer for thirty minutes. It wasn't a lot of time for what he planned to do, but it would have to be enough.

Before leaving the hotel, White and Sarazin had met in his room and pulled up Adaliya's neighborhood on Google Maps. Although White had spent hours in the neighborhood, it had been mostly at night. He wanted to familiarize himself with how it looked during the day. Using the free software, White had virtually walked the streets several times, which was much safer than physically wandering around Adaliya's house. Once he was sure he had grasped the basic layout of the neighborhood and Adaliya's property, he'd gone over his plan with Sarazin one last time. The roadwork a block away was a surprise, but it shouldn't impact the operation. Truth be told, White didn't mind a little background noise.

What he was about to do next was illegal. Combined with the fact that he was carrying a prohibited firearm, White was taking a big risk and would face significant jail time if caught. It wasn't a decision he'd taken lightly, but he estimated he had no more than a day or two before his former colleagues and the FBI picked up the trail from the flip phones and started breathing down his neck. White's fear was that Adaliya would see them coming from a mile away and would once again disappear. The best way to protect Veronica wasn't to place Adaliya under arrest. Her expensive lawyers would tell her to stay silent, and she would clam up. It would take months, maybe years, to figure out who her contacts were and how deep her network was. The best way for White to get the answers he wanted was to shock Adaliya, to catch her unprepared and with her guard down. And for that to work, it was imperative that he be the first to get to her.

Dressed as he was, White wouldn't have fit in the neighborhood if he'd come after 5:00 p.m. during workdays or on weekends. But now, he fit perfectly and even exchanged a couple of nods with other workers as he walked toward Adaliya's residence. Contrary to common belief, most nonviolent break-ins happened during daylight hours. There was a simple reason for that: most people weren't home. At night, people's natural defenses were up, but that wasn't the case during the day. In fact, people who acted as if they belonged were rarely suspected. With that in mind, White exited the park and jogged across the street toward the side of Adaliya's house.

"I'm about to go in," he said into the tiny microphone clipped to the collar of his coveralls.

"Understood," Sarazin replied. "I have a direct view of the driveway and will advise if I see anything. Good luck."

White looked both left and right and once over his shoulder. Seeing no one, he didn't hesitate. In two fluid movements, he jumped over the fence and landed on the other side. As he had expected, the backyard was well groomed and complete with a large patio with ample space for seating. The medium-size lap pool he'd seen on Google Maps was drained for the winter. To his left, a door led to a small mudroom. White pulled a lock-picking set out of his bag and went to work. The knob lock took a full minute to defeat, but White was out of practice and lock-picking was a perishable skill set. The dead bolt took much longer, and by the time he opened the door, beads of sweat had appeared on his forehead despite the chill.

"I'm in, Pierre," White whispered.

"Copy that. Nothing to report on my end."

White stepped into the house and slowly closed the door, happy it didn't squeak. He pulled his pistol out of the backpack and screwed the suppressor to the end of the barrel. He waited a long minute, listening for sounds of occupancy, but his heartbeat was too high. He slowed his breathing until he had it under control, then strained his ears for any sound that would tell him where the bodyguard was. No such sound came.

White tightened his grasp around the PAMAS's grip and began to clear the stately house, moving with trained efficacy as he swept each room. Entering the dining room, he spotted a large table on which sat an array of cereal boxes next to a bunch of empty bowls. Was it possible that he was alone in the house? White didn't think so. He had seen the little signs on the front lawn indicating that the residence was protected by an alarm system. If the house had been empty, White assumed he would have heard the chirp of the burglar alarm. The bodyguard was probably in the basement, enjoying a few minutes of alone time before Adaliya and the rest of his team returned.

"Ground floor is clear," White said. "On my way to the second floor."

"Ground floor is clear," repeated Sarazin. "Got it."

White reached the staircase, which had narrow steps and was closed in by walls on both sides. He climbed the carpeted steps almost silently, taking his time so his footfalls wouldn't carry. He checked all the bedrooms, keeping the master for the end. Adaliya's bedroom was by far the largest and most luxurious of the six. It had a light brown wooden floor and a large red carpet beside the unmade king-size bed. Original paintings were hung on the walls, and a beautifully crafted chandelier was suspended in the center of the room. White could see three sets of french doors. The first was open and led to a home office, the second to a small balcony overlooking the backyard—which he identified as a potential escape route—and the third to a walk-in closet. White skipped the office and the walk-in closet and continued toward the en suite bathroom. One of the bathroom's sinks was wet, just like the shower, confirming that Adaliya had indeed spent the night in her house. Returning to the home office, White stowed his pistol in the backpack and took in the small space. Three walls were lined with bookshelves filled with business, art, and self-help books. A laptop computer was on the white writing desk. A cell phone was connected to it via a USB cord.

White picked up the phone and confirmed it was password protected. Pulling intel off it would take hacking tools he simply didn't have. Still, maybe there was something he could do. He grabbed a paper clip from the desk and bent one of its ends. He inserted the end of the paper clip into the SIM card tray hole and gently applied pressure, making sure not to twist the metal. The tray popped open, and White used his phone to take a picture of the SIM card. With some luck, Veronica would be able to track down Adaliya's phone with the subscriber identity number inscribed on the SIM card. Then he closed the tray and turned his attention to the laptop. It too was password protected. The laptop's hard drive probably contained a lot of the answers he was looking for, but he didn't have the proper tools to uncover them.

White spent the next five minutes thumbing through mail and receipts, taking pictures and video of everything he thought might be important both in the home office and the walk-in closet. He flipped through the papers on Adaliya's desk and dug into her drawers, his eyes probing.

Then White froze. He held his breath as he listened, his heart banging inside his chest.

There it was again, the distinctive and panic-inducing sound of creaking footsteps on the hardwood floor. The footsteps were near, approaching fast, and didn't belong to someone trying to hide their presence. White pulled the pistol out of his backpack and waited, hoping that whoever was coming would bypass the master bedroom altogether. His prayer went unanswered as the footsteps stopped only a few strides away.

White heard a voice, deep sounding. Was it Afrikaans? White wasn't familiar enough with the language to confirm. The man was on the phone, and he didn't sound alarmed. On the contrary, he was soft spoken, almost serene. He had no idea White was hidden ten steps away from him. The man disconnected the call.

C'mon, move along. Nothing to see here.

Then Adaliya's phone rang, loud and strident in the silence of the bedroom. Its chime startled White, who briefly glanced at it. His attention lapse didn't last more than one second, but it was enough for the man to move from the doorway of the master bedroom to the home office. When White turned to face the incoming threat, he was shocked to recognize the huge bodyguard he had seen the day before at the school. This time, the man wasn't dressed in business attire; he was wearing a black tracksuit.

White had been wrong about him.

The man was big, yes, but he was fast too.

For a fleeting moment, their eyes met, and the bodyguard's mouth fell open in surprise, his big round face a study in confusion. White, who'd been holding his pistol in the low-ready position, didn't have time to raise the PAMAS G1 before the man locked gigantic hands on his wrists, keeping the pistol down and aimed away from his vital organs.

The next thing White knew, he was being headbutted. Because the bodyguard was six to seven inches taller than him, the blow landed on White's forehead. It came down with such force that White's knees buckled. The room around him started to spin, and he saw stars. He felt himself falling backward, but the bodyguard pulled him up with one hand while keeping his other locked on White's wrists. A knee connected with White's solar plexus, knocking the wind out of him. As White doubled over in pain, the big man stepped forward and grabbed White's pistol with both hands, twisting hard, trying to wrest it away. White yelled in pain as his wrist bones threatened to break. He battled to keep control of his gun, but it was a lost cause.

The other man was simply too strong.

Out of desperation, White swung an elbow and hit the man on the chin. It wasn't enough to knock the big man down—far from it—but it was just powerful enough to make him loosen his grip on the pistol. White fought back his dizziness, and with all his remaining strength he slammed the heel of his left foot to the side of the man's knee. The man grunted, and his grip on the pistol loosened more.

White struck again at the man's knee.

This time there was a loud crack, and the man yelled in pain as he let go of White's gun. He fell to his side, his left leg no longer able to support him. White could have shot him right there, but it wasn't like him to shoot an unarmed man. Seizing the advantage, though, he kicked the bodyguard squarely under the chin. The man's head snapped back. The power White had put behind his kick would have easily broken any other man's neck, but not this one's. The bodyguard struggled to his hands and knees.

"Stay down, goddamn it," White told him, his PAMAS G1 pointed at the man's shaved head. "Don't give me a reason to shoot you, dumbass. Make sure I see your hands. Got it?"

The man spat at White's feet, but he stopped moving. He was a fighter. White saw it in the man's eyes. As soon as he got the opportunity, the big man would get back in the fight.

White keyed in his radio. "I got into a little scuffle, but I'm okay," he said. "Give me a sitrep of what you're seeing."

There was no reply. "Tout va bien?" White asked, switching to French. "Dis-moi ce qui ce passe."

Still no answer. What the hell? White quickly checked his radio, making sure he hadn't accidentally switched frequency during the fight. He hadn't. Then why in hell was Sarazin not responding?

CHAPTER THIRTY-SIX

London, England

Reza had been surprised when the Mercedes and Range Rover he'd assumed were carrying Clayton White and his team had not returned to Adaliya's house. One hour after the garage door had closed behind the Escalade, Reza had deployed all his men in hopes they would spot the American spies.

They hadn't.

To make matters worse, one of his teams had been pulled over by the Metropolitan Police Service. The whole operation could have turned into a nightmare if his men had been forced to kill a police officer. Luckily, the officers had let them go, apparently satisfied they weren't about to blow up the London Bridge.

Reza had stopped counting the number of hours he'd watched that damned monitor. He rubbed his eyes with the palms of his hands and blinked a few times. His vision cleared, and so did his focus.

Where were the damned Americans hiding? They were close. They had to be. Or had they come to London only to conduct preliminary reconnaissance? Was it possible they wouldn't be back again before a few weeks—or a few months?

Reza shook his head slowly. No, they were here, biding their time— just like he was.

There.

Reza noticed someone jogging across the street. There wasn't anything unusual about the man's appearance. He looked like the ten other coverall-wearing laborers he had seen that morning carrying their lunch in their backpack. But, for a split second, Reza had a glimpse of the man's face in profile.

Reza enlarged the video feed coming from that camera. He slowly zoomed in but realized that camera three was going to lose the man to camera two. He brought up the feed from camera two and watched the monitor with renewed intensity. There it was again. The man looked left and right and then once more over his shoulder before climbing over the fence.

Reza pressed the pause button, rewound the video, and zoomed in. Reza stared into the man's eyes.

Clayton White. *Inshallah.*

Reza grabbed the radio and began to give his men instructions.

CHAPTER THIRTY-SEVEN

London, England

Reza had to give credit to his five-man team. Although he hadn't seen their facial expressions while briefing them over the radio, he could feel they wanted Clayton White dead as much as he did. They were focused, and proud to serve at the tip of the Iranian spear of war.

Reza had been honest with the members of his team, telling them exactly why he—as their commander—was about to risk all their lives. He hadn't given them the option to opt out. It would have been disrespectful to do so.

They understood.

Major General Mohsen Ashtari had been his father, but even more critical, he'd once been the inspiration behind an entire generation of Iranian fighters. Alexander Hammond might have given the order, but it was Clayton White who with his blade had robbed the Iranian people of the man who could have brought peace and wealth to their country.

This morning, Reza would strike a blow that would rejuvenate the Iranian fighting spirit that had been lost eight years ago. His father's murder had gone unpunished long enough.

It was time.

Reza grabbed the biggest of the two leather sheaths from the table and strapped it to his calf. He picked up the ESEE fixed-blade knife and slipped it into the sheath. He took the second sheath and clipped it inside his waistband. In this one went his three-inch Karambit-style blade, his favorite. There was something to be said about a knife that was shaped like a claw. He pulled his Browning Hi-Power from its holster and did a press check to confirm he had a round chambered. He then returned the pistol to its holster and placed it inside his waistband at the small of his back. The three extra magazines went to his coat pockets. So did the suppressor.

He was ready.

"To all call signs, this is Domino-One. I'm on the move. Confirm you're in position."

"Domino-Two and Three copy. We're in position and ready to go."

"Same for Four and Five."

"Six is mobile and ready to respond."

"Domino-One copy all," Reza replied.

Satisfied his teams were where they were supposed to be, Reza stepped out of the apartment. Within the next two hours a MOIS support team would come and take care of the logistics regarding the two apartments and the rental cars. The cameras his team had installed would be left behind, but it didn't matter. They were nondescript and could be bought in any high-end electronics store in the city.

Reza looked at his watch. Clayton White had been inside Adaliya's residence for eleven minutes. Had White become acquainted with Dandre, Adaliya's lead bodyguard? Dandre, contrary to all the other members of the security team, lived in house. As far as Reza could tell, Dandre never took part in the daily morning escort to the school. Reza hoped Dandre, who was the most physically impressive man Reza had ever seen, hadn't killed White.

"Domino-Four from One," Reza said once he was one hundred meters north of Adaliya's house. "What's the status of the Range Rover?"

"No movement, One. The vehicle is still two hundred or so meters south of the driveway. I've been keeping my eyes on it for the last five minutes, and I haven't seen anything moving inside. It's hard to believe there's someone there."

"Copy that, Four. That's about to change. Trust me."

Reza's plan was simple, but sometimes unpretentious plans were the most effective and tended to stay on track longer. The key was to be in and out in less than two minutes.

As Reza neared Adaliya's residence, he spotted the Range Rover. That was his cue.

"To all call signs, this is One," Reza said, his heart pumping with excitement. "Stand by. Stand by. Execute! Execute!"

As his teams began to move, Reza continued to walk nonchalantly on the sidewalk, heading toward the Range Rover. Exactly fourteen seconds after he'd given the order to begin the first phase of the operation, Reza observed Domino-Two stop his rental car—a light gray Skoda Octavia—about one hundred meters behind the Range Rover—well in range of the military-grade signal jammer his man carried. The jammer would stop all incoming and outgoing radio and cell phone communications within a two- to three-hundred-meter radius.

Moments later, Domino-Four drove his black Peugeot 3008 into Adaliya's driveway and climbed out of the midsize SUV. Domino-Five did the same from the passenger door, and they pulled their wool balaclavas down over their faces almost in unison. Reza sidestepped to his right and took refuge between two parked vehicles twenty meters away from the Range Rover. He scanned left and right, and, not seeing anyone paying him any attention, he pulled the Browning out of the holster and took a moment to fasten the suppressor.

Your move, Reza thought, keeping an eye on the Range Rover.

CHAPTER THIRTY-EIGHT

London, England

Pierre Sarazin spotted the light gray Skoda as it entered the driveway. *Damn.* Who the hell were these two guys? They weren't part of Adaliya's protective detail. That much he knew. Although he hadn't seen any weapons, the men's intentions were clearly not friendly. Sarazin had watched them pull down their black balaclavas and rush toward the front of the house, and then he had lost sight of them.

"Clayton from Pierre," he called out on the radio. "Come in, Clayton."

No response. "Clayton, two men are coming around the front of the house. Do you copy?"

Still nothing.

"Merde, Clayton! Réponds-moi, bordel de merde!" he shouted, reverting to French.

Things were rapidly getting out of control. Sarazin's mind was spinning, trying to figure out what this was all about. What was he supposed to do? What would Clayton do?

Sarazin tried to reach White again over the radio but had no luck. He tried his cell phone, but he couldn't get any signal.

What the hell? Getting a strong signal had never been an issue before. He'd been texting back and forth with Veronica less than one hour ago. Bile started coming up his throat.

Sarazin opened the rear passenger door of the Range Rover and stepped onto the sidewalk, waving his phone in front of him. It took a moment for his eyes to adjust to the sun. He squinted and looked at his phone. Still no bars. He was about to close the SUV's door when he remembered that he had stowed his pistol in the seat pocket at the back of the front passenger seat. He reached for it with his left hand, but quickly looked around to see if anyone was watching before pulling it out of the seat pocket.

Fifteen meters away, a tall, well-built man sporting a neatly trimmed beard was walking toward him at a leisurely pace. The man was dressed in a pair of jeans and a navy blue coat. What grabbed Sarazin's attention was his black wool hat—it was the same type the men who had climbed out of the Peugeot SUV had been wearing.

Sarazin's stomach clenched.

The man had a shy smile on his lips, but his eyes were alert and predatory, like a snake watching an injured bird he was about to chow down. In one smooth motion, the man brought up a long black pistol.

Sarazin, who still had his left hand wrapped around the PAMAS G1 grip, snatched the pistol out of the seat pocket and leaped to his right at the same moment the man fired his first shot. Sarazin didn't hear the shot, but he felt something pluck at his left leg as he landed hard on the sidewalk, his right shoulder taking the brunt of it. Sarazin saw a muzzle flash. Then another. His breath whooshed out as a round slammed into his chest. A millisecond later, his left knee exploded just as he was pulling the trigger. The man disappeared from his line of sight, but Sarazin fired again.

Then his vision blurred and a terrible, suffocating pain set in. For some reason, he couldn't get a breath in, which accentuated his state of terror. He used the last of his energy to painfully roll onto his back.

Sarazin found himself staring at the blue, cloudless sky. A spasm rippled through his entire body, and as he closed his eyes, the dim shape of a man loomed over him.

CHAPTER THIRTY-NINE

London, England

White was sure he had just heard two gunshots coming from outside the house. It could have been construction noise, but he'd been around firearms his entire adult life. He knew what he'd heard.

Pierre was in trouble.

The big bodyguard seized the moment to push himself up with his good leg and launched at White with surprising agility, his massive hands aiming for the PAMAS G1. White, who had anticipated the move, sidestepped to the left and cracked the bodyguard across the head with the butt of his pistol, knocking him unconscious. White hurried to the walk-in closet and grabbed a couple of leather belts, which he used to secure the big man's hands behind his back. There was no need to tie his feet; with his fucked-up knee, the bodyguard wasn't going anywhere.

White stepped out of the bedroom and scanned the hallway leading to the other bedrooms. He tried reaching Sarazin over the radio once again, but the Frenchman didn't reply. White took a moment to look at his phone. There were no signal bars showing. White cursed. He moved to one of the bedrooms on the other side of the house, the one with a window overlooking the street where Sarazin had parked the Range Rover. White carefully looked out the window, making sure to keep his silhouette hidden.

What he saw made his blood run cold. A man dressed in jeans and a navy blue coat was shoving an unconscious Sarazin—White hoped he wasn't dead—onto the back seat of the Range Rover.

Shit.

White couldn't see the man's face, only his back, but he had a black wool hat on his head. The Range Rover was about two hundred meters away, too far off for the PAMAS G1, whose effective range was fifty meters. White left the bedroom and headed for the stairs, leading with his pistol. He was halfway down the narrow steps when he heard the scuff of a shoe on the marble floor. White stood still. Whoever had done this had realized their mistake, because they stopped moving. White was in a terrible position, caught in the middle of the stairs.

Damn.

He'd have loved to retreat upstairs, but with Sarazin in dire need of his assistance, he couldn't afford to. Had the newcomers heard him too? A sudden commotion coming from the master bedroom surprised White. It was as if a large fish was wriggling and flapping on the floor, looking for oxygen.

The bodyguard. The large man had regained consciousness. The intruders downstairs must have also noticed the sound because White heard the approaching footsteps of at least two men—men who were no longer trying to hide their presence. The sounds coming from the bedroom continued to amplify, and White wondered if the bodyguard had managed to free his hands. With the continued commotion, he was convinced the two men would come up to investigate. In a way, that was good news for him. If they were in a rush, they wouldn't be as careful as they'd been only seconds prior.

Since there was only one way up, the intruders would have no choice but to take the stairs.

And White would be waiting for them.

CHAPTER FORTY

London, England

Reza threw the small man's body inside the Range Rover. He picked up the phone and the pistol the man had dropped next to the curb and put them in his coat pocket. He then pushed the man's legs deeper into the SUV so that he would have enough space to sit in the rear seat, and closed the door.

Reza frisked the man, and his hand came out bloody. One of his bullets had grazed the man's calf, but another had shattered his knee. Reza doubted the man would ever walk again—at least not without a cane. And that was only if Reza decided to let him live. His third shot had hit the man square in the chest, but his bulletproof vest had stopped it. Given how the man had moaned when Reza had searched him, the impact had probably fractured a few ribs.

"The Range Rover is secured," Reza said into his radio. "Domino-Two and Three, go help Four and Five."

"Two and Three copy, One. We're on our way."

Reza watched as the Skoda drove past the Range Rover and made a left into the driveway. Turning his attention to the phone he'd picked up, Reza was pleased to see the screen was unlocked. The man must have been using it when he'd exited the Range Rover. Reza placed his own phone next to it and launched a MOIS-conceived application that would automatically clone the man's phone and store it in a cloud server he could monitor with an application on his phone.

The man let out a long, pained moan. Reza hid the two phones inside his coat, then leaned toward him, grabbing a fistful of hair. Another moan. Reza pulled hard and lifted the man to a seating position.

"Have a seat next to me," Reza said in English.

The man was terrified. His eyes were the size of doughnuts, and beads of perspiration had formed on his forehead. His entire body was shivering. He was going into shock.

"What's your name?" Reza asked.

The man didn't reply. His eyes moved from Reza to his destroyed knee, then back to Reza. For a second, it looked as if the man was getting ready to spit into Reza's face.

Reza was quicker. He balled his fist and smashed the side of it hard into the man's face. Twice. Blood spouted from the man's nose and lips.

"What's your name?" Reza repeated.

Tears were running down the man's bloody face. "Pierre," he mumbled through his broken teeth.

Reza cocked his head. "Are you American, Pierre?"

No answer. Reza sighed. With his left hand, he grabbed Pierre's injured knee and squeezed. Pierre howled in pain as he spat blood and a couple of teeth, which landed on the Range Rover's plush carpet.

"I . . . I'm French," Pierre said in French, his hand to his nose. "I'm on vacation—"

Reza, who was fluent in French, looked at Pierre and shook his head from side to side.

"I don't have time for this," Reza said, driving the butt of his pistol hard against the side of Pierre's head.

Pierre's head tilted forward, coming to rest on his chest. There was a deep and bloody gash on his right temple.

Reza's phone pinged once from inside his coat, indicating that the application was done uploading Pierre's data. Reza scrolled through Pierre's text messages. His last exchange had been with someone named Vonnie. Reza read the exchange with growing interest—especially the part about Emily Moss.

Now Reza understood why the team of Quds Force commandos Nader had sent to New York had been unable to find the reporter. The little whore had traveled to Chicago to see a former boyfriend. But she had now returned to New York.

Reza clicked on the name and pressed the media tab. Numerous photos of Vonnie appeared on the screen.

"Hello, Veronica Hammond," he whispered. "As soon as I'm done with your fiancé, I'm coming for you and your pretty friend."

CHAPTER FORTY-ONE

London, England

White stood still, holding his pistol high in a combat grip. He saw the tip of a black pistol first, then the hands of its owner, then the forearms. White liked the forearms. They were a bigger target. White squeezed the trigger. The bullet ripped through the man's forearm. His pistol clattered to the floor, but the man wasn't able to stop his forward momentum in time. Half a second after he'd fired his first shot, White pulled the trigger again. The bullet struck the man's head, but White couldn't tell exactly where since the man was wearing a black balaclava. Before the man's body had even hit the floor, White was on the move, going down the stairs two at a time. He had to regain control of the fight. By opening fire, he'd lost the advantage of surprise. Now, he needed to press the attack.

The moment his feet touched the ground floor, White spun low and to the right. The second man was twenty feet away, shuffling back, his pistol pointed where White's torso would have been if he hadn't spun low. White saw the muzzle flash and felt the bullet zip harmlessly inches above his head. Before the shooter could adjust his aim, White fired two rounds in quick succession and dropped the man onto the marble floor. White scanned for more targets, then cleared his six. Satisfied he wasn't about to be shot in the back, he advanced toward the man he'd shot and kicked the suppressed pistol out of his reach before checking if the man was still breathing.

He wasn't.

One round had cleaved a path through the man's neck, and another had entered the top of his forehead, the hole in the black balaclava evident. White used one hand to pat down the body and found a spare magazine and a radio. White removed the balaclava, looked into the man's ear, and found what he was looking for. He grabbed the man's radio and put it in his backpack. He then inserted the earbud he'd found on the dead man into his own left ear.

Two different voices crackled in his ear one after the other. White didn't speak Farsi, but he recognized the language.

What the hell? Were these men Quds Force? MOIS? Or even criminals who had a beef with Adaliya?

White disregarded the last option, remembering the man who'd shoved Sarazin into the Range Rover. They had jammed White's comms with what he assumed was military-grade equipment. They had found Sarazin, and they'd most probably seen him enter Adaliya's house. This group knew what they were doing. They weren't thugs. Had he fallen into an elaborate trap? Was it possible that Adaliya had more resources than White had given her credit for?

He inserted a fresh magazine into his pistol and put the half-spent one into his coverall pocket. Although all the shots had been fired with suppressed pistols, White knew more men were about to enter the house since the first two-man team had shared the same radio frequency they were on.

But he had no idea through which door they would come. His eyes shifted back and forth between the front door, which was about ten meters behind him, and the side door he'd used to come in, which was about five meters to his left. As much as he wanted to hurry to Sarazin's assistance, he couldn't rush what was about to transpire. There was no doubt in his mind he was about to get into another firefight. He just didn't know how he would go about it. He quickly moved to the kitchen and took cover behind the island. He took long, deep breaths, knowing his body needed the oxygen for what was to come.

For a few seconds, everything was quiet. Even the flapping sound coming from the master bedroom had stopped. White guessed that the big bodyguard had heard the muffled shots and taken shelter.

Then the front door flew open and a man—also wearing a black balaclava—burst into the house, his pistol in front of him.

CHAPTER FORTY-TWO

London, England

Reza lifted Pierre's head with the tip of his Browning Hi-Power. The man's face was pale, but his chest was still heaving up and down as each labored breath came in and out. The bullet hadn't penetrated Pierre's bulletproof vest, but a rib might have punctured one of his lungs.

The chatter in Reza's ear suddenly turned from professional to downright panicky. What was going on inside the house? He shifted his weight so he could get a better view. From where he sat, all seemed normal, and since the police hadn't showed up yet, Reza assumed that Pierre's two unmuffled shots had been interpreted as part of the incessant and cacophonic construction noise emanating from the neighborhood.

"Domino-Six from One," Reza said, cutting through the chatter. "Go take a look at what's going on inside the house and report back."

More flustered verbal exchanges. From what Reza could make out, Domino-One and Two were down, and Four and Five were in a firefight with Clayton White, who they had successfully pinned down in the kitchen.

Good.

"I'm on my way," Domino-Six replied during a break in the comms.

With White pinned down and Domino-Six on his way, Reza was confident Clayton White's life was about to end.

Finally.

He wished he could have seen White's life drain away from his eyes, but Reza took pride in knowing it was his plan—his ruse—that had ended Clayton White.

It was time to go and move on to his next targets. Reza placed the tip of his Browning Hi-Power's suppressor on the bloody gash on the side of Pierre's head and began to take the slack from the trigger.

CHAPTER FORTY-THREE

London, England

Before White could engage the newcomer at the front door, another figure—this one armed with what looked like a suppressed H&K UMP—appeared out of the mudroom. The man fired a short burst at White, who ducked behind the kitchen island as bullets tore holes in the drywall.

Fuuuck!

White was pinned down, and the two shooters were now aware of his position. The tactical situation couldn't get much worse. He was outmanned, outgunned, and pretty much out of options. Another burst told White that the shooter with the UMP had moved toward the staircase, probably to check on his fallen comrade. White crawled on the floor, doing his best to keep the island between him and the shooters. The shooter with the UMP yelled something in Farsi. Maybe he was letting his partner know that their friends were dead? White, who was still lying prone on the floor, glanced past the island but retreated back immediately as the other shooter fired in his direction, his rounds bouncing off the marble floor and piercing the cabinet doors inches from White's face.

Shit. Too close.

The only good thing White could think of was that the men hadn't thrown a grenade yet. That wouldn't have been a pleasant experience.

White moved to his knees and popped up from behind the island, firing three quick rounds to keep the shooters honest. His first two rounds missed, but he got lucky on the third as it struck the pistol shooter while the man was attempting to carry one of his dead teammates. White ducked back behind the island as the shooter with the UMP fired a long two-second burst. White's heart was racing. The adrenaline had sharpened all his senses. Around him, chips of marble and stained wood flew off. Above the kitchen island, hanging from intricate ceiling hooks, copper and uncoated stainless steel pots and pans took a lot of hits, producing a cacophony of clinks and clunks. The moment there was a lull, White popped up again, knowing that the shooter had emptied his magazine. White fired two quick rounds in the general direction of the shooter, but the man dove behind a large wooden antique buffet. White switched his aim toward the man he'd injured moments ago, but he had moved out of sight.

White saw movement behind the buffet and squeezed the trigger four times, sending bullets thudding into the top of the heavy wood, one of them hitting a porcelain lamp. Seeing an opportunity to escape through the mudroom, he darted out from behind the island and sprinted toward it, firing one handed toward the buffet to keep the shooter's head down. White made it to the mudroom at the same time that the slide of his pistol locked back, indicating a spent magazine.

He ejected the empty magazine and was reaching for a new one when the mudroom door opened, hitting White hard on his shoulder and making him lose his balance. The full magazine slipped from his hands just as he came face to face with a tall bearded man. Clearly the man had rushed in and not taken the time to look through the door's four small square windows, because he looked as surprised as White. He swung his pistol in White's direction, but White stepped in and deflected the gun by hitting the man's right forearm with his own. The pistol coughed once, but the round flew out of the mudroom and into a kitchen cabinet that had somehow remained unscathed until now.

White drove the muzzle of his pistol into the man's gut and followed with a right elbow aimed at the man's jaw. The elbow glanced off the assailant's shoulder and did little damage. The man tried to back away to give himself the distance he needed to raise his gun again, but White didn't let him. He rushed the man with all his remaining strength, pushing him toward the opened doorway that led outside.

As they crossed the threshold, one of the assailant's feet caught, and he pitched backward, landing on his back with White on top of him. But the man was strong, and he managed to hold on to his pistol. White had dropped his during the fall. He used his left arm to pin the man's gun hand to the ground, making sure he couldn't point his pistol at him. White drove his knee over and over into the man's groin and thigh, but nothing really connected the way he was hoping. The gun barked again, and White heard the ping the bullet made as it ricocheted off the iron fence.

White threw an elbow toward the man's throat but missed, the momentum of his strike putting him in a precarious position that the man immediately took advantage of by punching White hard in the right ear. Yellow lights of pain exploded at the side of White's skull, and his strength wavered. The man pushed his advantage and bucked his hips upward and to the side and threw White off him. White managed to keep a hand on the pistol as both men got up. The man was strong and fresh and knew how to fight. He shoved White into the brick wall and then sent a jumping knee into White's solar plexus. White gasped for air but refused to let go of the man's right wrist. From the corner of his eye, he saw the left cross flying toward his jaw. He lowered his head and took the punch on top of his skull, hearing a cracking sound as his assailant broke his hand. Both men yelled in pain, but White recuperated first and punched his adversary in the throat. The man's knee buckled.

Seeing that the man's finger was still inside the trigger guard, White brought his right hand on top of the pistol. With his two hands on the gun, White stepped in and twisted hard and outward. The man screamed as the bone inside his trigger finger snapped in two. White, now in possession of the gun, crashed the butt of the pistol on the man's forehead. The shooter fell on his back, and White sent the heel of his shoe down on his throat, crushing his windpipe in a shockingly loud crunch.

For a moment, White stood there, panting hard, completely exhausted, rubbing the side of his throbbing head. There was a faint scuff behind him—a small rock wedged in the sole of a shoe scraping on a stone slab. White just had time to duck his head and start leaning to his left when something smacked him hard on the head. His hand took some of the force out of the blow, but White still went down, face first onto the large stone slab. He tried to roll out of the way, expecting another crack at the top of his head, but he didn't have the strength.

Then he heard a click behind him, the hammer of a pistol being cocked.

White sighed. During his fight, he'd lost his tactical awareness and forgotten about the two other shooters. And now he was going to die because of his mistake.

"Don't you dare move, Clayton White, or I'll execute you the same way you killed my husband," Adaliya Oxley said. "With a bullet to the head."

But White hadn't heard the last sentence. He'd already passed out.

CHAPTER FORTY-FOUR

London, England

Reza resisted the urge to pull the trigger. Pierre was going to be more useful to him alive than with his brain splattered on the side window of the Range Rover. Inside the house, the firefight was still raging. Domino-Four had been hit in the leg, and Five had taken cover. Reza groaned in frustration.

"Entering now," came in Domino-Six.

Reza considered ordering Six back, but Clayton White had proven harder to kill than most. Six was going to be the man tilting the balance in Reza's favor; he was sure of it. In any case, all his men were *deniable assets*, a term his father had liked to use.

The roar of Cadillac engines startled Reza as two white Escalades sped past the Range Rover. White had entered the house less than twelve minutes ago; it was impossible that Adaliya and her crew were already back.

Unless Dandre is still alive and reached out to her, Reza thought.

"All call signs from One," Reza called out, his voice calm but assertive. "Finish this now and get out of there. Incoming security personnel will have the house surrounded in less than twenty seconds. Follow your individual exfil protocols. Domino-One out."

Reza removed the suppressor from the barrel of his pistol and leaned forward in order to put the Browning back in the holster. Looking out the window, he scanned for anyone who'd be close enough to see him get out of the SUV. Leaving Pierre in the back seat, Reza climbed out and replaced the Frenchman's phone where he had found it—between the curb and the front right wheel of the vehicle. This way, odds were no one would find out that Pierre's phone had been compromised.

Reza took one last look at Adaliya's house, then tucked his hands in his pockets and walked in the opposite direction.

CHAPTER FORTY-FIVE

London, England

White's eyes fluttered open. Each beat of his heart stabbed the side of his head where he'd gotten whacked by what had felt like a steel pipe. He was seated in an armchair similar to the ones he'd seen in the dining room. His sore hands were bound behind him with steel cuffs. Both his ankles were duct-taped to the chair's legs. He looked up and blinked a few times. His vision cleared. He was in Adaliya's garage, which was bigger than White had imagined. The two Escalades were parked side by side, occupying a good portion of the space, but White was in a twenty-foot-by-twenty-foot area at the back. The armchair on which he was seated was in the middle of a large and very thick plastic tarp.

Not a good sign.

In front of him were six fifty-five-gallon black steel drums. The five on the left had been closed with aluminum lids. The drum in front of White wasn't. White watched as a member of Adaliya's security team opened the rear hatch of an Escalade. Another man walked into White's peripheral vision and helped the first one load a steel drum into the back of the SUV.

"These are the men you killed, Mr. White," Adaliya Oxley said, her voice calm and soothing, as if her men were simply loading bags of potatoes and not steel drums packed with human bodies.

White cleared his throat. "I killed three men, not five."

Adaliya walked in front of White, the plastic tarp unable to swallow up the decisive and sharp clicks of her high heels hitting the garage's cement floor. She looked at him with her large, sparkling dark eyes, her hands resting on her hips. Then the corners of her lips hooked up into a strange smile.

"Yes, you're right, of course," she said.

Adaliya was a tall, slim woman who carried herself with the practiced elegance of a runway model. She had long jet black hair that rippled down her shoulders. She was wearing a pair of close-fitting blue jeans and a military-style black-and-gold velvet jacket over what seemed to be a white T-shirt.

"Before we get down to business, I thought you'd like to know that a doctor friend of mine is taking care of our mutual acquaintance," Adaliya said.

The last time White had seen Sarazin, he was being shoved into the back of the Range Rover. There was no point in hiding the fact that he was here with the former French spy.

"Will he live?" White asked.

Adaliya nodded.

Something told him she was being truthful. White thought it was a bit weird that despite the unfortunate situation he found himself in—knowing he was about to get shot in the head or, even worse, tortured, then shot in the head—a huge weight had just been lifted off his shoulders. He was happy his friend was going to make it.

White's thoughts switched to Veronica. She'd miss him. He knew that. He had cherished every moment he had spent with her. There was no doubt in his mind that he'd become a better person because of her. She was a special woman, and she deserved to be loved and treasured every hour of every day. From the bottom of his heart, he hoped she would one day find someone else that would be able to make her laugh.

Seems like I won't be running after our little ones after all, White thought. *Sorry, Vonnie.*

Raising his gaze to Adaliya, he said, "Make it quick, will you?"

She cocked her head to one side, and again that weird smile appeared on her lips. Behind her, men were loading a third drum into the Escalade. She turned around to the youngest of the two, a short, barrel-chested fireplug of a man.

"Once you're done here, I want you to help the cleaning crew," she told him. "I want my kids to sleep in their beds tonight. Understood?"

The man gave Adaliya a curt nod; then his gaze stopped on White, pure hatred emanating from his sharp green eyes. Adaliya put her hand on his shoulder. "Go now."

The man reluctantly stepped away.

"He's pissed at you," Adaliya explained. "You really messed up his father's knee."

"The giant?" White asked, curious. "It can't be. The man's almost seven feet tall, and this guy isn't even . . . whatever."

Adaliya shrugged, then looked into the empty drum for a few moments. Then she observed White from the corner of her eye before returning her attention to the drum.

"You know we'll have to cut off your legs to make you fit in this one, right?"

"Either that or you'll have to fold me in two," White replied, not missing a beat. "These drums are about thirty-five inches in height, and I'm just over six foot. So there you go."

Adaliya took a few steps toward him. "You're an interesting man, Clayton White," she said without a hint of malice. "And I'm glad you understand how precarious your situation is. It's gonna make the rest of our little chat together much easier."

White wasn't sure where this was leading, but at least he was still breathing. So he didn't mind listening to her rant.

"I'll make a deal with you," she said. "I'll ask you a few questions. Answer them honestly, and you'll get out of here. Easy enough to understand?"

"That's your way of telling me you'll kill me quickly?"

A look of impatience crossed her features. "I don't play games, Mr. White," she barked. "Neither should you."

Adaliya took a deep breath and seemed to regain her composure.

"But lie to me just once," she said, showing him one finger to emphasize her point, "and I'll make you pay for all the hell you've brought to my life. And yes, in case you're wondering, you'll die slowly, and you'll end up at the bottom of the English Channel like the rest of these assholes."

She gestured toward the drums that had now all been loaded into the Escalades. "Simple enough?"

White swallowed a smart-ass reply and nodded.

"Dandre told me you could have killed him if you wanted to," Adaliya said, not wasting time. "Why didn't you? Because you certainly weren't shy about killing everybody else, it seems."

"I came here for you, no one else," White said. "That's why I waited until your children were off at school."

Adaliya frowned. A muscle twitched in her jaw.

"How nice of you," she hissed. "So you were going to wait for me? Kill me in my bedroom?"

"It depends," he said.

"On what?" she shouted at him.

Something snapped in White's head, and he replied in kind, not caring about the consequences. "What the fuck did you expect? You ordered the assassination of the vice president of the United States, Adaliya! And you tried to kill my fiancée. If you really think I was going to sit idle while you plotted your next attack, you're fucking delusional!"

Adaliya took a small step back, as if his words had pushed her away from him. The bodyguard who had stayed in the garage was on White a second later and whacked the barrel of his pistol across White's cheek, drawing blood. The bodyguard then placed the tip of the suppressor an inch away from White's forehead and looked at Adaliya for further instructions. White spat blood from his mouth, the red liquid landing two feet in front of Adaliya's high-heeled boots.

Adaliya looked momentarily stunned; then understanding crossed her face. She waved away her bodyguard. The man grunted but obeyed, returning to his spot a few feet behind his employer.

"Let me be crystal clear about this," Adaliya said. "I think whoever's behind the two Florida operations should be applauded. My hatred for Alexander Hammond knows no bounds, and I rejoiced when I learned his precious Heather was killed, because from now on, and for the rest of his miserable life, he'll feel the same pain I have to live with every hour of every fucking day. But I didn't do it. I swear it on my children's lives. I'm done with all that shit. I'm trying to build a good life for my kids. Can you understand that? I have no desire to relight a feud with one of the most powerful men in the world. Sure, I could get lucky and win a few rounds, but I'd eventually lose the war. And then what? My kids would be orphans."

White wasn't sure if he was supposed to say something or not, but he remained silent, which seemed to be the safest option.

Adaliya began pacing back and forth, shaking her head and waving a long finger at him. "I'm no fool, and I'm no victim. I know my husband launched an unprovoked attack against Veronica Hammond last year in San Francisco," she finally said. "When Roy shared his plan with me, I wasn't happy about it. I tried to dissuade him from going that route, but his mind was set. You have to understand. We had so much going on at the time, and we were so, so very close to our objective. It's no excuse for what he did, but if we'd sold Roy's shipping company to Le Groupe Avanti, we could have changed millions of lives in South Africa. You hear me? Millions."

White had to admit he hadn't expected such a passionate speech from a woman who had been married to a confirmed sociopath for almost two decades.

"Then came that beautiful, intelligent fiancée of yours with that mobile application that could see through the oceans," Adaliya continued, resuming her pacing. "And Roy couldn't allow that. He just couldn't. He was sure it was Alexander Hammond's way to screw him over."

"I know all of this," White said. "Your husband told me, remember?"

"I was already back in England when you came to South Africa. I have no idea what you two discussed, but I'm sure he talked to you about your father, yes?"

White felt his heart pinch. "I know Hammond collaborated with your husband to kill my father, if that's what you mean," he said. "I've known for a year now that Hammond allowed his chopper to be shot down by people paid by your organization."

Adaliya's look softened to something like compassion, if she was capable of any.

"I'm sure it wasn't easy for you to accept," she said. "Have you told your future wife?"

White didn't think it was Adaliya's business to know what he shared or didn't share with Veronica, but then again, he didn't want to end up in a fifty-five-gallon drum either. Plus, he liked the fact that Adaliya had used the words *future wife*. That meant he still had a chance to get out of England in one piece, didn't it?

"I haven't told her, and I'm pretty sure Hammond isn't aware I know his darkest secret either."

"Agreed," Adaliya replied. "'Cause if he knew, you'd most probably be dead. Anyhow, that's quite a powerful weapon you're holding in reserve, Mr. White. I hope you'll one day have the chance to use it."

"You're speaking as if I'll live another day," White said.

Adaliya locked eyes with him, her face only inches away. She was so close he could smell her perfume, or maybe it was just the scent of the flowery soap she'd used that morning.

"Did you believe me when I told you I had nothing to do with the Florida attacks?" she asked.

"I do now."

Adaliya seemed satisfied by the answer.

"That means someone set you up," White added.

"Yes," she said. "Someone did."

"Then it's too bad you had to cut these guys up to fit them in your steel drums," White said. "I bet they could have enlightened us."

She flashed him a smile. "Oh, but they did, Mr. White. They did."

CHAPTER FORTY-SIX

Sixteen Hours Later . . .
Over the Atlantic Ocean

White was seated next to Veronica in one of the two comfortable love seats inside the cabin of the Gulfstream G550—the call sign of which today was Air Force Two since Vice President Hammond was aboard. Hammond was seated alone at the back of the plane while Special Agent Albanese and the rest of the protective detail were at the front.

The gash on the side of White's head where he'd been hit with a steel pipe had required eight stitches, and two more had been needed to close the laceration on his cheek where Adaliya's bodyguard had whacked him with his pistol. White's right ear had mushroomed to almost the size of a junior hamburger at McDonald's.

"Thanks again for being here," he said to Veronica, squeezing her thigh.

"As much as I hate to admit it, it was my dad who made it happen so fast," she said; then her mouth opened as if she wanted to add something, but no words came out.

"What is it?" White asked.

"I . . . I'm not sure," Veronica said. "He seems . . . different? He's . . . I don't know. It's hard for me to put into words. I've spent the last forty-eight hours with him in Washington, trying to bridge things up, you know? But it's hard for me to trust him."

"I get it," White said. "He's gonna need you to get through the next few weeks, and you might need him too, Vonnie—and that's okay."

Veronica nodded and rested her head on his shoulder. Then she said in a tired voice, "I miss her so much, Clay. And I'm so damn mad."

"I know," he said, kissing the top of her head. "It will get better."

They stayed silent for a good while, and White thought Veronica had fallen asleep when she said, "I wish we could have taken Pierre with us."

"Let's just be happy that he's alive, okay? The doctors said he'd be able to fly back to the US in ten to twelve days. It could have been much worse."

"I know, but it still sucks."

White felt the same way, and a fair amount of guilt too. Sarazin shouldn't have been there. White had missed the mark on this one. He should have insisted on going to London alone. The former French spy had his heart in the right place, but he didn't have the proper training. White wondered if he'd been selfish in allowing Sarazin to tag along, knowing from the start that Sarazin's contacts in England could greatly improve his chances of success.

From the moment White had contacted Veronica, it had taken eleven hours until the wheels of Air Force Two had touched down at Northolt, the older Royal Air Force base. RAF Northolt was located approximately six miles north of London's Heathrow Airport. Adaliya had driven him personally to the airport, but she had made a quick stop at a warehouse along the way to drop off five fifty-five-gallon steel drums. The drive to the airport had been surreal. Adaliya's last words before leaving him at the airport's gate had been to remind him to tell Hammond that as far as she was concerned, the issue between them was settled.

"Clayton," Hammond said, standing in front of White. "A word?"

White opened his eyes, realizing he had dozed off. Veronica's head was still resting on his shoulder. He gently laid her down on the love seat, joined Hammond at the back of the plane, and took a seat in front of him.

"Sorry I couldn't get to you sooner," Hammond said. "Heather's funeral arrangements are getting more complicated by the minute."

Despite his personal opinion of Hammond, White was deeply saddened by Heather's death. She had been a great mom to Veronica. Her death had left a void that would take years to get over—if ever.

"I'm—"

Hammond raised his hand. "I know how you feel about me, Clayton. I wasn't looking for your sympathy," he said. "Now, tell me what the fuck happened in London?"

For the next thirty minutes or so, White did exactly that. When he was done, Hammond was shaking his head, visibly upset.

"Iranian intelligence? No, Clayton, you got this wrong. It can't be them. That bitch Adaliya lied to you," Hammond said. "The Iranians don't have the guts to pull such an operation on US soil. They have way too much to lose. You going to London was a waste of time—"

"I'm telling you, it's the MOIS," White said, interrupting Hammond and getting to his feet. Adaliya had warned him that Hammond wouldn't believe her. He headed back to the love seat where he had left his backpack. He pulled out a phone and a pair of earbuds, then returned to his seat facing Hammond, who looked annoyed.

White powered on the phone. Once the device had booted up, White clicked on the photo and video app. He gave the phone to Hammond along with the earbuds.

"There's only one thing on this phone, nothing else. Double-tap on the video and listen carefully."

Hammond did. He spent the next five minutes watching the interview Adaliya had conducted with the intruder White had shot in the leg. White had watched it numerous times and had been stunned to see Adaliya physically appear in the video. She had risked a lot by recording the enhanced interrogation on the Iranian officer. If that video were to leak to the press or the police, she'd spend the rest of her life behind bars.

When the video was over, Hammond looked at White.

"Mohsen Ashtari? That fucking cockroach," he said. "He's still messing with us, eight years after we killed him."

"What we need to know is if his son Reza is acting alone and supported by a bunch of rogue agents, or if it's the entire MOIS and Iranian leadership behind him," White said.

"That's the billion-dollar question, isn't it?" Hammond replied. "I'm the one who put the Mohsen Ashtari target package together for the president. I recall that Mohsen had two sons. One was Reza, the Quds Force officer, but the other, Nader, was an intelligence officer at the MOIS."

"I'll look into it," White said. "See what he's become, what he's doing, and—"

"How? You have no official position," Hammond interrupted, waving him off with his hand. "No, Clayton, you'll stand down on this one. I think you've done enough."

"What's wrong with you?" White asked. "I thought you were going to open doors for me. Not shut them in my face."

"Relax. I'll share with you anything of interest that comes up," Hammond said, removing the earbuds and returning them with the phone to White. "There you go. Now if you'll excuse me, I have calls to make."

White, irritated at being kept on the sidelines, took the earbuds but not the phone.

"Adaliya wanted you to keep it as a gesture of goodwill," he said.

Hammond frowned, and a flash of worry crossed his features. "Why?" he asked, dropping the phone into the interior pocket of his sport jacket. "Could be dangerous for her."

White waited a beat before answering; then he said, "Mutual assured destruction."

Hammond's mouth opened, then closed, his eyes once again casting a worried look. White had caught him off guard.

"I'm . . . confused," he said.

"No you're not. You're wondering what Adaliya Oxley told me. It's okay, Alex, I know you're a curious man. I'll tell you this. Adaliya and I had a very long and very honest talk with each other."

"I'm . . . I'm glad you did," Hammond said.

"We talked about many things," White continued, his cold eyes drilling into Hammond's. "One of them being what really happened to my father."

The vice president tried to force a smile, but the result was more akin to a grimace. White recognized it for what it was. A crack in Alexander Hammond's facade. White continued to stare at the vice president for a very long time, enough that even though he was trying to play it cool, a thin layer of perspiration formed on Hammond's forehead.

Hammond closed his eyes for a brief moment and sighed.

"So, what now?" he asked.

"Tell me the goddamn truth."

Then, surprising White, Hammond started talking.

CHAPTER FORTY-SEVEN

Over the Atlantic Ocean

White wondered what had pushed Hammond to open up. Could it be that the assassination of his wife had made him conscious of his own vulnerability? Or could it be that his conscience had finally woken up? In the end, it didn't matter why, because White would never forgive him. He just wanted Hammond out of the vice presidency. His murderous ass didn't deserve to be seated in that office.

When Hammond finally stopped talking, he looked deflated.

"You committed murder. You committed treason," White whispered through clenched teeth, jabbing a finger toward the second-most-powerful man in the United States. "You betrayed your best friend because he wanted to do the right thing. You don't deserve the privilege of your office; the American public deserves better than you. Your daughter deserves better than you. Despite all of your medals, you're just a fucking coward. Let me ask you this, Mr. Vice-fucking-President. How can you wake up every morning and live with yourself?"

Hammond remained silent for a long time, his head buried in his hand. White didn't mind. They wouldn't reach Washington, DC, for another five hours. When Hammond ultimately met White's unwavering gaze, he said, "I would do it all over again."

White felt his face turn crimson. "What did you just say?"

"Let me explain, Clayton," Hammond said. "There isn't a day I don't think about him. I loved that man like a brother."

"But you killed him regardless," White said, his voice saturated with contempt.

"I did. I gave Roy Oxley's man Maxwell's flight plan and—"

"Enough!" White hissed. "I know all of this. I've listened to the recordings."

"The recordings?" Hammond asked. "What are you talking about?"

"I've known about your betrayal for a year now," White said.

"I see," Hammond said, a hint of a smile appearing at the corner of his lips. "So it was Roy Oxley who told you, not Adaliya."

"I didn't want to believe him, but I read the emails, and I listened to your conversations. It was you."

"Then you know I was threatened. They would have killed my Heather and Vonnie if I didn't do what they asked."

"Don't bullshit me," White said, his face twisting with anger. "You were the commanding officer of JSOC. You had plenty of other options at your disposal. You took the easy way out. That's it. It isn't more complicated than that."

"I assume you've kept the recordings in a safe place?" Hammond said after a short pause, his eyes calculating.

White kept his mouth shut. He wasn't about to tell Hammond what he had done with them.

"It doesn't matter," Hammond said a few seconds later. "Keep them. Do whatever you want. Adaliya has copies too, I'm sure. Mutually assured destruction, right?"

Hammond fell quiet as White pondered what to do next.

"Why haven't you told Vonnie any of this?" Hammond asked, as if it was an afterthought. And maybe it was. "Don't you want her to hate me for the rest of her life for what I've done? Wouldn't that make you happy?"

For the first time in his life, White looked at Hammond with pity. "You've known me since I was a boy, and that's what you think? I love her more than I hate you."

Hammond's features were suddenly tortured, as if all his well-built barriers had toppled, but White knew better than to fall for it completely. As sincere and disarming as Hammond could make himself look, he was still a master manipulator.

"Vonnie's lucky to have you in her life," Hammond said. "You make her happy. It's easy to see. I know what I've done is unforgivable, so I won't insult you by begging for your forgiveness, but I'll ask you this: Time. Give me time, Clayton."

Hammond's strange request surprised him. "Time?"

"Give me enough time to find the bastards who killed Heather. Give me the time I need to put them six feet under."

"Then what?"

"I'll resign," Hammond said simply. "You have my word."

"Your word? Isn't that ironic?"

"I need the power of my office to do this," Hammond said. "Help me, Clayton. Help me find Reza Ashtari and whoever else was involved in the attacks. Help me protect Veronica. Once I'm done, I'll leave."

White studied Hammond's face, looking for any suggestions that he was lying, but found none. He gave Hammond a slight nod, then headed to the love seat where Veronica was still sleeping, wondering if this time Hammond would keep his word, or if he would once again break it.

CHAPTER FORTY-EIGHT

Ministry of Intelligence and Security
Tehran, Iran

Nader pushed himself off his chair and yelled into his phone.

"No, Reza! You will not contact our assets in Mexico. And for the last time, you're not going to New York! I want you to head back to Tehran immediately. That's an order!"

Silence.

"Reza? Reza?"

Realizing his brother had hung up on him, Nader smashed his phone onto the polished wooden surface of his desk. Then, in an uncharacteristic fit of rage, he threw it across his office, but watched in horror as the phone hit the wall only inches below the supreme leader's picture.

Nader breathed a sigh of relief and sank back into his chair, emotionally drained from the conversation he'd just had. Had Reza completely lost his mind? Had he gone mad? He couldn't believe his brother was on his way to the United States. Apparently, Reza had cloned the phone of one of Clayton White's associates and had found out about an upcoming meeting between Veronica Hammond, Emily Moss, and a *New York Times* editor. It was even possible that White would be in attendance too. And Reza, without authorization or any kind of backup or support, had decided to go to New York City to kill them all.

Unbelievable! This time, his brother had really lost it.

Nader buried his face in his hands, knowing he was partly to blame for his brother's fall from grace. For years, they had been a great team. They had worked together almost flawlessly. He planning the missions, and Reza executing them.

Reza Ashtari had participated in more missions than any other MOIS field operative before him. Reza was the most precious covert weapon in the entire MOIS arsenal.

But this was to be no more. Not after what he'd just told Nader on the phone.

Nader shook his head. Angry at himself.

I should have known this was coming. He should have seen the signs. He should have pulled his brother out of the field after the failed Florida Keys operation—the worst operational failure since Nader had assumed the role of deputy director of the Foreign Operations Directorate—but he had not. He'd been blinded by Reza's promise to avenge their father by killing Clayton White. And Nader had fallen for it.

No later than yesterday, the supreme leader had even compared the failed Florida mission to the successful 2018 raid Israeli intelligence had conducted at a closely protected warehouse in Tehran. The Mossad operation had seen more than one hundred thousand documents, images, and videos related to Iran's nuclear plans fall into Israeli and American hands.

It was that bad.

Emily Moss was in possession of critical photos that could jeopardize Iran's strategic partnership with China. There was one golden rule that had to be respected at all times when dealing with the Chinese. Under no circumstances were you to embarrass them.

Unfortunately, photos proving the existence of the arbitrary executions of over ten thousand prodemocracy civilians in torture chambers run by the MOIS in Syria would surely do just that. If China was to officially distance itself from Iran, it could very well be a blow the Islamic Republic would not recuperate from.

Adding to his stress level, Nader hadn't shared the details of the London operation with the minister of intelligence. Nader's authority was sufficient to order such operations, but the rules were clear: the minister had to be read in to a foreign operation involving a member of the MOIS no later than twenty-four hours after it had started. Nader had failed to do so. On purpose.

And now, his neck was on the chopping block.

What he couldn't allow, couldn't tolerate, was his brother's refusal to come home. The London operation was a failure of epic proportions. Five MOIS covert operatives had been lost in a single mission. Never before in the history of the MOIS had something like this happened.

On a more personal level, and to add fuel to an already hot fire, Reza had been incapable of killing Clayton White in London, and he had almost dismissed the deaths of the five operatives—his colleagues!—as something of little importance. His brother, the greatest and fiercest warrior Nader had ever known, was no longer fit to lead, no longer fit to operate.

It was evident to Nader that his brother was blind to his failures. By refusing Nader's order to come in, Reza had placed him in an unsustainable—and very dangerous—position. That being said, Nader hadn't climbed all the way to the very top of the MOIS by playing fair. He still had one last card to play.

Nader got up from behind his desk and walked to where his phone had fallen. The screen was cracked, and the battery had popped out on impact. Nader reinserted the battery into his phone, waited for it to power up, then dialed his assistant's number.

"Bring my car around," he said. "I need to see the minister."

CHAPTER FORTY-NINE

The Office of the Supreme Leader of Iran
Tehran, Iran

Nader Ashtari's armored sedan rolled up to the outer-perimeter security checkpoint of the Iranian leader's walled compound. The driver handed over his credentials to the uniformed guard while mirrors were run under both sides of the vehicle. Soon the sedan was moving again. It stopped a few moments later at the bottom of the marble staircase that led up to the official residence of Iran's septuagenarian spiritual guide. As Nader waited for his bodyguard to open his door, he couldn't help but wonder whether he had kissed his children and hugged his wife for the last time. To say that he was nervous would be an understatement.

He was petrified.

Many people had disappeared after being summoned by the supreme leader. Business leaders, members of the Iranian Parliament, and general officers of the armed forces had simply vanished following their meetings. By law, the supreme leader was never wrong. He was *inviolable*. Former colleagues of Nader's had been arrested for simply questioning one of the supreme leader's decisions.

Nader's door opened, and he stepped out of the vehicle, where he was met by a protocol officer. The man was serious, unsmiling, but greeted Nader with a deferential nod. Nader followed the man up the steps to the first of many armed security checkpoints. Nader was cleared through rapidly and continued his journey through multiple corridors and additional checkpoints before being shown to a lounge area just outside the private offices of the supreme leader.

"It will only be a few moments, Deputy Director Ashtari," the protocol officer advised him. "Coffee?"

Nader shook his head and ran a finger around his collar, wishing he hadn't knotted his tie so tightly. A small layer of perspiration had formed along his hairline.

"Do you know if the minister of intelligence has arrived?" Nader asked.

"Yes, he's inside," the protocol officer replied, nodding toward the massive vaulted double doors that led to the inner sanctum of the most powerful man in Iran.

Nader forced himself to remain calm. He was here now. He had nowhere to go. But if he played his cards well, he might just get out of this mess unscathed. If he didn't, his efforts would be rewarded by a bullet to the back of the head.

One of the doors to the office opened, and two men came out. One stayed behind, his broad shoulders taking up most of the space in the doorway, and the other headed directly to Nader. The men were dressed identically in standard attire of green combat fatigues and black boots. There was no insignia of any sort on their uniforms. Nader, who had personally briefed the supreme leader on five previous occasions, recognized them as part of the supreme leader's personal protection detail. Nader rose to his feet, his diminutive stature apparent against the other man's bulk.

"Deputy Director, please follow me."

Nader did as he was told and shadowed the bodyguard into the supreme leader's office. The door closed behind them and was locked by the second bodyguard. In contrast to the grandeur of the Iranian prime minister's office, the supreme leader's office was austere, with a simple writing desk at the center of the room and three wooden chairs. The only luxuries were the thick—and very expensive—Persian carpets that covered two-thirds of the office's floor. The supreme leader was seated behind the desk, stroking his long gray beard and staring at Nader. He was dressed in a light brown robe and black turban. From where Nader was standing, he could see the man was barefoot. The only item on the desk was a black paper folder. Across the desk and to the supreme leader's left, the minister of intelligence sat upright in a chair, his spine straight as an arrow. He glanced over his shoulder at Nader.

Nader tried to read their faces, especially their eyes, but got nothing, which didn't help with his already sky-high anxiety.

"Come join us, Nader," the supreme leader said. "Please sit."

Nader sat in the chair. It was even less comfortable than it looked.

"The minister has shared with me the details of your meeting with him," the supreme leader started, his eyes drilling into Nader's. "Is it true? Is Reza on his way back to the United States? Has he gone rogue? Or mad?"

Nader relaxed and inwardly sighed with relief. The minister had told the supreme leader exactly what Nader had shared with him at their meeting earlier that day. *Perfect.*

Nader took a deep breath and said, "No, Supreme Leader. I'm afraid you've been misinformed."

The minister's head snapped in Nader's direction, and he opened his mouth to say something, but the supreme leader raised a finger, silencing him.

"I've been misinformed? By whom?"

"By me, through the minister. This admission comes with my sincere apologies to you, Supreme Leader," Nader said, then turned toward the minister. "And to you, Minister."

The minister seemed to relax a little, but his eyes indicated he had no idea what Nader was talking about. As far as the minister was concerned, Reza had defied a direct order by returning to the United States. For now, though, the minister seemed willing to play along.

"Explain yourself," the supreme leader hissed, his eyes narrowing with an evil very few men could muster.

"Since I last spoke with the minister, I had the chance to once again speak with Reza," Nader lied.

"And?" the supreme leader snapped.

"Reza admitted his failures," Nader continued. "He regrets his ill-conceived actions. He's ashamed, and embarrassed, to have put his own needs above those of his nation. Consequently, he knows he has lost your trust and mine, Supreme Leader. And yours too, of course, Minister."

"Then why isn't he coming back to face the consequences?" the supreme leader asked. "I'm not a merciless man like some have suggested, and that's particularly true in this situation, when one's goal was to avenge the murder of one's father, who you both know was a great friend of mine."

"He knows that," Nader replied quickly. "But he believes he could make amends by serving you and the Iranian people one last time."

Nader's last words had obviously caught both the minister's and the supreme leader's attention. The supreme leader leaned forward, his elbows now resting upon the edge of the desk.

"How?" he asked. "Tell me."

"Please allow me to start at the beginning," Nader said. "The reason we sent Reza to America was to silence the journalist Emily Moss by any means necessary."

The minister nodded in agreement. "Once that Syrian military officer had shared with her the pictures of the torture chambers we built, she had to be eliminated. Reza was the right man for the job."

Nader took the plunge, knowing there would be no return after what he was about to say.

"I gave Reza way too much latitude for this operation. And because of my lack of judgment and my blind trust in Reza's abilities to perform,

I didn't keep an eye on him," Nader said, shaking his head while praying the supreme leader was going to swallow his lie.

The supreme leader seemed to consider Nader's explanation for a long minute. Nader's chest tightened, certain the supreme leader could hear his racing heart from across the desk.

"Don't be too harsh in your self-assessment, Nader," the supreme leader finally said. "Reza's a calculating soldier. That's why he's been so successful and valuable to us for so many years. For this operation, he's been two or three steps ahead of you the entire time. Maybe, Nader, it is you who's losing his edge."

All the built-up pressure in his chest released, and Nader realized he'd been holding his breath for the better part of sixty seconds.

"Apparently so," he conceded.

"What happened to this Syrian traitor?" the supreme leader asked.

"A Quds Force commando paid him a visit," the minister replied, coming to Nader's assistance. "He'll never talk to a reporter again."

"And what about the . . . facilities Emily Moss obtained pictures of?"

"Destroyed," the minister replied. "As of two days ago. We're presently in the last stage of the cleanup operation."

Nader relaxed some more. This was good news.

The minister continued, "We made it look as if the destruction had been the work of Syrian rebels—"

"Terrorists!" shouted the supreme leader.

"Absolutely. I misspoke," the minister said, bowing his head.

"With the facilities gone, and the Syrian officer dead, Emily Moss is like a shark with no teeth," the supreme leader said in a much quieter tone. "She can write and publish whatever she wants; she won't gain any traction."

"You are once again correct, Supreme Leader," Nader said. "The Americans and some European countries might whine about it to the United Nations, but as long as they have no hard evidence, the Chinese will back us and will dismiss their complaints."

"If I may add something," the minister said, looking at the ayatollah. The supreme leader gave him a curt nod.

"Our friends in Damascus aren't happy about this. They've asked us to intervene, which is what we're doing as we speak. Our forces in Syria are raiding multiple known terrorist compounds. And we will rebuild the destroyed facilities, too, of course, but it will cost significant capital we don't necessarily—"

"Enough," cut in the supreme leader, visibly upset. "Syria remains a priority. Whatever the cost, but I don't want our military intervention to become a direct confrontation with the United States."

"Yes, Supreme Leader."

Then, turning his attention to Nader, the supreme leader pointed a bony finger at him and said, "You see, Nader, this is why I wanted Emily Moss eliminated. Reza's failure to do so is already negatively impacting many of our other projects. The funds we'll need to reinvest in Syria will have to come out of other endeavors important to our nation."

"I can assure you that Reza is well aware of the dire consequences of his actions," Nader said. "As for the Americans, I'm positive—and I'm sure the minister will agree with me—that with the present chaos in Afghanistan, and with the Taliban back in power, the Americans don't want a confrontation with us either. They don't have the stomach for it."

"So you believe they'll leave us alone in Syria?" the supreme leader asked.

"I'm persuaded that if we can offer the Americans something concrete, something that would prove to them we have no hostile intent toward them and that the attacks in Florida were the work of a lone wolf, we would achieve our objective in Syria with little or no long-term negative consequences from the Americans."

The minister snapped his head in Nader's direction, visibly shaken by what Nader was proposing.

"Are you suggesting that we admit our participation in what could be considered an act of war against the United States? Have you lost your mind, Nader?"

Nader didn't bother replying; his eyes were on the supreme leader, who was looking right back at him, intrigued.

"A lone wolf, you said?" the ayatollah mused.

Nader nodded.

The supreme leader rose to his feet but signaled to Nader and the minister of intelligence that they should remain seated. The ayatollah slowly walked to the lone, tiny bulletproof window of his office. He had his hands behind his back.

"I know where you're going with this, Nader. I presume this is the moment when you'll share with me what Reza has in mind, yes?" the supreme leader asked, gazing out the window.

"To make amends for his mistakes, Reza has offered to become a martyr," Nader said.

Nader heard the rush of air entering the minister's mouth as he gasped in surprise. The ayatollah, though, remained immobile.

"How?" the supreme leader asked.

"Reza is presently on his way to Mexico to meet with our contacts," Nader said. "He'll wait for further instructions a few miles south of the American border. If you give him the privilege to proceed, he'll cross the border and make his way to New York City."

The supreme leader angled his body so he could look at Nader. "New York City?" he asked.

"Three days from now, Emily Moss and her friend Veronica Hammond are scheduled to meet with an editor of the *New York Times*," Nader said.

"How did you come up with this information?"

"I can't take credit for it. Reza got it for us. He cloned the phone of one of Veronica's friends," Nader said, keeping it short.

"And this intelligence . . . is it valid?" the supreme leader asked, returning to his seat behind the desk. "Would you bet your family's life on it?"

Nader didn't flinch. He'd known all along it might come to this.

"Yes, Supreme Leader. I would."

The ayatollah smiled. "Good, good. Please, Nader. Tell me more about what Reza has in mind."

———

Fifteen minutes later, Nader and the minister were escorted out of the supreme leader's office. They walked alongside each other through the corridors but didn't speak until they'd reached the marble steps outside of the building. The sky was a crisp, distant blue, and even though the sun was high and the temperature had risen a little since they'd arrived at the compound almost an hour ago, it was still cold enough for their breath to fog in front of their faces.

"You're a cunning little man," the minister murmured. "You're playing a very, very dangerous game, Nader."

Nader looked at the minister and shrugged. "It's the nature of the business we're in, isn't it?"

"Your brother has no clue you've thrown him to the wolves, does he?" the minister challenged.

Nader didn't reply. He started down the steps toward the armored sedan idling at the bottom of the stairs.

CHAPTER FIFTY

Three Days Later . . .
New York, New York

Lying prone on an elevated homemade sniper nest inside the modified cargo area of a gray minivan, Reza Ashtari adjusted the scope of his Dragunov sniper rifle until he had a clear view of the entrance. Through monitoring Pierre's phone, he had learned that Clayton White had somehow survived his men's assault on Adaliya Oxley's house.

That was unfortunate.

The silver lining was that White was now in New York City. In a few minutes, he would walk through the restaurant's entrance with Veronica Hammond and that bitch Emily Moss.

The minivan's windows were heavily tinted, and its back windshield had been replaced with a high-end isinglass-like material that would allow Reza to fire through it without much sound. With its engine turned off, the inside of the van was cool, but Reza was used to being uncomfortable. Thirty minutes ago, he had spotted the Secret Service two-man advance team. They had secured the interior and the immediate vicinity of the restaurant, then had chatted with the maître d' for a few minutes before taking position under the porch. The pretty, petite brunette editor from the *New York Times* was next to arrive. She talked with a special agent for a while, then was escorted deeper into the restaurant—and out of Reza's sight—by the maître d'. Reza wouldn't have to wait much longer.

The Dragunov wasn't his preferred precision rifle, but it had been the only option available to him. Luckily for Reza, he was quite familiar with the weapon since Iran's own Nakjir 3 sniper rifle had been built with almost the same specifications. Anyway, it wasn't as though he had been in a position to be picky.

Reza had breathed a sigh of relief when Nader had called him back to let him know he had changed his mind about the operation. Reza had been prepared to run the mission by himself, but it would have been much more difficult to pull off if his brother hadn't green-lighted it. The United States–Mexico border had been more treacherous than Reza remembered from previous missions. The MOIS assets embedded with the cartels had provided invaluable assistance during the crossing. The assets were now standing by in El Paso for further instructions.

All of this—the van, the sniper rifle, the exfil protocol—wouldn't have been available without his brother's assistance. Thanks to Nader, Reza actually believed he had a shot at both completing the mission and at getting out of the United States alive.

After he had hung up on his brother following a heated discussion, Reza had seriously doubted that Nader would have the guts to authorize the New York City operation. But Nader—like so many times before—had once again come through, which made Reza chastise himself for being so skeptical about his brother. Nader had certainly grown into a force to be reckoned with since he had taken over the deputy director position. He was now operating at the strategic level, and it suited him rather well.

Still, it was a gutsy move, and there was a fair share of risk involved. The potential rewards, though, justified rolling the dice—at least they did for Reza and his brother. Their father's honor demanded it.

God was giving him a second chance.

And this time, Reza wouldn't miss.

CHAPTER FIFTY-ONE

New York, New York

White lay alone in the king-size bed of the spacious suite he was sharing with Veronica, watching the ceiling and wearing only his underwear. His head was pounding with the worst headache he'd ever experienced. It felt as if the right part of his brain was being squeezed out of his ears. He knew the headache would eventually leave, as the others had. They'd occurred on and off since his return to the States. White had taken it easy for the last forty-eight hours, nursing his injuries by sleeping in, watching a bit of television, and reading Don Bentley's newest thriller. He'd even offered to help Veronica with her mom's funeral arrangements, but she'd politely declined.

The gash to the side of his head had started to heal, but his right ear still didn't look pretty. The doctors had assured him it would return to its normal size within a week or two. As for the headaches, the brain surgeon had said it could take up to four weeks for them to disappear completely.

He had yet to hear from Hammond in regard to the investigation into the Ashtari brothers. White would give him a couple more days; then he would start pushing for answers. Reza Ashtari was still in the wind. Nobody had seen him. It was possible he had returned to

Iran—or whatever shithole he had climbed out of—to lick his wounds, but White had his doubts. Reza had been a step or two ahead of them in London, and his trap had almost worked. It had been a brilliant idea to leave pointers leading to Adaliya Oxley. White had fallen for it, and it had nearly cost him his life.

He and Veronica would have to remain vigilant for the foreseeable future.

Veronica came out of the bathroom, a towel wrapped around her. She looked at him, visibly annoyed. "We're leaving in ten minutes, Clay. Get dressed."

But he didn't move. He stared at the towel snugged tightly around her curves. If he had his way, he'd yank the towel off her and make love to her—but he didn't have the energy.

She seemed to realize he wasn't feeling like his usual self. She adjusted her towel and sat on the bed next to him.

"Another headache?" she asked.

He nodded.

"You don't have to come to the restaurant if you don't feel well," she said, massaging the bridge of his nose. "Stay here. Rest. It shouldn't take more than two or three hours."

"Thanks, baby. I think that's what I'll do if that's all right," he said, keeping his eyes closed, enjoying the massage. "It's too bad, though, 'cause I read the reviews. It's a pretty cool place you're going to. Please tell Emily I'm sorry, and I wish her luck."

"I'll do that." Veronica kissed him gently on the lips before heading to her open suitcase. "I'm picking her up at her parents' apartment in Yorkville in twenty minutes. Then we're off to SoHo for our meeting with the *New York Times* editor."

The map of Manhattan flashed in White's mind. "Our hotel isn't even five minutes away from the restaurant. That's one hell of a detour."

"I know," she replied, walking back toward the bed wearing an elegant blue long-sleeved dress with a low neckline. "But we have some girl talk to do."

White opened one eye. "Girl talk?"

Veronica beamed at him. "She thinks Angus is about to propose to her. How about that? Zip me up, will you?"

CHAPTER FIFTY-TWO

New York, New York

White was half-naked, strapped to a gurney. His father, Maxwell, was standing next to him, pumping his chest and screaming at him to wake up. Behind his dad, Alexander Hammond smiled as he slowly raised a pistol and aimed it at Maxwell's head.

Bang!

White woke up, covered in sweat. Disoriented, he sat up in bed and attempted to clear his mind.

A sound startled him.

The nightstand. His phone. It was vibrating.

He grabbed it, looked at its screen. It was a New York City number he didn't recognize. He glanced at the clock. Veronica had been gone for about half an hour.

"Yes?" White said.

"Good afternoon, Captain White," a man said, his perfect English tinted with a slight British accent. "My name is Nader Ashtari. Does the name ring a bell?"

White rose up from the bed, a surge of adrenaline rocking his body.

Nader Ashtari. One of Major General Mohsen Ashtari's two sons.

"How did you get this number?" White asked, putting the phone on speaker and scrambling to pull up the correct application to record the call.

"Reza, who happened to be in London last week at the same time you were, cloned your friend Pierre's phone," Nader said.

White froze. "Say that again?"

"You heard me, Captain—"

"I'm no longer a captain," White said, cutting the man off and finally finding the application he was looking for.

"Ah, but you were when you pushed your knife into my father's heart."

Could this man be the real deal? Very few people knew what he had done in Iraq eight years ago. White had written an after-action report about the mission, but it had been classified as top secret. It could have been leaked. Odds were against it, but he guessed it was possible.

"I don't believe you," White said.

He heard a loud, impatient sigh coming from the man at the other end of the line.

"Moments before the helicopter took off, you punched my brother unconscious," the man said. "In the chopper with you were Lieutenant Mustafa Kaddouri, an officer with the 1st Commando Battalion, and Technical Sergeant Oscar Pérez, who was killed a few days ago in Miami.

"And in case you're wondering, Lieutenant Kaddouri is no longer among the living either."

White stopped breathing, but the man continued to speak.

"When my father was admitted to the Medical City Hospital, it took the doctors longer than it should have to correctly identify his cause of death. When my brother and I realized it was your knife that ended his life, you were out of our reach."

White's heart was pounding in his chest.

"Are you still there, Mr. White?"

"What do you want?"

"I want you to know that I moved on, but my brother didn't. He still very much wants to kill you."

"I'm aware."

"Yes, but did you know he is in New York City?"

"What?" White couldn't believe it. How did the Ashtari brothers know he was in New York City?

"Are you with Veronica Hammond at the moment?" Nader asked.

White didn't reply, stunned by Nader's words.

"Are you with your fiancée?" the Iranian repeated, this time with more urgency. "This is important, Mr. White. I know you're supposed to be eating with her and Emily Moss at a restaurant in Tribeca.

"It's a matter of life and death," added Nader. "And the clock is ticking."

"I'm not with her," White conceded.

"Then if you want to save your fiancée's life, I suggest you listen to what I'm about to tell you very, very carefully."

CHAPTER FIFTY-THREE

New York, New York

Reza was able to guess exactly when Clayton White and Veronica were about to arrive. The two special agents posted at the front of the restaurant became alive. Their eyes scanned the rooftops, looked left and right, and took an extra second scanning the vehicles driving by the restaurant.

Any second now. Lying prone behind the Dragunov, Reza held the rifle steady, satisfied that he had the right angle on the target and that his position was solid. He tracked the two-SUV motorcade as it came to a stop in front of the restaurant. White, Veronica Hammond, and possibly their friend Emily Moss would be seated in the first vehicle. The second car was a security car filled with three or four additional bodyguards. The drivers stayed in their vehicles, but the bodyguards fanned out around the motorcade to provide a physical barrier for their protectees. One of the bodyguards from the security vehicle opened the rear passenger door of the lead car.

Reza's finger moved to the trigger, hoping that White would be the first person out of the SUV, which would allow Reza at least one more shot to take out either of the women. Reza took a full breath, briefly rested at its peak, then exhaled just as Veronica Hammond climbed out of the SUV. A second later, it was Emily Moss's turn to leave the vehicle, and then, to Reza's shock, one bodyguard positioned himself behind the reporter.

What? Where was Clayton White? Why wasn't he there?

Reza refused to give in to the emotions running wild inside him. It was possible that White would get there late. But even if he didn't, Reza still could get the women when they exited the restaurant. It wouldn't give him the same satisfaction. But it would do.

CHAPTER FIFTY-FOUR

New York, New York

White, wearing only his running gear and a black fanny pack, rushed out of his hotel room, looking for the Secret Service special agent he knew was keeping an eye on the door. The special agent, a new guy White had never seen before, was sipping a bottle of water two doors down.

"Flower's in danger. Omega! Omega!" White shouted at him, using the code word for an immediate evacuation.

"What? I didn't hear—" the special agent started.

But White was on him in two strides. "Wake the fuck up and do what you're told," White barked. "I can't reach Veronica on her cell. She probably turned it off. Get the guys moving. I want her out of that restaurant and into a safe house *now*."

White didn't wait for the man's reply. He crashed through the door leading to the staircase and raced down the steps three at a time. He reached the lobby from the third floor in less than twenty seconds. He raced across the lobby and spotted another special agent who was standing outside the main entrance. A cute female valet parking attendant was trying to get his attention, but the man had his hand on his earpiece, focused on what was being said over the air.

"Do you have a car?" White asked.

"It just left with two other agents toward Tribeca. We have an Omega situation at—"

"I know," White said, cutting him off. "Give me your radio. Now."

Although White didn't know the special agent, the man did as he was told and unclipped his radio.

"I don't need the earpiece," White said as the man began to remove his suit jacket to access the wired earpiece.

"Link up with the agent on the third floor to know what's going on. I want you guys to stay here and make sure the lobby is secure in case we have to come back. Understood?"

"Yessir."

White turned to the young valet parking attendant. She had a pair of keys in her hand. White snatched the keys from her grasp.

She looked at him with wild eyes but didn't seem overly bothered by the fact that he'd just taken a set of keys from her.

"You're Veronica Hammond's boyfriend, right? Oh my God. Big fan. What's going on?"

"Which car?" he asked, holding the keys.

She pointed toward a white late-model Maserati Levante Trofeo. "Can I have a selfie?" she asked, but White was already gone.

He unlocked the Maserati SUV and started its engine. The big Ferrari-built V8 engine purred to life, its exhaust sound loud enough that people across the street noticed it. White buckled his seat belt, worked the paddle shift, and raced out of the hotel's semicircular driveway. He had left his room sixty-eight seconds ago.

He turned up the volume on the portable radio. The Secret Service was in the process of evacuating Veronica and Emily, but they had to hold inside the restaurant until the motorcade circled around the block. The two-car convoy was two or three minutes away, stuck in traffic.

Shit.

Driving with one hand, White keyed the radio.

"To all units, this is Clayton White. Be on the lookout for a gray minivan. I say again. Be on the lookout for one gray minivan. Probably within two hundred meters of the restaurant. It's being used as a mobile sniper nest."

The special agent in charge of Veronica's protective detail replied instantly.

"White, this is Flower's detail. Good copy for the gray minivan. How many shooters?"

Nader Ashtari had sworn there was only one, but White didn't trust him. "Unknown."

"Unknown number of shooters. Check," the special agent replied.

As he sped through traffic, White wished he had a police car. The Trofeo was a beast, but at lunchtime in New York City, having 590 horsepower was a bit redundant. Still, he managed to incur the wrath of dozens of drivers and pedestrians, but he didn't care, continuing to push the Maserati through the tight, congested streets while treating the traffic lights with little or no respect.

When he was less than two minutes away from the restaurant, the portable radio cracked to life.

"Motorcade's ten seconds away," a special agent said.

"Copy. Site is clear. I see you."

C'mon guys. You got this. Keep your heads on swivels. Stay focused.

Seconds later another voice came in. "We're coming—"

"Break, break, break. Get Flower and Moss back in, I've spotted a potential—" another special agent started, but he never finished his sentence.

The next sound White heard was a bloodcurdling gargle.

"Agent down! Agent down!" another agent shouted.

White slammed his fist against the steering wheel. "Goddamn it to hell!"

Looking at the Maserati's navigation system, then at the traffic in front of him, White grabbed the portable radio and his fanny pack, put the transmission in park, and climbed out of the vehicle, leaving it in the middle of the traffic lane.

Then he sprinted the last three hundred meters to the restaurant.

CHAPTER FIFTY-FIVE

New York, New York

Reza observed the special agents standing outside the restaurant through his riflescope. Something was going on. There was a light in their eyes that hadn't been there seconds ago. Both men had reached for their radios at about the same time—and Reza believed it was to turn up the volume.

Whatever had been said on the radio had agitated them. Their guns weren't drawn, but they had each opened their coats for easier access to their firearms. Could it be that Clayton White was on his way? That thought didn't last long. Movements inside the restaurant drew his attention.

Veronica Hammond and Emily Moss were being escorted to the vestibule. Why? An uneasy feeling grew in his stomach. Had he been spotted? If that was the case, a mix of police officers and Secret Service special agents would have already rushed the van. No, it was something else.

Then it hit him. He muttered a curse. He'd been betrayed. Federal agents had probably arrested the smugglers in El Paso. To save their skins, they had given him up. But wait. That didn't make sense either. The smugglers didn't know where he was going. They didn't know his final objective. Only Nader did.

After all they had been through together, had his own brother turned on him? Reza's gut churned, and he clenched his teeth until his jaw ached. A keen sense of betrayal threatened to overwhelm him.

Nader, my brother. What have you done?

Reza's thoughts were interrupted by the sight of a special agent approaching the minivan. Reza swore. He shouldn't have lost his focus. Whatever his brother had done, he would deal with it later. The agent was fifty meters away. His pistol was drawn. Reza peered through his scope back at the restaurant. Veronica was coming out, but Reza didn't have a clear shot. One of her bodyguards had suddenly stepped in front of her and was pushing her back inside.

Reza fired. The 7.62 mm round smacked into the bodyguard's back, and he pitched forward. Even though the Dragunov was suppressed, the round still gave an unmistakable *crack* as it broke the sound barrier. Reza swung the Dragunov toward the nearest agent. The special agent was now less than thirty meters away, and Reza wondered why the man hadn't started emptying his magazine into the van. As he pulled the trigger, he remembered that American police officers had very tight rules of engagement. If they couldn't see their targets, they were told to hold fire.

That suited Reza just fine.

He pivoted his rifle back toward the restaurant, looking for a target of opportunity. Veronica's two-car motorcade screeched to a halt in front of the entrance, so Reza altered his aim. He still had a direct view of the entryway between the two SUVs.

Come out. Come out, Reza willed. The man he had first shot was still alive, and he was in the process of crawling back toward the restaurant, leaving behind him an impressive amount of blood. Reza could shoot him again, the angle was right, but he preferred to wait a few more seconds to see if another agent would come out to assist the injured man.

But the Americans didn't bite.

Their first priority was the protection of their dignitaries, even if it meant leaving one of their own to die. As a former military officer, Reza understood better than most how much courage it actually took to stand down when one of your brothers-in-arms was dying in front of your eyes.

So be it. Well done, he thought, squeezing the trigger. The top of the man's head exploded. Now convinced Veronica and Emily Moss wouldn't come out, Reza emptied the rest of his magazine into the restaurant, hoping for a lucky shot.

He left the Dragunov where it stood, grabbed his phone, and climbed out of the minivan through the sliding door. Multiple police sirens were getting louder. Within seconds, the entire area would be swamped with officers. His getaway car was four hundred meters away, and with luck, he would be able to get to it without being stopped. But just in case, he opened his coat for easy access to his knives and Browning Hi-Power.

CHAPTER FIFTY-SIX

New York, New York

White stopped running and transitioned to a walk, holding the portable radio against his ear. There were now two agents down in the streets, and one more was injured inside the restaurant, but his wound wasn't life threatening. White knew he was close because everywhere he looked people were screaming and running. A few brave—or very stupid—folks had their phones out, trying to record what had been the source of that sudden chaos. All around him police sirens echoed off the buildings.

"To all units, possible male suspect spotted exiting a gray minivan," a special agent said over the radio. "Tall, well built, wearing a gray jacket and a gray hoodie. Last seen walking west on Beach Street."

Beach Street. White quickly turned down the volume. He was on Hudson Street, less than twenty feet away from Beach Street. *Damn.* He'd probably walked or run right past Reza. He scanned left and right, then over his shoulder.

Shit.

He unzipped his fanny pack and wrapped his hand around the Glock, making sure to keep his finger outside the trigger guard. In his running jacket's pocket, his phone began to vibrate. Two short bursts followed by three longer ones. It was Veronica. White pulled out the phone, looked at the screen to confirm it was indeed his fiancée, and brought the phone to his ear.

"Clayton!" Veronica shouted. "Where—"

Then, just off Beach Street and turning in his direction, White saw him. The problem was, Reza Ashtari had seen him too. And they were only ten feet apart. The flash of recognition on the Iranian's face was instantaneous. And so was the pure, unadulterated hatred in his eyes. White saw him reach behind his back, and he threw his phone at Reza's head, hoping it would buy him the extra second he needed to draw the Glock from the fanny pack. The throw was spot on, but the Iranian had quick reflexes—White's phone sailed over Reza's head as he stepped in toward White and ducked to his right. White's Glock was still half-inside his fanny pack when Reza crashed into him.

White just had time to angle his body to the right. Taking advantage of Reza's forward momentum, he threw the Iranian over his shoulder.

———

Reza landed hard on his back and bit off a curse. He quickly jumped back to his feet and realized he no longer had his pistol in the small of his back. That was the bad news. The good news was that Clayton White had also been forced to let go of his.

For a moment the two men stared into each other's eyes. White was about his height and weight. Reza could tell that every single pound had been refined for strength and agility. He did a quick survey of White, searching for signs of a wound he could exploit to his advantage, and noticed that blood ran from the right side of White's head. His right ear was swollen and mixed with the blood from his head wound. White's eyes were something else, though. They were disturbingly empty of any expression. They conveyed nothing. No fear. No anger. No rage.

Reza struck first with a lightning-fast front kick aimed at White's sternum. White rotated his hips to the left, and Reza's foot missed the mark; he realized too late he'd gotten sucked in too close. White never stopped his movement and delivered a powerful strike toward his neck. Reza ducked just in time, catching only a glancing blow at the top of his skull. Before he could mount a counterattack, his breath exploded out of his lungs when White's fist plowed deep through his abdomen. Then it was as if a sledgehammer hit him on the chin. Reza's vision blurred and his eyes flooded with tears. He stumbled back a few steps and blinked them away. He looked at White. The American winced, but his expression hadn't changed. He didn't even look tired. Around them, onlookers had gathered, many with their phones in hand. Behind White, maybe sixty or seventy meters away, uniformed police officers were running toward them.

Rage erupted inside of him, and he unsheathed his knife. White mirrored his action, pulling a six-inch blade from his fanny pack.

"Don't," White said, his voice calm, almost compassionate. "Or you'll die in the streets of New York."

"But not before I gut you," Reza said. Then he launched at White, thrusting his knife straight at the American's neck.

———

The pain inside White's head suddenly became much worse, but he didn't dare show any sign of it on his face. Reza was holding his knife at chest level, standing with his feet shoulder width apart. His knees were bent slightly. Not a good sign for White, since it didn't look like this was his adversary's first knife fight.

Reza rushed forward, his knife heading straight toward White's neck. His speed was astonishing, and White barely had the time to dodge backward as the blade sliced the air millimeters from his neck. White slashed at Reza's exposed arm, but the Iranian had already pulled back. Reza's next attack came a second later with a slash toward White's abdomen. White hadn't anticipated the move, so he missed his block. Reza's knife cut through his jacket and skin alike.

White grimaced at the pain as he ducked under another slash aimed at his neck. He retreated a step as warm blood poured out of him, soaking his shirt. He didn't think the wound was deep, but he could feel it tearing more every time he moved. More importantly, Reza had seen him wince, and that was exactly what he'd wanted. When the Iranian struck again, White stepped in and knocked Reza's blade with his left forearm, accepting a cut and feeling the hot sting as the steel of the knife bounced off a bone. But he was where he needed to be. Reza's eyes widened as White plunged his knife deep into his abdomen, then twisted with all his strength, and pulled out his blade in a wide slash across the man's stomach.

Reza gasped, then fell to his knees, looking at White. His eyes moved to his right, toward the pistol that had slipped out of his waistband. He reached for it.

White plunged the sharp steel of his knife a few inches into Reza's chest, then slammed his free hand into the back of the hilt to drive it through his heart.

As New York City's finest arrived, White got down on his knees and raised his hands above his head.

EPILOGUE

Six Weeks Later
Key West, Florida

White squeezed Veronica's hand as she sat down next to him.

"Sorry," she whispered in his ear.

"Are you okay?" he asked, concerned. It was the third time she'd gone to the bathroom in the last two hours.

She smiled at him, her eyes sparkling. "Yes, I'm totally fine," she said, kissing the back of his hand.

Seated to White's immediate left was Alexander Hammond, who'd flown in only an hour ago. Emily Moss and Pierre Sarazin were also present. Since White had spent the entire afternoon out fishing with Sarazin, and Veronica hadn't felt like cooking, they'd decided to order in some food. The feast on the round table was spectacular: platters filled with lobster tails, shrimps, scallops, and mussels. Not to be forgotten were the four dozen fresh oysters Sarazin had personally selected at Alonzo's—a well-known oceanfront oyster bar on Front Street. A huge garden salad—thanks to Emily—full of cherry tomatoes and freshly cut cucumbers she had picked from her garden completed the spread. Five long-stemmed wineglasses sat next to two exquisite—if White was to believe Sarazin—bottles of French chardonnay.

"Too bad we didn't catch anything today, Clay," Sarazin said. "Raw tuna would have complemented the chardonnay perfectly."

"There's always tomorrow, mon ami," White replied, winking at his friend.

Following two weeks in a London hospital, Sarazin had been allowed to fly back to the United States. Courtesy of Alexander Hammond, all his hospital bills had been taken care of. The surgeons had been able to rebuild his knee, but Sarazin would never walk normally again. Still, it was better than the alternative. More troubling was the hit he'd received on the head. It had caused massive internal bleeding, and the brain surgeons who'd worked on him had warned Sarazin that he had probably sustained irreparable damage—but they didn't know what kind of aftereffects he would suffer. Only time would tell.

"Allez, Pierre, open the bottles," Emily said, laughing.

As White observed Pierre uncorking the first bottle of chardonnay, he wondered what Veronica thought about her best friend once again traveling overseas for a new assignment. Following the shooting in Tribeca, and citing exceptional security concerns, the *New York Times* had withdrawn its offer on Emily's article about Iran's involvement in Syria. To soften the blow, the newspaper had offered her a full-time editorial position, but she had turned it down, preferring to continue her career as a freelance journalist.

"Emily, remind me again where you're headed next," White said, going for the biggest oyster on the platter.

"I'm going to Monaco, but not for two months. In the meantime, I've got plenty of work to do in New York. Angus is moving in with me," she said with a big smile between two bites of salad.

"Glad to hear about you and Angus, but Monaco?" Hammond asked as he plunged a big piece of lobster meat into a not-so-small bowl of garlic butter. "Why?"

"To cover the Yacht Show, of course," Emily replied. "Can you believe it? They're actually paying me top dollar to splurge on caviar and champagne."

"Well deserved, and good for you, beautiful lady," Veronica said, wrapping her arm around her friend's shoulders. "I'm thrilled for you. I truly wish Clay and I could join you."

"Why don't you? You're too busy at SkyCU?" Emily asked. "C'mon, girl. If Clay's the reason you can't come, he can stay behind, you know? I don't care as long as *you* are there. No offense, Clayton."

White laughed. "None taken."

After dinner, once the dishes were done, White pulled the screen door open and joined Hammond, who had stepped out onto the balcony, a glass of American whiskey in hand. White leaned over the handrail, his arms resting on the railing. Both men stood in silence as they watched the glitter of the ocean. Below them two Secret Service special agents and a local K-9 unit were patrolling the shoreline.

"Thank you, Clayton," Hammond said, keeping his voice low. "You're a man of your word."

"So you're done?" White asked. "It's over?"

"I spoke with Iran's supreme leader earlier today," Hammond said. "He has once again apologized for his rogue agent. He said he was glad we were able to deal with him in time."

White's mood turned darker. "In time? Did you tell this jackass about the two special agents who were killed?"

"Of course I did," Hammond growled, visibly offended White would think otherwise. "But what am I supposed to do about it? If it wasn't for Nader Ashtari's tip, there's a good chance Veronica would be dead. You get that, right?"

"So you believe the ayatollah now?"

"I believe that Reza Ashtari and his brother planned the first two operations together. I have a feeling the ayatollah didn't know about it. But I could be wrong."

White considered this for a moment. "So all of this was retribution for what we did in Iraq?"

Hammond shrugged. "You did slide a knife into their father's heart."

White nodded. "So when the first operation failed, and their plan B in London nose-dived, Nader Ashtari decided to cut his losses and save his neck by giving up his brother. That sound about right?" he asked.

"That's the most logical conclusion," Hammond said.

"Why wait all these years? I don't get it."

"I've been asking myself the same question," Hammond conceded. "And I haven't found the answer."

"What of Emily's piece about Iran's involvement in that massive genocide in Syria? The *Times* might have gotten cold feet about publishing it, but it doesn't mean what's in it isn't true. Have you looked into it?"

"The CIA did. They didn't find anything to substantiate Emily's reporting."

"What? That's Emily we're talking about here," White said, almost whispering. "She wouldn't have made that up. I saw the pictures."

"Pictures are easily doctored," Hammond said, taking a long sip of his drink.

"Ah, c'mon. Those photos were given to her by a former Syrian military officer who'd worked in the torture chambers. They weren't doctored."

"I don't know what to tell you, Clayton," Hammond said. "As I said, the CIA looked into it. That Syrian officer you're talking about has vanished. They couldn't find him."

"Vanished? Sounds like the MOIS had him killed."

"Maybe," Hammond replied.

"What about the facilities, then?" White asked, getting angrier by the minute.

"I asked the National Reconnaissance Office to take a look."

"And?"

"Whatever buildings were there aren't anymore. The analysts think they were burned down."

"Shit."

"Yeah. Exactly."

"I feel like I've played a game of chess without even knowing there was a match going on," White said.

"I don't want to sound paternalistic, but that's often the case," Hammond said. "And honestly, right now the US has bigger fish to fry than what's going on in Syria. Emily seems to have let it go. Maybe you should too."

White was about to reply when the sliding door opened and Veronica squeezed herself between them. "I hope I'm not interrupting?"

"Not at all," White said.

She took a long deep breath. "God, I love the ocean," she said. "Just like Mom did."

"She sure did," Hammond said.

White wrapped an arm around Veronica's shoulders and gave her a light squeeze. He could see his fiancée was on the verge of tears, her eyes moist in the dim light cast by the moon.

"When you're done here, please join me inside. There's something I want to show you," Veronica said a minute later.

"Clay and I will be right there, Vonnie," Hammond said.

Veronica gave White a peck on the cheek and returned inside the apartment.

Hammond brought his glass to his lips and knocked the rest of the whiskey back in one gulp. "I'm resigning the day after tomorrow. It's settled," he said.

"You told the president?"

"I'm flying back to Washington in the afternoon. I'm meeting him at the White House just before dinner."

"All right. That's for the best," White said, with not a hint of compassion. He wondered if Hammond had hoped he would change his mind about the vice presidency. He guessed he'd never know. As far as White was concerned, the matter was settled. Not that he didn't want to see Hammond go to jail for his father's murder, but the chances of that happening were almost nil. There was a big difference between knowing someone had done something and being able to prove it beyond reasonable doubt in a court of law. And like he had told Hammond in the Gulfstream on their way back from England, he loved Veronica more than he hated him.

———

Inside the apartment, Veronica gathered everyone in the small living room.

"Okay, Vonnie," White said, not sure what was going on. "We're all here."

His fiancée had acted strangely all afternoon. For the last few days, she'd been on back-to-back conference calls for eight to ten hours each day, and that wasn't counting all the online sessions she'd done with Brad at SkyCU Technology and government representatives at NOAA. White couldn't remember the last time he'd seen her so happy. Visibly, tonight was when they would all learn about Veronica's next big project.

Veronica smiled at him, then cleared her throat.

"As you guys know, the last year and a half hasn't been easy. There's been some ups—big ups, even—but the downs definitely won. Still, I believe in the future, and I'm the kind of woman who looks forward, not back. With that in mind, there's something I'd like to give Clayton."

White sat straighter in the sofa at the mention of his name. "Me?" he asked, confused.

Veronica handed him a small white box she'd kept behind her back.

"What is it?" he asked, his heart beating faster for some reason now that all eyes were on him.

"Open the box, Clay," Veronica pressed him. "It won't bite."

White pulled open the top of the box. Inside was a photo of an object he at first didn't recognize. Then he did, and his eyes watered. His hands started shaking uncontrollably. The box fell out of his hands. Only the picture of the positive pregnancy test remained. He looked at his fiancée. She was crying too.

"We're pregnant?" White asked her.

She nodded, wiping her tears with the back of her hand. "Yes."

He took Veronica in his arms and kissed her as everyone clapped. "How long have you known?"

"Three weeks," she said.

He held her tight in his arms, hoping he'd never have to let her go.

Then, without warning, the mood was shattered as the front door burst open and Special Agent Albanese rushed inside. His gaze stopped on Hammond, and he made a beeline for the vice president. White watched as Albanese whispered something into Hammond's ear. Two more agents entered the apartment.

Hammond nodded, a stern expression on his face.

White made his way to Hammond, and Albanese squeezed past him, barely acknowledging White's presence.

"What's going on?" White asked.

Hammond looked at him. "I need to get back to Washington immediately. I'm sorry, Clayton. And congratulations."

Hammond turned to leave, and White was about to grab his elbow, but Veronica stepped in. "Dad? What the hell?"

Through the open sliding doors, the sound of approaching helicopters reached the apartment's living room.

Hammond placed his hands on his daughter's shoulders.

"The president had a massive heart attack, Vonnie. He's dead," he said, speaking just loud enough that only she and White could hear.

Hammond kissed his daughter on both cheeks. "Sorry to have ruined the party."

And without another word, Hammond followed Albanese out of the apartment.

Veronica looked at White. "Oh my God. I can't believe this."

"Yeah," White said, "me neither."

ACKNOWLEDGMENTS

I hope you enjoyed reading *The Last Sentinel* as much as I enjoyed writing it. I have the privilege of writing for Thomas & Mercer, a true publishing dream team. I'd like to thank my editor Liz Pearsons, who once again pushed me to go further. Thanks, too, to Caitlin Alexander, who understood what I was trying to achieve and helped me get there. Thanks to Gracie Doyle, Sarah Shaw, and the rest of the formidable team of publishing professionals at Amazon Publishing.

A great many people have offered encouragement throughout the writing of this book. I'd like to thank Marc Cameron, Jack Carr, and Mark Greaney for providing me with exceptional blurbs for my Clayton White series. Thanks to Ryan Steck of *The Real Book Spy* and to Sean Cameron, Chris Albanese, and Mike Houtz—the three very talented writers from *The Crew Reviews* podcast—for their support. Big thanks to my friends and fellow writers Joshua Hood, Don Bentley, K. J. Howe, Jeffrey Wilson, Brian Andrews, Kyle Mills, and Brad Taylor for their support.

I'd be remiss if I didn't thank my agent, Eric Myers of Myers Literary Management. Thank you, my friend, for always being in my corner.

I also want to thank my two children, Florence and Gabriel, who make me so, so very proud. And finally, an enormous thank-you to my wife and coconspirator, Lisane. Without you and the kids, none of this would mean anything.

ABOUT THE AUTHOR

Photo © 2013 Esther Campeau

Simon Gervais was born in Montreal, Quebec. He joined the Canadian military as an infantry officer and was commissioned as a second lieutenant in 1997. In 2001, he was recruited by the Royal Canadian Mounted Police and became a federal agent. His first posting was in Toronto, where he served as a drug investigator. During this time, he worked on many international drug-related cases in close collaboration with his American colleagues from the Drug Enforcement Administration. His career switched gears in 2004, and he was placed with a federal antiterrorism unit based in the Ottawa region. During the following years, he was deployed in several European and Middle Eastern countries. In 2009, he became a close-protection specialist tasked with guarding foreign heads of state visiting Canada. He served on the protection details of Queen Elizabeth II, US president Barack Obama, and Chinese president Hu Jintao, among others. Gervais lives in Ottawa with his wife and two children.